SIDESHOW

in the Center Ring

Books and stories by Marian Allen

Novels
Eel's Reverence
Force of Habit
SAGE Book 1: The Fall of Onagros
SAGE Book 2: Bargain With Fate
SAGE Book 3: Silver and Iron
Sideshow in the Center Ring

Short Story Collections
Lonnie, Me and the Hound of Hell
Turtle Feathers
The King of Cherokee Creek
MA's Monthly Hot Flashes: 2002-2009

Visit the author at
http://MarianAllen.com

SIDESHOW
in the Center Ring

Marian Allen

Per Bastet

Sideshow in the Center Ring

Copyright © 2014 Marian Allen

Published by Per Bastet Publications LLC, P.O. Box 3023 Corydon, IN 47112

Cover art by Stacy Garrett
Photo Image by Sheri Wright

ISBN 978-0-9899711-4-0

Dedicated to the Southern Indiana Writers Group, who all said, "Ewwwwww!" in the right places.

SIDESHOW

in the Center Ring

Chapter 1

It started with parties and ended in blood. I'm not a violent woman – who would have thought it would end in blood? Maybe it started on Helena Street. If you go back that far, maybe the blood makes sense.

Helena Street was where I was born and raised: a thousand feet of narrow, broken, asphalt that we called Hell Alley. It ran from Market Street to the service entrance of 63 Andriot, a block of condominiums, overpriced for the upper class. We were a century into the New World Order, and a quick flip through a history book showed a pretty familiar picture. The Haves did, do, and always will; the Have-Nots didn't, don't, and won't. Helena Street was for Have-Nots.

"Connie!" my mother would call me in that fingernails-on-chalkboard voice: part panic and part rage. "Cornelia Phelan! You get home!"

I would grin and roll my eyes at my grade-school cronies and give them a slow wave. I'd stroll across the street and up the three feet of "walk" between the pavement and our front porch. When I got into the house, Mom would pinch my shoulder between her thumb and her fingers and shake me hard enough to make my head whip back and forth on my neck.

"Your Daddy will be here any minute and just look at the mess you left me. You expect me to do it all myself? I count on you, girl, and you let me down!"

It didn't do any good asking Mom what she'd been

doing all day when I'd been at school – she didn't have a job – not one listed on the National Register, anyway – or why she counted on an eight-year-old to do her work for her. That just would have made her wild, and Daddy would have asked where I'd gotten a split lip, and I'd have had to dodge to keep from getting another one from him. One thing you had to say for my folks – they had the spirit of stick-together, those two.

So, we'd get the house picked up in time, and Mom would open a couple of cans of stew and put a plate of bread and a tub of margarine on the table and a six-pack of beer for them and a Big Red for me. Daddy would come home with beer already on his breath and kiss us both and drop his shirt on the floor and we'd partake of our gracious family meal. Afterward, I'd go out back and play on my rusty swing-set, left over from the last family who'd lived in our particular rat-hole, and I'd kick the back fence as I swung forward and try not to kick the wall of the house as I swung back. Low profile – that was the ticket.

We shared the Alley with rats and other assorted vermin. We dodged pimps, pushers, and gangs. When we got old enough, some of us entered one or more of these bands. I never did. Just wasn't a joiner, I guess.

Hell Alley consumed most of the kids I grew up with, but it was the making of me. Insult humor– Slapping, in our lingo – was very big in Hell Alley. I was good at Slapping.

A guy would say, "Hey, Girl! Good Girl! Come here and let me tell you something!"

And I would say something like, "If I was as good as you are ugly, I could work a miracle. What I'd do is turn your face inside out so nobody but you would have to look at it."

And so on.

~*~

Slapping was only one of our favorite sports. Another was going to church. Mom and Daddy didn't go to church; up too late Saturday to see much of Sunday. That's how it was with a lot of the kids. My Aunt Bootsie – a sister of my Mom's – used to drive down to the Alley in her purple electric mini-van and cram it full of us half-washed sinners. She'd take us to St. Philemon's Cathedral uptown, near her two-story shotgun house, and line us up in the front pew where she could keep an eye on us from the choir. Afterward, she took us to Joe and Sinkers for doughnuts and then back to Helena Street. I'd go in and see if Mom and Daddy were up yet. If they were, she'd come in and visit. They usually weren't, and she'd go home.

We'd go through St. Philemon's hymnals looking for material to use in another of our games. We'd get a packing crate or an appliance box out of the big dumpster behind 63 Andriot, do one-potato to choose a kid to be "it," put the kid in the box, and sing one of those hymns. Then we'd cheer and dance around for a while and sit down and eat whatever cookies or chips we'd scrounged for the game.

Our favorite hymn was "Flesh is My Portion." You know:
Flesh is my portion, blood is my cup,
Through these, Life is mine .
At this, Your feast, I eat and I sup
Flesh and blood Divine.

The grown-ups would all beam and say, "Ain't it cute, the kids playing church like that? Baptism and communion and everything?"

They never caught on. We were playing Cannibal.
~*~

Every school has its pecking order, and the Alley kids

were at the bottom of ours. People who talk about how children have to be taught bigotry have never been sent to school wearing the Wrong Clothes or, in our case, uniforms made out of the Wrong Material. Now and then, one of us would get fed up and fight back, and it was usually me. I don't like being stepped on, and I don't like people stepping on my friends. For the purpose of argument, everybody who got stepped on was automatically, if temporarily, my friend.

Like I said, I'm not a violent woman, and I wasn't a violent kid. I slapped with words, when the choice was left to me. Some people have no sense of humor, though: if it wasn't some upscale moron taking a swing at me when she couldn't think of a comeback, it was a teacher shaving points off my grade because I participated in class discussion "not in a way conducive to the learning experience." I got sent to the principal's office so often, they printed me up a permanent hall pass. I kept it in my wallet, in one of those plastic pockets you're supposed to use for pictures.

By the time I left fifth grade, the name Cornelia Phelan meant something: Troublemaker.

Middle school was better. Playing hooky and pitching bull weren't listed in the curriculum but, as they say, "We learn by doing."

I mean, being class clown is fun, but it doesn't pay anything, and I was tired of being poor. Not ashamed of it – tired of it. So I started cutting classes one or two days a week and taking the El into the city, telling jokes on street corners for the tag ends of credit books. I did all right. Tag ends add up. I opened a bank account. Got a job walking dogs at 63 Andriot to cover where the credits were coming from.

Then, one day, when I was hitting on all cylinders on the corner by the Milky Way Chili Parlor, there stood Aunt Bootsie.

I had outgrown church about the same time I'd outgrown Cannibal, but I'd seen Aunt Bootsie every Sunday when she'd come for her weekly load.

Now she just stood there, looking at me, her arms crossed, her eyes half-closed.

My tongue seized up on me and my wits froze and I closed my mouth and stared back at her.

"I'm taking you home. I'll call in to my office from there and tell them I'm taking half a personal day today. It's time I had a talk with your parents."

"About me cutting school? They don't care."

I didn't have any brothers and sisters. Had to be a low sperm count, it sure wasn't abstinence, and nothing was planned in my family. Mom and Daddy were their own pack of brats.

"I want the girl," was what Aunt Bootsie had to say. "Either she comes with me, or I see to it that you both do time for neglect."

"The gummint talk big," Daddy said, "but they don't care—"

"I do. I'll see to it. You know I will."

Mom and Daddy acted like they were thinking it over, but they were glad enough to see me go. Sure, they'd have to clean up after themselves and get their own meals, but they wouldn't have to spend any money on me, probably wouldn't report I was gone so they could still claim the tax credit, and they wouldn't have my existence reminding them that they were supposed to be responsible adults.

"Don't nobody ask my opinion!" I remember saying.

"That's right, nobody's asking your opinion!" Daddy said. "This is for grown-ups to decide."

"I see one," I said, pointing to Aunt Bootsie.

The old man gave me a black eye, but it was the last one he ever gave me, and I bloodied his nose for him while we were at it. So.... I packed my things in a couple of grocery bags and climbed into Aunt Bootsie's purple van.

I never saw Mom and Daddy again. Never heard from them, never looked for them. Sometimes I wonder when and how they died. They must be dead, or they'd have touched me for money by now.

~*~

Aunt Bootsie bored holes in my head with fossilized maxims and poured in some sense. She drove me to school and dragged me to Mass. She made me take some business courses in high school, but I always told her I'd never work a permanent job in an office. I didn't, either. The Friday night after I graduated from Day High, when my little schoolmates were drinking themselves green at the Prom and driving onto other people's lawns, I did my first routine in a comedy club.

I got asked back. I got asked back with pay. I worked my way up from low joint to trendy dive to nightclub to cabaret. I wasn't any household word, but I was working steady, and doing what I liked.

Twenty-one, and still Slapping. I Slapped 'em upside the head, and the harder I hit, the more they pulled their hair out of the way and drew targets on their cheeks.

One of those "talent hunt" shows caught my act and put me on worldwide holovision. I clicked.

TerraNet signed me to play the wise-cracking waitress on that comedy about the space station diner, PIE IN THE

SKY. I took that show away from the guy who was supposed to be the star; I ate him up alive.

So TerraNet gave me my own show, and I buried anybody the other nets put against me, and I was In.

At least, I thought I was In. Then I went to my twenty-year class reunion. I was the only one of the Alley rats who showed up; maybe I was the only one who made good.

That was okay with me; it wasn't the Alley rats I wanted to crow over, it was the classier-thanthou cliquesters. I mean, I was pulling down major credits, dictating contract terms to one of the Big Three nets; I figured I had some ego-strokes coming from the knew-me-when kids.

No. They weren't going to give me that. They were doctors, lawyers, professors, CEO's, entrepreneurs, and other such high-powered types.

"Still clowning around?"

"Rough life – ha ha!"

"I was just telling my husband–" marriage had recently become trendy, "–what good friends we were in high school, how I took you under my wing, and all that."

And I said, "The only time I remember you taking me under your wing was the time I said, 'If you had to rely on your memory instead of your ability to read at a distance, you'd never pass a test,' and you got me in that headlock–"

Not the success I had planned. I stayed long enough to collect some new ammunition, and got a little of my own back before we called it a wrap, but I was given the old school set-down, and we all knew it.

I needed to tell Aunt Bootsie about it, and get some down-home, hard-nosed advice. I called her house, and a neighbor answered.

She was crying. Aunt Bootsie was dead.

"Those people you sent to clean her gutters? You know how she was – she sent them away and climbed up there herself. She fell off the ladder. She seemed all right, just a little dizzy; I helped her in and called the ambulance. She died before they got here. Last thing she said was, 'I'm not as young as I used to be.'"

She had never let me do a thing to pay her back; not a house, not a car, not a coat, not a thing. She left me what little she had. I donated it all to the church. By the time the media got through sanctifying me, I wished I had torched it.

~*~

And now come the parties.

TerraNet threw one for my second Top of the Net award. Everybody had been invited, and everybody brought somebody.

Lester Mayrick, assigned by the studio to ride herd on me, kept busy reminding me of names I hadn't forgotten.

Some names, though, were new to me, and some of them had Lester overawed.

"Socialites," he whispered. "You know, with a capital S. The Good Society."

"The which?"

"The Good Society. Very exclusive."

"Oh, yes. They go to nightclubs and the management lets them say who gets in and who doesn't. This is that bunch?"

"Yesssss."

"So what's so 'Good' about them? They sponsor a charity or something?"

"The Good Society is what the press calls them, dearest. They don't call themselves anything; they don't have to."

"Money, money, money?"

"Some of them, yes."

"Socially prominent?"

"Some. One of them's a countess. They don't have to be rich, though, or important, or anything else. If they're in with that group, they're Something, just because they're in with that group."

"Oh, really? And how does one get in?"

"They let 'one' in, I guess."

"Well, did you ever," I said. "How too, too utterly divine."

Lester shook his head. "Are you just trying to be different, or do you mean to tell me you aren't impressed, being in the same room with these people?"

"Can these people get me canned?"

"No."

"Then I'm not impressed. —Who's that with the bones? Her face looks familiar, but I haven't seen a skeletal structure like that outside of the Smithsonian."

"Shhhhhhh! That's Marissa."

"Who?"

"Marissa! Marissa del Hueso. 'The Face.'"

"Ohhh. No wonder she looks familiar." I'd seen that face done in everything from enameled copper to mashed potatoes, and on everything but the sides of milk cartons. It was a well-built face – overbuilt, I might even say – olive-colored, heart-shaped, strong cheekbones, big amber eyes, full lips. But it was small and closed—a face like a fist, if you want to know what I think of it. It was worth a million credits – since her press agent had insured it for that amount.

Notice he didn't insure her body. Marissa had the frame of a rhinoceros. She kept herself thin, but that hardly helped: everywhere she took off a pad of fat, she exposed a lump of bone. She was Marissa, so it really didn't matter, don't you know.

"She's supposed to be some kind of classic beauty, right?"

"Not 'supposed to be.' She is. The world's top artists– photographers– what-have-yous – line up to beg her to model for them."

"I would have guessed battle tank engineers."

"Stop it, Connie. This is great! Studio's getting fabulous pictures for the prospectus – Marcus Vadny's here, too."

Even I had heard of him. "An actual, certified, card-carrying zillionaire playboy? At my party? What is he, slumming?"

"Well, yes. They all are. They don't mix much with ordinary people."

"Geez, I'm surprised they didn't come in sterile bubbles." Something was cooking inside me. It was just on the boil; the sound it made was, "This is my party," but it smelled like, "In with that group."

"So," I said to Lester. "You know who they are; you know who I am." I batted my eyelashes. "Introduce me."

"Oh, no. Not I. You just snicker at them from afar, like a good little peasant, and don't make your Uncle Lester blush."

"Sure. Okay."

I waited until Lester detached himself from me for a minute, and I drifted over to Marissa del Hueso. Something was going to give, here; even in Hell Alley, we had enough manners to come say hello to the guest of honor, and none of these people had even looked at me. They were going to look at me, now.

"Hiya Face," I said. "Having a good time?"

"Lovely," she said, her "classically beautiful" face immobile. "I'm so sorry I can't stay longer."

The dear little fairy – I'd frightened her away with my rough, peasant manner.

"Just dropped in on your way to somewhere else?"

"Yes."

"Well, great, I'm glad you did. This party needs some class. Say, have a beer before you go. –Hey, Lester! Let's have a beer over here for The Face!"

Marissa turned red, and then ... she started to giggle.

It surprised me, but I'm not a pro for nothing. "Come on, Lester," I said, "get the lead out!"

Lester brought a splash of beer in a sherry glass, and avoided my eye as he handed it over.

Marissa took her beer and tossed it off. Everyone applauded. She loved it.

And I found myself invited for a weekend cruise aboard Marcus Vadny's yacht. Not invited by Marcus Vadny, worse luck, but by the group in general.

I accepted.

~*~

This was after my Aunt Bootsie died, of course. Aunt Bootsie would have said, "Put it in tin, or put it in gold with diamonds on it – look at it close. If it's trash, it's trash."

But Aunt Bootsie was dead, so I went on the yacht. I didn't kid myself; I knew I was there as a novelty, and because I had made Marissa laugh. I made 'em laugh on the yacht, too. I was invited to two weeks in Hanna Hobbs' island villa off the coast of Uruguay. After that, they took me for a month of skiing in the Altai Mountains.

It was a kick, at first. Then it was a goal. I was with them, but I wasn't one of them any more than a poodle is a pet owner just because he's at a dog show. And I wanted to be one of them. I deserved it. I wasn't a "good little peasant"– I wasn't any kind of a peasant at all. I was Cornelia Phelan, and I was as good as anybody. That nagging little voice telling me that "trash is trash" got a pat on the head and a patronizing smile.

I learned the Inner Circle's names and relative status quos, and the hooks that held them in place.

Jocelyn Demmarie: she composed and sang intimate little songs, accompanied herself on her Yamaha Lasernova, and never performed publicly, only for friends. Hurst Sandbourne: He had written one book ten years earlier that was so – I believe the word is "dense"– that several careers and a small industry were based on trying to figure out what the book had meant. He was always "working on" another, but it had never materialized. Ivor DePere, who made obscene amounts of money ruining good paint and canvas. Zizi Takana, CEO of GreenSink, Inc. Hannah Hobbs, ex-wife of three entertainment moguls. Rula Urka, Lester's countess. Marissa, The Face, the Queen Bee of them all.

And Darryl. Darryl Moran. He'd been a poor boy on a token scholarship when he'd started selling free-lance art criticism to small presses and local papers. He'd known his business, and he'd become a Power in the art world. That was when he'd started using his reviews as sticks and carrots. He had never said anything good about Ivor, which was a point in his favor. Of course, Ivor was bulletproof – he could sell a nosebleed if he signed it–so it hardly mattered.

I despised Darryl for the way he trashed something precious: the respect of people who trusted his judgment. And then there was the way he treated his so-called "lover," Honey Clayton. True, she begged for abuse, as long as it came from him, but that didn't excuse him for obliging her.

He was 5'8", wiry, with fine glossy hair and skin the color of bitter chocolate. His eyes were as black as the Pit, his lips were thin and wine-colored, his nose was long and narrow. He thought he was hypnotically handsome. So did Honey. I thought he was a low-down, sadistic, rat-faced, overrated, self-important lump of digestive waste.

I took against him the minute I saw the round-headed weasel. The first words he'd said to me were, "I don't watch much holovision, but I saw your show last week. Then I remembered why I don't watch much holovision."

I had answered, "Write it down, so you won't forget again. If you ever developed an artistic sense, it could ruin your career as a critic."

But, he was one of Them, and I put up with him and bided my time, intent on getting above him on Status Mountain, and rolling a few rocks his way.

In the meantime, I was holding my own; not one of the Inner Circle, but not a flunky, either. That took strategy and diplomacy, a little soft soap, and a sure hand at targeting my Slaps where they'd do me the most good.

~*~

The last thing I was looking for was a "bes' frien'" to give me big-eyed disappointed looks while I worked. That's what I got, though, and a more unlikely pal I could not have imagined.

It was Lester's countess, Rula Urka, who introduced me to Jackie. I had won a couple of performance awards, and the Good Society had granted me something like Most Favored Minion status. The countess was particularly adept at dealing out treats like the Herringmaster at SeaWorld.

"I hope you take no offense, Connie," the countess said one day, "but – who dresses you?"

"Who dresses me? Well, Nanny used to do it, but she was hitting the bottle, and we had to let her go. What do you mean, who dresses me?"

"Who has the dressing of you? Or are you buying your wardrobe ... in the stores?"

The way she said it made it sound like, "Do you pick your clothes out of the garbage?"

"Well, in the stores, yeah," I said. "Golly, you can get some really neat stuff at the Goodwill."

Understand, I dressed nice. I dressed very nice. I paid plenty, and I was considered a fashion plate in most of the company I kept.

The countess nodded, as if my joke had confirmed a suspicion and said, "I am on my way to see Jackie. I will take you with me. Jackie Eastman. You will have heard of him, of course – of his public businesses – but this is something quite different. We do not go to the Jackie Eastman Fashion Outlet."

Rula smiled at the thought. "We do not go to Eastman's in New York City. He is here, in this city, now, at the Tarlton Hotel, in the Lindauer Suite on the twentieth floor. Someone has phoned me, to let me know, and I have agreed to an appointment. My measurements, Jackie has by heart. He will take yours, ask you questions, and he will undertake the dressing of you."

A young woman of twenty or so let us into Jackie's suite. She greeted both of us by name. She smiled and said, "The countess is a dear and valued customer, and everyone knows Cornelia Phelan."

I pointed at her. "You," I said, "get a tip."

"Jackie's in the other room," she said. "Through there."

I expected Jackie Eastman to be a slim and sensitive gentleman with artificial waves in his hair.

When I saw the real Jackie, sitting on the couch, scribbling on a 26 X 30 pad of newsprint, I thought he was the cutter.

He was fat, fortyish, and funny-looking; about 5'7", white as a beached fish, with a fringe of dark hair around a flat and freckled top. His eyes were brown and warm, but too close together. His nose was small but blobby. His tongue was too large for his mouth; it made his jaw look loose and his lips look soft and, I learned when he spoke to the countess, it gave him the slightest lisp.

He had one of those 80mm "good tobacco" cigarettes burning in an ashtray on the coffee table. The ashtray was full of stubs.

He threw down his pad and came over to us. "Countess! Who've you brought me?"

I run into a lot of people who like to pretend they're so out of the mainstream they don't even know the year, much less who I am. When they turn that phony blank look on me, I have this urge to paint graffiti on it with my nails. Jackie's look wasn't blank, though; it was brassy.

The girl who'd answered the door said, "It's Cornelia Phelan, Jackie. She's been on HV for years. She's very funny."

"Thanks," I said.

"Jackie," said Rula, with heavy impishness, "these girls, they get younger all the time. You should be ashamed."

"Why? —Oh, I get it. Countess, shame on you. You should have your mind washed out with soap. Mina, do I make passes?"

The young woman laughed and patted Jackie's arm. "He says he likes his women all grown up."

"I'm a saint," Jackie said. He retrieved his pad and pencil. "Now, let's do business."

Rula chose some fabric and some designs for herself, and left. I was instructed to stay, to be measured by Mina and questioned by Jackie about my tastes and needs and so on. It was like being interviewed and groped simultaneously. The attempt had been made before, so I recognized the similarity.

The truth is, although Mina tried to put me at ease, and Jackie was as common as an old shoe, service this personal seemed unnatural to me, and it was obvious, and it put my back up.

When we were finished, I said, "Now I have a question: How much is this bag of rags going to cost me?"

Jackie lit a cigarette. "That depends on what you're willing to pay."

"I'm willing to pay something, I'm no cheapskate, but a dress is a dress, no offense."

"I'm not offended." Jackie picked up a pencil and began sketching something with swift, light strokes. "Nobody is going to send you a bill."

"What is it, a free will offering?"

"The countess is taking care of it."

"She is?"

"Enjoy it while it lasts."

My stomach clenched and my fists kept it company. "You think it won't last?"

"Like I said, that depends on what you're willing to pay for it. They pick you up, they put you down."

"Maybe," I said, "and maybe not."

"That's right. And you know what it is that you can't put down once you pick it up?"

"Yeah, I know. That's not what I mean. I'm no parasite. You send me a bill. I only asked what it would be, that's all. You send me a bill for all of this, you hear?"

He didn't. When I came in for my first fitting, he told me everything had been taken care of. I asked how much; he wagged a finger at me and said it was rude to ask the price of a gift. I told him I wanted to buy an exact copy of everything for my evil twin; he laughed. I wrote him out a check for more than I thought the stuff could possibly be worth; he donated it to UNICEF in my name.

Finally, he said, "The Fashion Outlet has prices. The salon in New York has prices. For my private clients, clothes cost what I say they cost. What I charged the countess has nothing to do with you. For you, call this one on the house."

"Why?"

"I like you."

"Why?"

"God knows. Maybe you remind me of a real person." He lit one of the cigarettes he smoked like smoking was a second career and winked.

Now, I've been winked at more than once. Dirty, flirty, and Harmless Bertie – I've seen a lot of types and felt a lot of reactions. Jackie's wink, though, was like Jackie: one of a kind. It was like a kiss on my heart.

Like I said: Who needed it? I didn't need that. I didn't.

~*~

So it started with parties, and Darryl Moran, and Honey Clayton, and Marissa the Face, and Jackie Eastman. If I had to put a finger on the top of the long slide, I guess it would be that party just after I closed production on SYBIL WRITES, a dramcdy about a psychic mystery writer who finds the solutions to unsolved cases as she turns them into short stories. Jackie rarely came to Good Society parties, but he came to that one.

Darryl attached himself to me, all provocative smiles and smoldering looks. He knew he made my skin crawl, which is what made it fun; that, and because it killed Honey Clayton's soul.

When he was sure Honey had maneuvered close enough to hear, he leaned over to me and murmured, "That dress is ravishing."

"I'll ask Jackie to make you up one. It couldn't look any worse on you than what you're wearing."

He took his arm from my shoulders. "This suit? This suit–"

"You're right, it isn't your tailor's fault. You can't put a suit on a jackass and expect it to do either of them credit."

Honey moved to his side and put a hand on his arm. He drew her closer and kissed her forehead, his open eyes on me.

"Lucky girl," I said, moving off in a parody of desolation. "Lucky, lucky girl."

Now, this Honey Clayton had been one of the most beautiful women in the Terran Union – once upon a time: close to six feet tall, slender and curvaceous; complexion the color of coffee with lots of cream; hair like honey mixed with butter, and long, and silky-looking; eyes a soft, clear green – I had seen the pictures.

By the time I met her in person, Darryl had begun his work, and she had begun to fade. Now she was overblown; not obese, but puffy, like a rose about to start dropping petals. She was an unhealthy red from the nose across the cheekbones – most of the day; in the mornings, she was greenish-gray. Her eyes always had a dull glaze. She'd cut her hair, curled it, streaked it, done anything to it Darryl admired in anyone else's hair, until it was fried lifeless under its expensive dressing. All this for love.

Honey was one of Jackie's models; a live model, though she worked with holographers, too.

Darryl Moran had seen her at Eastman's in New York

and had charmed her stupid. When he had whistled, she had come. When he hadn't whistled, she had worried. He had played mind games with her until her head was inside out.

She still worked for Jackie. When she had started to, shall we say, "flesh out"? from moving too fast and drinking too hard, Jackie had put in a line for the full-figured woman and kept her on at top pay.

But she still came when Darryl called, like a rat in an approach/avoidance experiment. There was a glint in her eye tonight, and all of us who knew her could see this was going to be one of her more flamboyant toots.

Jackie joined me at the buffet. "I can't stand to see him touch her. Or, worse, her touch him." He grimaced.

"It is kind of like seeing a snail in the petunias, isn't it?"

Jackie laughed. "That was funny, what you said about the suit."

"That's what I'm here for."

He lit another "good" tobacco cigarette, frowning again. "That's nothing to be proud of: being some kind of Society pet."

I didn't like his tone. "You aren't?" I said.

"I'm a vendor. And that's as close as I want to get to them. If you're smart, you'll keep your distance, too."

"Who said I was smart?"

"Maybe you're right. Maybe you aren't."

"No, no, no; you weren't supposed to agree with that one. How about if I make a signal?"

He wasn't in a joking mood. These even-tempered, good-natured types are grim when they get broody. "You're not the only one I've seen it happen to," he said. "Trapped in the old neighborhood. You think the only way you can get out is to climb out over everybody you see, but that won't work, because you'll always see somebody else you think you have to climb over. I'm here to tell you, the only way out of it is just to turn your back on it and walk away."

Instead, I turned my back on him and walked away. Started to, anyway.

"Honey won't listen, either," he said.

I turned back. "Listen, Bub, don't put me in a box with Honey. You won't see me making like a sheep, letting a pack of dogs drive me over a cliff. That's one thing you never have to be afraid of."

"I'm not. I'm afraid I'll see you making like a dog."

Well, that didn't even deserve an answer. Trapped in the old neighborhood? I wasn't trapped in the old neighborhood; I carried it with me, like a custard pie looking for a face.

I was on the other side of the room, talking to Marissa and Hurst, when two arms slithered around me from behind. One went around my waist; the other tried to go higher, but I blocked it.

Darryl chuckled in my ear and moved so close I could feel his body from his shoulders to his knees.

"Doctor," I said, "I have this wart on my back."

Darryl pressed his pelvis closer and said, "A sizable wart."

"A corset would hold that in for you."

"I meant this," he said, pressing even closer.

"I know," I said, "but I never speak ill of the dead."

He was about to let me go when Honey swayed up to us. He kept his hold when he saw her.

Honey's flush covered her face and neck down to her shoulders. Even her ears were red. She clutched her drink so tightly her fingers were white and her veins stood out through the puffy flesh. I could almost hear her teeth grind.

We stood there, frozen and silent, for an hour's worth of thirty seconds. Then Honey pulled back her glass and flung the contents at my face. The glass was empty.

Darryl stepped back and roared with laughter. He threw his arms around himself and all but doubled over. Everybody wanted to know what was so funny, and he was just tickled to death to tell them.

Some of the other Socialites laughed, and some of the toadies. Not everybody. Certainly not Jackie. Certainly not me.

Honey's unhealthy flush drained away. She looked defenseless without it.

Much as I despised her, I wished sincerely that she'd had something in that glass. I'd have poured my own drink over my head if it would have done any good.

I went over to her and spoke so only she could hear me. "Laugh, you idiot," I said. "Laugh with them, so they can't laugh at us. And let's move on, fast."

She didn't laugh, but she focused on my face.

"At least smile," I said, pretending to share a private joke with her. "And let's start walking."

The model in her responded, and she smiled charmingly. I put an arm around her waist, and guided her to the bar.

I left that party, then. As I went out the door, I turned and scanned the room for Jackie. Instead, I saw Honey clinging to her drink with one hand and Darryl's arm with the other. She whispered something; Darryl looked at me with eyes that glinted malice, and mouthed a kiss.

That was really the beginning, I think.

Chapter 2

So, I really needed a problem, right?

There was this new product on the market; they called it Black Lightening Beauty Elixir. Now, I was no hag at this time: My skin was sort of a sandy bisque; my hair was thick, coarse, and black with reddish highlights – I should have left it at that.

The gimmick with this Elixir was: it worked on the enzymes that enhance or repress the various pigments in your skin, and changed your skin color. You could go anything from porcelain white to canary yellow to roan to licorice. Your hair could grow out anything from white to black. The skin changed overnight; the hair sort of snuck up on you.

The package insert said it was harmless, you could take it forever if you liked the look your "personal metabolism" created, or you could stop anytime and fade back to your natural coloring.

Almost no chance of side effects. AMA approved, satisfaction guaranteed or double your money back.

Everybody was talking about taking it. Marcus Vadny and Hanna Hobbs and Ivor DePere went on and took the plunge. Marcus just went darker, to a brown the color of a buckeye shell. Hanna turned a sort of yellowish-gray, which she tried to pass off as chic. Ivor turned a vibrant ballet pink.

So I took it, too, and went to bed wondering which way my enzymes would jump. They jumped, all right, every which way. When I woke up and looked at myself, I thought it was a joke. I even checked the apartment day book – scanned the electronic butler's automatic register of incomings and outgoings, to make sure nobody had sneaked in during the night and pranked me.

I was every skin tone possible. In swatches of different sizes. All over my body. Even my hazel eyes – one now set in a patch of ebony and the other in a patch of tan – looked different shades. At least my lips were one solid color. Black.

Sweet Liberty, what a monster!

I called my doctor, Dr. Candace Embry, and begged for an emergency run. I wouldn't tell her what had happened, I wouldn't turn on the visual, and I refused to step out of the apartment. Bless the woman, she agreed to come right over, before she started her rounds.

She's understated, Dr. Embry. When I opened the door to her she wrinkled her nose and said, "Oh." She came in, sat, and folded her hands in her lap. "You sounded a little panicky over the 'phone."

She was calm. I went cold with relief.

"So you've seen this happen before?" I said.

"Nnnno, I can't say I have."

"But you know what happened? You can fix it?"

"I know what happened, but I don't know why. There was an AMA bulletin about it just last week; I wish you'd called me before you took this stuff."

"So do I."

"As for fixing it, that's kind of iffy."

"Iffy? What do you mean, iffy?"

"Mmmm." Dr. Embry didn't approve of my agitation. It wasn't accomplishing anything. Neither was her sitting there, staring at me, saying, "Mmmm," but let that pass.

She took samples of my blood, plugged her little black box into my wall jack, and called the readings in to the lab.

I sweated. Iffy. TerraNet wasn't going to honor a contract on the basis of "iffy." By damaging my appearance, I'd damaged what was legally TerraNet property. We had just signed a new contract; I got to create this show; I got to develop it; I got to control what I said and who I was and what I did.

My manager had really put the screws to them on this contract. TerraNet was probably thinking better of it now; they'd probably be glad of a chance to back out, probably be even more glad of a chance to show me what they thought of people whose managers put the screws to them. I'd be lucky if they'd let me buy my way out and go into hiding till this passed off.

I could kiss the Good Society goodbye, too. And I'd been so close. So close.

We had spent about a month gambling in a one-horse country called Sennarette; the countess had borrowed heavily from me, and had finally stopped mentioning repayment. Before long–this was the fantasy – I'd be getting my own bills. Then, some night, we'd be out somewhere, and somebody would spoof the common folk and say, "Another round! Whose turn is it? It's Connie's turn." And I would say, "No, it isn't. It's Marcus' turn. Next round is mine," and I would know I was In.

Now? Wouldn't happen now. The most I could hope for now would be Freak-of-the-Month, and that was unacceptable – that would be worse than nothing.

"Connie?" Dr. Embry held a sheet of paper. I hadn't even heard the printer going.

"Good news?"

"Well, partly. I'll leave you this name and number. She's done wonderful work with trauma victims."

That was the good part. As for the rest, it was as bad as could be. Well, I'll be fair, it wasn't quite as bad as could be. There could have been liver damage, and there wasn't. No other enzyme activity had been interfered with. But it wouldn't go away. It would never get any better; I should be glad it wouldn't get any worse – except that I had yet to see what my hair would look like when its roots grew out.

Dr. Embry had only been gone a minute when the doorbell rang. I thought she had forgotten something, so I hit the remote and clicked open the door.

It was Lester. "It was such a beautiful day, I thought I'd come take you to breakfast." Then he saw me. "Jesus, Mary, and Joseph."

"No," I said, "it's me."

He laughed. The longer he looked, the harder he laughed.

"I'm glad you're taking it so well," I said.

"I love it! What is it, body paint?"

I told him what it was, and he didn't love it anymore, and he stopped laughing altogether.

He sat beside me and thumped gently on my thigh with his fist.

"Connie.... Why, why, why? You looked great before. Of all the times to try something new with your looks, why now?"

"All the other kids were doing it." A feeble crack but – to my shame – true.

"This voids the contract. I think TerraNet would be safe in saying this voids the contract."

I'd rather have had them void it than make me eat it, but I had to kick, out of sheer perversity.

"Why?" I said.

"Look at you!"

"I have been looking at me. I think I look pretty funny. So did you, when you thought it was paint. How come it's funny if it's paint and not if it's skin? I think we've got a civil-rights case, here. Maybe a class-action discrimination case."

"Connie, be reasonable. You promised TerraNet a concept for a workable show with you as the star. A workable show. Whatever you were planning to pitch – how can it work now?"

"Lester," I said, "don't you get it? This is part of the show. I meant to do this. I expect this new show to run forever. If it doesn't, I'll build another show around The Look. It might even start a fashion trend."

Lester looked unconvinced, the skeptic.

"You didn't do this on purpose," he said. "You don't have a show concept built around this."

"When is that meeting?" I said. "I'll have one by then."

And so CLUB CALIBAN was born; a farce about the great-granddaughter of the monster from Shakespeare's play THE TEMPEST: Tallulah Caliban's island will be seized by the Government unless she pays taxes on it. Although she hates people, she can only pay the taxes by opening and running a successful pleasure resort. There's this corrupt official masquerading as a tourist. He's trying to ruin her so he can throw the island (and her) to a friend of his who's into animal experimentation: the wild and crazy Dr. Moreau.

TerraNet loved it, loved me, bought the show and honored the contract.

While we were waiting to go into production, my new hair came in. Some of it stayed black. Some of it was a tawny red. Some of it was gray, some white.... You get the picture. We left it alone till the day before production, then cut it down to the new growth. The effect was ... unique.

TerraNet decided the best thing to do about my "condition" was tie flags on it and run me up the flagpole. I made personal appearances. I gave speeches, warning young people against anything any public service organization could tack to me. I hosted a telethon for the cosmetically disadvantaged.

The Black Lightening people offered half their kingdom and the hand of the princess if I'd settle out of court. I settled, and used the payment to set up a fund for my fellow victims of the pursuit of beauty.

The media was saturated with pictures of me accepting two checks: One for the Fund, and one for double my money back.

The public ate it up. CLUB CALIBAN was – you should forgive the expression – a monster hit.

As for the Society.... I kept myself under wraps until I could make my pitch to TerraNet. After that, I was busy with the show and the "crusade." When I was ready to start accepting Society invitations, none came. What did come was a draft on Marcus Vadny's bank for the credits Rula owed me. No note from her, or from him.

But Jackie Eastman called me. He called when the first supermarket tabloid hit the stands.

I took his call with the visual transmission off.

He held up a paper. The headline screamed, over a grainy flatphoto,

TRAGEDY STRIKES COMEDY STAR
–CONNIE VICTIM OF MYSTERY DISEASE
–NEW EPIDEMIC ON THE WAY?
–TOP DOCS, PSYCHICS, PREDICT.

"What is all this?"

"Understatement."

"Come on, Connie, this is Jackie you're talking to. Is it a gag, or what?"

"You have such a way with words." I hesitated, then clicked on the visual.

"Good God!"

"That's a matter of opinion," I said. "I guess I know why you're calling. The free ride is over. Or am I still even a personal client?"

"Personal– Why wouldn't you be?"

"Then I am? Have they said?"

Jackie tossed the paper aside. "I choose my own personal clients. Put that thing on wide-angle and step back a little bit. Now turn around, slow."

I did.

"Wow," he said. "What a physique!"

I had to laugh. I wanted to cry, but I just had to laugh.

"I'll be right over."

And he came, and I felt like a human again until he left and I caught my reflection in a mirror.

~*~

I still didn't hear from the Socialites.

Jackie kept designing my clothes. Simple lines, plain cuts, not much detail, solid colors or monochrome patterns or, at the busiest, tiny little designs on a light background.

"What are you doing?" I asked him, some months and a new wardrobe later. He was back in town, in the Lindauer Suite. I wanted desperately to camp there, partly for his humanizing effect on me and partly in hope of running into the Countess or Marissa. "Are you putting in a new line? For Freaks Only, or what?"

"You don't like it?"

"I love it. TerraNet loves it. I wore a couple pieces on the show– We got fan mail for the clothes."

"I don't know why. Your character looks like she shouldn't be wearing clothes. She looks like she should be wearing a harness and a snap-proof chain."

I lifted my arms. "What can I say? I'm type-cast."

"Stop it! You want to know what I'm doing? I'll tell you what I'm doing. Look at yourself in the mirror. Pretend it isn't you. What do you see?"

I had stopped looking into mirrors. Jackie always had one in his suite when he came to town, of course. I always kind of casually threw something over it whenever I came to see him. Now he took the something off and dropped it to the floor.

"What do you see?" he said again.

I saw a monster. I saw a clown. I saw a freak. I saw a thing that used to be a woman.

Lifting my head, as if I felt entitled to, I said, "I see a Star. In a nice little dress."

Jackie didn't think it was funny. He covered the mirror again and sat down on the couch.

When he didn't say anything, I said, "They haven't.... Nobody's said anything to you?"

Jackie picked up his pad and pencil. "No, they haven't."

I watched him draw for a while. I thought I might as well leave, but I didn't want to leave. I wanted to watch Jackie draw for a while.

He flipped a page and started a new sketch, then stopped and lit a cigarette. "If they don't call you, it would be the best thing that could happen."

"Says you."

"What do you need them for? Do they control your show? No. Do they control your fans, or your credits? No." He put a hand on his chest and said, "Nanny will still dress you, with or without them."

"Thank you, Mary Poppins. But that isn't it, at all. Lots of people have hit shows, and fans, and credits; and you have more private customers than just the Good Society."

"'Good Society.' There's some irony that just isn't funny."

"Yeah, well.... Whatever you call them, they're the ultimate 'In group.' You and I might think of this crowd as so many slugs in sequins, but there's not one kid who spit on me in high school who could pay money to wash any of these people's feet."

"So you want to be one of them, so you can look down on people, too."

"That's right."

"Don't kid me, Connie. You look down on people now. I bet you always have."

"Jackie, Jackie, what's the good of being a Superior Person if nobody knows it or admits it? I want there to be no question. I want there to be no doubt. I want the people whose dogs I used to walk to see my picture in the paper, hobnobbing with people who wouldn't let them carry the Pooper Scooper. I want to be In, Jackie. Not just run with them; BE one of them. I want to be THE One of them. I want somebody to name a perfume after me."

"There are other nuts to crack, you know, if it's a challenge you want. Not just anybody can be a nun, either. Why don't you join a convent?"

What a funny guy.

~*~

So the TerraNet production season drew to a close and the Good Society Off-Planet Fun-Time season drew closer, and still no word. Then....

We shot exteriors on Carcel Island, just off the South Carolina coast, but we did the interiors in a theater, before a live audience.

This was the last scene we had to get, and the kid who played Ariel, the bellboy, tripped up the stairs. Tripped, as in fell flat on his face. Instead of calling for a retake, I shambled over to the kid and pretended I was switching his shoes to the other feet. The kid got my idea, stood up, wiggled his feet, grinned, and made it up the stairs this time. I shambled back to the registration desk while the audience did what the "applause" sign said, and we were through.

Marissa del Hueso was waiting in the lounge.

Here we go.

Marissa stood when I came in, and shoved a cheekbone at me. I kissed the air above it.

"Connie! I haven't seen you for ages! Where have you been?"

Headlined just about everywhere.

Out loud, I said, "I've been around. Working."

"Too busy for your old friends?"

"I'm always available to my friends. Anyone knows how to reach me during production."

"I thought you'd been calling everybody, and you hadn't called me."

No, she hadn't. She'd known I was being held out of the boat with a ten-foot pole until it was clear whether I'd sink or swim.

I was practically walking on water now so, since it looked like I didn't need it, my pal Face was throwing me a flotation device. If I didn't take it, the boat would go without me. If I seemed too eager, my pal would cut the lifeline, and the boat would go without me all the same.

"I haven't called anybody," I said, and let it go at that.

"You might have warned us."

"I figured Hannah and Ivor were warning enough."

Marissa laughed. She waved a hand at me and said, "Yet you..."

I shrugged, and she didn't care enough to pursue the subject.

"At any rate, after what happened to you, the rest of us had our enzymes tested. Then we decided we wouldn't take the elixir at all. So your suffering hasn't been in vain."

That was quite a comfort. "I come to it naturally," I said. "My parents were guinea pigs."

Some of the crew wandered in, then, and we hugged and joked around a little and made empty promises to get together during the hiatus. Marissa sat like a mannequin, her bee-stung lips pursed in a touch-me-not moue.

When they had gone, Marissa looked at me again, and said, "You do that so well," as if she were talking about baiting a fishhook or something.

Then she said, "We're going to Marner for the Season."

"To Marner? Furry people ... slavery.... That Marner?"

"Darryl's found the most marvelous resort."

I didn't say anything.

"You're not going to be tiresome about it again, are you? I've heard it before, and it's so pointless. If slavery suits the Marneri, who are we to object? We can't impose our own values and institutions on everyone in the universe. It wouldn't be right."

Ha, ha, ho, ho, ho. Much any of that bunch cared about right – or values, either.

"We're having a party at the Tarlton on Tuesday," she said. "Marcus has chartered a pleasure cruiser for the trip. We'll leave from the party. I'd like you to come as my guest. *Do* say you will."

Marissa's face was hard to read. She didn't move it much; I guess she thought it would last longer that way. Still, I knew what she was thinking: I would come to the party. If the rest of the Society gave me the freeze, so would Marissa. If the others accepted me—in whatever capacity – they'd be following Marissa's lead. She loved it when the collective whim blew up her back; it didn't bother her at all that her little gamble meant more than a giggle and a shiver to me.

But this was my chance. If I turned this down, I'd lost them. If I lost the Society, I was back in the sticks looking for breaks; back on the street corner, telling jokes to commuters.

So slavery was one of the few legal perversions I'd never learned to tolerate. So what? It was legal on Marner – had been, since long before we "discovered" the planet. They weren't going to emancipate everybody if I said I wouldn't come otherwise. I didn't have to buy anybody, and I could tip big.

"I'd love to come," I said.

~*~

I stepped out of the Rolls Silver Feather flier into the artificial brightness of the hotel roof pad.

Not bad, for a gutter-rat. Not too shabby, Connie, my girl.

The doorman offered his gloved hand to help me out. When I put my hand on his, he jerked, but he didn't pull away. Then he recognized me.

"Cornelia Phelan," he said. "It's really you. I thought it was some clown in Cornelia Phelan makeup."

"No, it's really me. It doesn't come off."

He looked at his glove. "Great. We have to pay to have these cleaned, you know."

"That's a shame." The flier eased off behind me.

"We never miss your show, at home. Wait till I tell the kids. We think you're the funniest thing on the box. I mean you still are. You always were."

I reached into my bag for his tip.

"No," he said. "No, really. It's an honor. My littlest girl, she has a birthmark on her nose, and she's the hit of the school."

"Well, bless her heart." *What a life.*

"Could I...." He reached into his breast pocket. "For her." He pulled out a notebook and flipped it to a blank page. "I wouldn't ask anybody else, it's not ethical, and bad business. They'd be steamed if they ever found out. But it's for her."

I took the notebook and the pen he held out with it.

"Relax," I said, wishing I could do the same. "Her name is...."

"Angela."

I wrote: "Angela– You and me, kid. 'They can kill us, but they can't eat us.' –Connie Phelan."

The doorman read what I'd written. "That's what you always say on the show," he told me. "Angela loves that. This'll really tickle her. Thanks."

"Give her my best."

The rooftop was still empty, except for the two of us. I no longer expected the media; I wasn't Big News anymore. Only one yellow-journalism rag still sent a goon around to try to snap me talking with my mouth full. It had been different just after TerraNet unveiled me, of course. Then, all I'd needed was somebody following me around yelling, "Peanuts! Popcorn! Crackerjack!" to have made my life a complete circus.

I hadn't expected fans, either. My fans wrote me letters it hurt to read and sent pictures of themselves it hurt to look at, but they didn't organize groups to go feed my ego every time I stepped out of a car.

I had thought maybe Marissa would leave the party to meet me, out of the kindness of her heart. Of course, she hadn't invited me to be kind. She hadn't gotten to be the reigning queen of the Good Society by being kind. She would be waiting in the Crystal Ballroom, strategically placed to watch my entrance and the others' reactions to it.

I started up the red all-weather carpet to the roof-top entrance. Before the doorman could pass me and do his duty, Jackie Eastman opened the door and waved him back.

God love the man.

He looked me over, smoking an 80mm "good" cigarette as if it were part of his brain.

I was wearing one of his frothier creations: a lime-green Teddy under a sleeveless white net gown.

"That looks great," he said. "You set it off."

And, for ten seconds, I was a beautiful woman. Then I put out my hand to take Jackie's arm and saw my patch-work flesh, and I was myself again.

Jackie threw the butt of his cigarette into a half-barrel of sand and held the door for me.

There weren't many people in the upper lobby at that time of the evening: a few guests, half-a-dozen staff. The elevators were all the way across the room. They would be. Somebody whispered my name. I glanced around; they were all looking; they were all smiling.

As we stepped into the elevator, I smiled back and waved, pushing the "close door" button with a clenched fist.

"Everybody stares," Jackie said.

"I know."

"Oh, you have that problem, too?" He winked, and got out another cigarette. "Are you tired of it?"

"Sort of. Sometimes. No."

The elevator stopped. Jackie positioned his lighter. When the doors opened, he lit up.

"Do you want to go in alone?" he asked.

He was offering me an escort, bless him. It was a nice thought, but the chic elite would have eaten me alive if I'd shown a hint of weakness.

"Alone," I said.

He nodded. "Much more effective. You look great."

"Thanks – and thanks for the offer."

"Good luck." He gave me an "okay" sign.

I gave him one back.

Jackie trotted down the hall and slipped back into the party by the service door. I'd go in at the front of the room, by way of the double-doors that opened onto a dais. As Jackie said, much more effective. I figured I'd have about twenty seconds to hit or miss, another ten to clinch it or lose it. And never another chance.

I had the stage-flumps. I took a deep breath and let it out slowly. And again. I looked at my watch. I'd go in when the sweep hit the 12. Wait for it... Now.

I opened the doors wide and stepped through. I stood there, pretending to look for Marissa, while I counted ten, slowly. I could hear them, drawing one another's attention to me, whispering. They began to laugh. Someone did a wolf-whistle and shouted, "Connie!"

I "noticed" the crowd's interest, then, and played to it, twirling and presenting myself, lifting my skirt to show my ruined legs and grinning like a monkey, as if I were revealing a treat. Someone applauded; I curtsied with a flourish. The applause grew, wavered, took heart and swept the room.

I flipped a salute and stepped down into the arms of the party, into the midst of my heart's desire, my soul's enemy.

I checked my watch. Thirty seconds. That's timing.

Chapter 3

So here I was at the party. They'd laughed at me, and I'd grabbed their laughter in a half-Nelson and wrestled it to the mat. I was In – but only on spec. I'd been a minor Somebody with them, before. I wanted that back. For starters.

Marissa was right where I'd expected her to be; close to the dais, where she could read the audience; her back to me, so she could pretend she hadn't noticed me come in. She'd oiled her hair for the party: the black foam of it glistened around her head. One lock, straightened, hung down the middle of her back. Another time, I would have tweaked that lock with a laugh and joined another group. This time, I couldn't. I was Marissa's guest.

Marissa turned, pressed her lips in her minimal smile, and held out an empty glass. "Refill, please Connie, darling."

Refill, please, Connie darling? So that was the tone she wanted to take, was it? Beulah, peel me a grape, was it? Well, she might be Marissa, but I was Cornelia Phelan, and....

And I was there by her invitation only.

Now, how could I do this without tossing either my chances or my cookies?

I spotted a waiter, put two fingers in my mouth, and whistled. When she (among others) turned to stare, I waved Marissa's glass. The waiter nodded, and threaded her way to me.

"Yes, Mem?" she said.

"Another one of these for Mem del Hueso, and keep them coming."

"Yes, Mem."

I turned to Marissa, dusting my hands against one another, rolling my shoulders as if I were loosening up after a bout of heavy lifting. "Anything else I can do for you, Boss?"

She shook her head, pretending to be embarrassed by the "unwelcome" attention I'd drawn to her, laughing deep in her throat, so she wouldn't have to move her facial muscles.

"Then I'll just go mingle, shall I?"

She lifted a glitter-dusted shoulder and blew me a kiss. This would give her a chance to huddle with the other caste quarterbacks – see how the score was shaping up.

It also gave me a chance to buttonhole various People who Counted and do a little low-key lobbying for myself.

I studied the room. There was Honey Clayton, holding up the bar; and there was Jackie, next to her, handing her a boiled shrimp every time she reached for her glass.

Nice try/good luck/no chance, I thought. She probably walked in with enough of a load on to last her through a month's drought. There's some camel blood in her, somewhere.

Mingle. Start with the easy ones, the fringe of the Upper Few. Work my way inward.

So, I let Hurst Sandbourne tell me how responding to all the scholarship on his now-twenty-year-old masterpiece was keeping him from writing another. I listened to Zizi Takana give a "he-said/I-said" report of her last shareholders' meeting, nodding knowingly when she – surprise! – came out on top. Then I smiled and swayed to the beat of Jocelyn Demmarie's Lasernova, and thumped her out a weird rhythm I picked up from an old man on Carcel Island.

Fingertips trailed across my bare shoulders. Darryl.

Jocelyn looked up to see why I'd stopped; I saw her glance across the room, then lower her head to her instrument again. I could feel Honey watching.

"Hello, Connie," Darryl said. "I was hoping you'd join my little excursion. Marissa told me she'd invited you; I was afraid you wouldn't have the nerve to come."

"Why? If they can stand looking at you, they can stand looking at me."

He laughed and put a finger under my chin, lifting my face. I hate it when guys do that.

"You have become a trifle–" he whispered, "–exotic. Exciting. Especially in that charming thing you barely have on."

"Spreading it a little thick, Darryl," I said. "You think I don't know I look like a set of desert camouflage fatigues?"

"Hardly that," he said. He began touching patches of my skin, murmuring color names as he did.

"Bronze. Umber. Jet. Cinnabar. Ocher. Ivory."

I brushed his hand away.

"I haven't finished," he said.

"Yes, you have."

He curled the corners of his mouth in what was supposed to be a smile.

"For now," he said. "You're right: This is too public–"

He finished the sentence to the air. I walked away.

And blundered into a knot that might have finished me: Ivor DePere, Hanna Hobbs, Marcus Vadny, and Marcus' new Currently Significant Other, Countess Rula Urka.

Ivor and Hanna had returned to their normal colors; Marcus was maintaining his enhanced good looks. Rula put a hand on Marcus' arm as I entered the group, and smirked.

I doubted she was waiting to shower me with belated thanks for almost making her my dependent.

I also doubted any of the Gang of Three appreciated the effect of my Dreadful Example: turning the cutting edge of a fashion trend into a cluck trap, with the four of us caught and everyone else seeming oh-so-wise.

Maybe it was time for me to honk my nose and squirt myself with seltzer.

I grinned and wiggled my mismatched eyebrows while the group had a titter at my expense.

"I have so much to thank you for, Marcus," I said. "New look, big hit.... You and Hanna and Ivor. I wouldn't be what I am today, if I hadn't been so hot to copy you."

"I suppose I should apologize," said Marcus, with a dimpled smile. "But, is it my fault you followed my lead?"

"Your lead?" said Ivor. "All you did was make what was good even better. I, on the other hand, turned into a creature of the most hideous delicacy. Of course," he said to me, "as you say, I got over it."

"And what about me?" asked Hanna. "I just looked like an old weathered walnut, and nothing else on Earth. I did."

"Why did you let it pass off?" I asked. "You could be making big money, like me."

Not needing to make big money by exhibiting themselves for pay, they laughed.

That's the ticket: take three people with egg on their faces and form the Egg-on-the-Face Club.

Presto-change-o, see them go from oddball to elite before your very eyes. Let them accept me as a mascot, and see if I didn't end up as president.

"What did you do when you first saw yourself?" Rula asked.

What an opening. I did ten minutes, including ruthless

parodies of the unflappable Dr. Embry and good old Lester.

Now, a fool would have taken all this attention as a sign of friendship, and slit her own throat by acting equal. I knew better. They'd make much of me if I'd make more of them; kind of like blowing up a pneumatic pillow to sit on. Little did they know: I was a human whoopee cushion. Great title for my autobiography.

Things were progressing well. If Marissa withdrew her invitation now, one of the newly-formed Egg-on-the-Face Club would invite me instead, and they'd spend the Season defining themselves as the circle within the Circle. That wouldn't do. Now, instead of pulling me out of her hat and seeing who would go "Gosh," Marissa had me hopping around loose, and she'd have to run like holy heck to make it seem like I was following her.

I wasn't the only guest, of course, and I spent some time chatting the others up: a pop singer, a politician, a stock-market wizard, a ballerina, and the author of a best-selling cookbook. They were all attached to one or another of the Socialites. Maybe I'd bring a guest, someday. Maybe I'd invite Lester – give the kid a thrill. Maybe I'd invite Jackie.

That reminded me: I wanted to say goodbye to Jackie before we left.

He was still at the bar, still next to Honey, though he seemed to have given up trying to transfer her addiction from alcohol to shellfish.

When I walked up, Honey turned away, gulping down her drink as if it were a magic potion, and Darryl would love her back if she drank it fast enough.

"You'll give yourself the hiccups," I said.

She gave me a glare that would whither cement.

"Hey," I said, "do you see me coming on to him? Do you? He just does it because it gets to you."

Honey plonked her glass on the bar. "No, he doesn't."

She gestured vaguely toward her glass; the bartender tilted his bottle. When Honey looked away, I tilted it back up. Honey lifted the nearly-empty glass and chugged it. She gave it sort of a what's-wrong-with-this-picture look and plonked it on the bar again. I held up one finger, sideways, and the bartender gave her another token splash.

At least she'd get some exercise.

"We should be leaving, soon," I said to Jackie. "I just wanted to say thanks and—"

"Didn't I tell you? I'm coming."

"Are you, now? No, you didn't tell me. Well, well; this is a first, isn't it? And whose little guest are you?"

"Don't sound so smug, Society Pet. Marcus released a cabin on the cruiser to me and I have my own reservations at the resort. I'm not In, and I don't want to be, so I don't have to worry about being thrown out on my can."

"Now who's being smug?"

"I am."

"So why are you going? Taking your Connie Phelan Freakwear line out on the road, or what?"

"I need a vacation." He glanced at Honey, but she was occupied. He moved closer to me. "I'm worried about Honey," he said. "I mean, seriously worried. She's a mess, and she's getting worse real fast. To let her go to another planet while she's like this, without a friend to look out for her a little bit.... Maybe you could—"

"Don't look at me, Junior, I'm not her friend. If you want to play nursemaid to a bar-fly, feel free, but don't try to hire me on as assistant."

"Gee, you're tough," said Jackie. "You can't imagine how impressed I am."

A loud, low-pitched hiss filled the room, as the cruiser shuttle pulled up at the balcony.

"Where's Darry?" said Honey. "Darry, darling, the shuttle's here."

And there was Darryl. And there was Marissa. Together. I should have known things were going too well. I should have played schoolgirl-crush with Marissa for a while before I made my play for independence. Bad timing.

I had this coming, and I took it with a smile. I let the effort that smile cost me show. You know how bullies are: if I didn't give them their payoff now, they'd just work on me till they got it.

"Connie," Marissa said, "since you don't seem to need me for moral support – and I'm glad; I really am – Darry and I are sharing my stateroom on the trip out, and you and Honey are sharing his."

Honey finished her drink and let the glass fall. "You don't seriously expect me to share a stateroom with a witless freak," she said, with too-perfect clarity.

"Why not?" I said. "They expect *me* to. Come on, Roomie, let's go choose bunks."

She jerked her arm out of my hand and walked, unsteady but alone, into the waiting bus.

~*~

Marissa and Darryl made sure everybody got the word that they would be an item, at least on the trip to Marner. It caused quite a stir; a suppressed stir, but a strong one.

Marissa was top dog in the pack just now, and Darryl ranked pretty high, too. It was simple straw-clutching when a couple of potential sinkers like the countess and Marcus Vadny teamed up, but Marissa and Darryl? What was the why of that?

Why Darryl would latch onto Marissa was obvious: He'd goose his own status by association. But why would Marissa let him latch? Not just to pen me up with Honey. I'd like to think I was important enough for Marissa to take desperate measures to keep me in my place, but I didn't. That might have been the icing, but the cake was something else.

I hoped she wasn't falling for Moran's oozy charm. I hoped she was setting him up for a fall. Leading him up the garden path, then kicking his keister into a pit of sharpened stakes. Just to show she could, you know. Just for laughs.

I sat myself next to Honey on the shuttle-bus. For both our sakes, I had to talk a little self-preservation into her.

"You look like you've just been elected Bride of Kong," I said. "It could be worse. I don't snore."

She leaned back against her headrest. She looked hollow, pale, and drained. "Shut up," she said.

"He isn't worth it."

She turned away.

"He's killing you."

She turned back. "Whose business is that? It's mine. It's my life. Why don't you stay out of it, you and Jackie? What if he is killing me? What's it to you?"

"Oh, right. Sorry. Go right ahead, throw yourself into a live volcano. I'll just stand on the edge with everybody else, and make bets on which catches fire first, your hair or your behind. Fine. The only thing is, Darry Darling and Marissa have entered you and me in the three-legged race; until that's over, if you go, I go. So, if you don't mind too much, could we please decide on a plan of action? We could both come out better off instead of worse. What do you say?"

"Shut up." She leaned back again and closed her eyes.

This was going to be a real fun trip.

~*~

When we got to the cruiser, I left Honey sitting there with her eyes closed. Let Jackie or Darryl or somebody else see that she got aboard.

The party re-formed in the cruiser's lounge. One steward mixed drinks while another gave us a brief talk on the theory of faster-than-light travel, and what to do in an emergency. We swarmed the bar and ignored the talk.

Someone tickled the nape of my neck. I turned to see Darryl grinning, his other hand running up and down Marissa's back.

"Jealous?" he asked.

"Why should I be? Marissa and I are just good friends."

Honey came up, then, holding a glass, her lips and eyes damp with the drink.

"Darry...." she said.

Marissa whispered something in his ear. He blew me a kiss and gave her his arm. They made their way out of the lounge, followed by chuckles and murmurs.

Jackie came up and put a hand on Honey's elbow. Honey jerked away, sloshing liquor over her hand and down the front of her dress.

"Take it easy," Jackie said, his eyes anxious over his soft-lipped smile. "That's no way to treat a masterpiece."

Honey frowned at him, as if she suspected even him of mocking her.

"That dress is one of my favorite numbers," he said. He might have been speaking to a real woman in a real situation, instead of Honey Clayton in the midst of a Society gathering.

"It's hand washable," he said. "Do you have a sink in your room?"

Honey's frown smoothed away, but she still didn't get

it. She still stood there, with everyone watching her while they pretended they weren't.

He looked at me.

I nearly said, "Why don't *you* go play house with her?" It stuck in my throat and, before I could spit it out, I had swallowed it.

"Oh, well, come on," I said, instead, to Honey. "Let's go back to the room and rinse out a few things. Then we can curl each other's hair, and paint our toenails, and look through some movie magazines. Maybe call the duty-free shop and ask if they have Prince Albert in the can, whatever that means."

I came closer; she scowled at me and walked away.

When I let myself into our stateroom, Honey was already in one of the double beds, fully dressed, out cold. She was soaked in sweat. She reeked of bourbon and herself. She tossed and squeaked and sighed.

We had been left a bucket of ice. I emptied it into the sink and put the bucket next to her bed, just in case. Also just in case, I sat up a while; she was in no shape to aim, and I was in no mood to smell the result.

By and by, she settled into a deep, natural sleep. I took some ice water from the sink and bathed her face and neck and arms before I hit my own sack.

I dreamed I was back in Hell Alley. All the pushers, pimps, and prostitutes were dressed in Jackie Eastman originals. Rats and roaches played around their feet, laughing at their jokes and fetching them drinks.

I tried to be invisible, but they saw me. I couldn't run. They took and put me in a big black cannibal pot filled with clear liquid. Darryl held me under with a canoe paddle. When

I couldn't hold my breath any longer, I pulled the liquid into my lungs. It was tonic water, and I could breathe it.

I could see through the pot, and I swam to the edge. I knew, any minute, Aunt Bootsie would come speeding up in her purple mini-van. She'd snatch me out of the pot and I'd be safe.

Jackie Eastman stood at the mouth of the street, with his arms held out to me. Although he was so far away, we could speak in normal tones and hear each other plainly.

"I don't want to come any closer," he said. "You come to me. Come on. If you're coming out, they won't bother you."

"I'm waiting for Aunt Bootsie," I said.

"Aunt Bootsie isn't coming. I'm sorry. She's dead."

"What?"

And I was alone, staring at a furry Marneri face on a 'phone screen.

"Your Aunt Bootsie is dead," the Marneri told me.

I woke up crying.

Chapter 4

Honey was still asleep. All her high color had passed off, leaving the greenish gray of her morning-after look.

I wished she were awake. I wished she were a person. I wished my Aunt Bootsie were still alive, or at least that she'd been alive in my dream. I wished Jackie Eastman, in my dream, had come into the Alley for me.

No, not for me; with me. After all, I wanted to be here, didn't I? I needed to start thinking seriously about moving from guest to Socialite. I could make a start on the trip out, if I could connect with a partner, one I could trust. We could watch each other's backs – keep us both out of the cannibal pot.

Marcus and Rula were a good team like that, I thought. Marissa and Darryl, on the other hand, had joined forces so they could get a closer look at one another's weak spots.

Was Hanna ready to put me up for junior member? She wasn't particularly trustworthy, but she was too dumb to be very dangerous.

Ivor? No, I'd been Ivor's guest on another trip, and he'd borrowed my favorite nightgown and never given it back. Heaven only knows what he'd ask to borrow if we were roommates.

One thing I knew: I couldn't spend three months in close quarters with Darryl Moran, which is what I'd be doing if Marissa decided they'd make a Season of it. I'd tear his throat out, or retch in his face, or sit down and start playing with my toes if I had to suffer him in intimacy and large doses.

I could, I supposed, move into one of the second-class cabins toward the back — the ones the Socialites called "steerage." That was where the general-purpose leeches and brownnosers hung their hats. Unacceptable. Worse than dodging Moran.

I decided to dress and go see who was stirring.

~*~

The cruiser was on Greenwich time, which meant that it was now 8:00 in the evening. It was noon in the time zone we'd left. Breakfast, lunch or dinner, I was hungry.

More people were up and about than I had expected. Ivor, of course, out of habit; he always painted in the mornings. He preferred to work by natural light when there wasn't much of it. That way, he was just as surprised as anybody at his latest production. He didn't work during the Big Season, of course; he needed three months to lose any skill he might have developed over the previous nine.

Hurst Sandbourne was in the dining room with Russell Griffith, his Significant Other, sitting with Jocelyn Demmarie and her guests, the ballerina and the politician.

Zizi Takana was chattering robustly with Spencer Stedman, the cookbook author. Both of them were drinking vegetable juice and wearing workout skins, pungent with pumped metal and virtuous fitness.

Zizi waved at me. "We've been to the gym. It was marvelous."

"Keep it to yourself," I said. "You're obscene."

She laughed. "Come join us."

"Well...."

What about Zizi? She was poisonous, but only in a casual sort of way. And Marissa set Zizi's teeth on edge; she'd love to get one up on Marissa by pulling a guest out from under her thumb.

Zizi was an organic chemist by trade. At 27, she had developed a method or process or something to form simple starch into a cutting edge – any shape, any thickness, any degree of sharpness. It held its edge for long enough to be practical, and disintegrated in 60 days out of its package. Cheap as dirt to produce and good for the garden. She had made a mint.

She had worked for her spot on top, and on top was where she was, most places. But Marissa seemed to have a lock on the Good Society, for some reason; probably because she was totally unproductive. Zizi couldn't understand it, and it drove her nuts.

I couldn't understand it, either but, then, I had never understood what made the "popular crowd" in high school the "popular crowd." Nobody liked them, but everybody followed where they led.

People.

So I sat. To be perfectly frank, composting isn't my topic of choice for table conversation, but that's what they were talking, and that's what I talked, too. I ordered the Vegetarian Special and a tall, frosty glass of carrot juice, and only smiled when Zizi made a snide comment about it.

"Listen, I have a question," said Spencer, Zizi's cookbook writer. He cut his eyes at her. She turned a palm up with the ghost of a shrug.

He hesitated, but decided to take that as a go-ahead.

"What do you think TerraNet would say to a CLUB CALIBAN cookbook? Where is it supposed to be set? What kind of food would Tallulah Caliban serve her guests?"

"Um.... Raw meat, I think."

Zizi laughed briefly. Spencer flickered a smile, not

sure whether or not he was being got at, and by whom, and for whose benefit.

"Well, is it, like, Caribbean?"

I had mercy.

"That's my impression," I said. "But why don't you contact Lester Mayrick? He's the Chief-Cook-and-Bottle-Washer on the show." I got out one of my cards and wrote Lester's name and E-mail address on the back.

"Thanks. Thanks a lot." Stedman tucked the card away.

Zizi nodded approvingly at me. I had, apparently, done the right thing.

Yes, Zizi was a definite possibility.

Jackie Eastman came in while Zizi and Stedman were gathering themselves to leave. He joined us.

I told him Zizi liked the Vegetarian Special, that I was having it, and that I recommended it, too.

"No thanks," he said. "What you're eating, I haven't eaten for years. I don't intend to start again, at my age."

"Vegetables?"

He shook his head. I got it, and pushed my plate away.

Zizi and Spencer finished grazing and left.

I asked the steward who took Jackie's order to bring me a steak and fried potatoes.

"You are such a phony," Jackie said.

"I'm not a phony. I'm a chameleon. Is a chameleon a phony because it changes colors to protect itself? No. So what makes me a phony?"

"I would say 'higher intelligence,' but I'm beginning to wonder. Where's Honey?"

"I left her deep in slumber, dreaming her self-destructive little dreams. I wouldn't tell this to anybody but you, but I did try to talk to her last night as if I actually thought it would do some good. It didn't. She wants the two of us to butt out of her life and let Darryl get on with his work."

"I know."

"So let's." I had a wonderful idea. "Listen, Jackie. You say you're a vendor and you don't want to get close to these people. Well, who's farther away from them, really, than each other? If you limited your client list and – let's say – 'didn't have time' to design for the others, you could swing quite a bit of power here. If I were your favorite preferred client, I'd swing quite a bit of power, myself. The two of us could carve out a nice little niche about midway up the status ladder, if you get my meaning."

"I don't want–"

"But wait, listen. Maybe then we could get Honey to come over into our household – convince her that it would make Darryl jealous, or something. Maybe we could break his hold on her somehow. What do you think?"

Jackie stared at me while the steward served our orders. "I think," he said, "that you think you're trying to run a game on me. I also think that you don't know yourself very well. You think you're pretty slick, but you're soft. You're soft, Connie, and you'd team up with me and try to save Honey's life, and you'd tell yourself it was to get a boost into the Society, but it wouldn't be for that at all."

I gave him a good long stare right back and said, "You're the one who's soft. In the head, you're soft," and tucked into my steak.

"Anyway," he said, "I won't do it. I said I don't want to be a part of this, and I meant it. Honey isn't going to leave Darryl, no matter what. I just want to be close enough to keep her from going splat when he finishes her off and tosses her over his shoulder."

"Why? I mean, why all the concern and tender devotion for a woman who just wishes you'd fade into the wallpaper? She's happy with the man she's got."

"I know."

I stopped eating. "So what is this, True Love?"

"If I loved her, I'd hit her between the eyes with an ax-handle and put her out of her misery."

"So what, then?"

He didn't answer for a minute, then he said, "You know."

I did know. My Aunt Bootsie would have called it "common decency."

"So?" he said. "What are we going to do?"

"About what?"

He took his fork in his fist and put his fingers around the edges of his plate.

"You going to move to another table?" I said. "Who can you sit with who's any better than I am?"

He gave one of those long, slow, headshakes that are usually accompanied by, "Tsk, tsk, tsk."

"I'm already sitting with somebody who's better than you are. Nicer, stronger, more guts, more brains...."

"Who, yourself?"

"No, you."

The laugh I came out with was so sudden I snorted potato, and had quite a time clearing the systems.

"You have a stubborn streak," I said. "Did you know that?"

"I've been told."

He ate silently for a minute, his eyes on me, but not seeing me. Then he said, "I want to tell you something."

I put down my fork and watched bubbles come off the ice in my water glass. "Is this something I want to hear?"

"Probably not, but I've never let that stop me before. It

isn't a dramatic revelation, if that's what you're afraid of. It isn't going to threaten to make a difference in your life."

"Oh, well, in that case..." I picked up my fork. "Tell away."

"You know Darryl was born on the wrong side of the tracks, like you?"

"No, Jackie. I was born on the wrong side of the tracks. Darryl was born under the wrong side of the tracks. –He was born poor and worked his way out; yeah, I know. Should I applaud?"

"Just pointing something out. I was born on the wrong side of the tracks, too. Did you know that?"

"No, but I'm not surprised. I kind of assumed it."

"Why?"

"Well, you're ... ordinary. I mean, not ordinary, but ... regular. Normal."

"Like you?"

"Well...."

"Like Darryl?"

"Well.... What's your point?"

"Believe it or not, I have plenty of Old Money and Middle-aged Money clients who are 'normal, ordinary, and regular.' It isn't where you're born, it's how far apart you place yourself and other people on the evolutionary scale. My first boss gave me a piece of advice once: He said, 'Be nice to people on your way up–'"

"Yeah, I know that one: 'Be nice to people on your way up; they're the same people you're going to meet on your way back down.'"

"No, he just said, 'Be nice to people on your way up.' Period."

"Not very snappy."

"No, he wasn't. But he was reasonably content with

himself. Are you?"

"Yes. Sure, I am. Why wouldn't I be? You're a very nosy guy, you know that?"

"Let's say I take a special interest in special people."

"You also have an elevated opinion of your fellow beings."

He looked around the dining room. "No," he said. "Not that."

Right on cue, Darryl Moran walked in.

He was alone. His boyish grin was a trifle strained. I wondered what the little vixen had done to him, to put such a dent in his self-satisfaction.

He sat alone. He stayed alone.

Finally, Ivor couldn't stand the suspense any longer. He leaned across the aisle and asked, "Where's Marissa?"

"She has a headache this morning."

"Too late," I said. "She needs to work on her timing."

"It's easy for you to make jokes about it," Darryl said. "She woke me up with her groaning and grunting. She wouldn't let me take her mind off it, and I finally had to dress and leave."

That was no headache, that was a migraine. Marissa got them, from time to time. Too much bone in her head, maybe. There's medicine for it, of course, but Marissa was allergic to the medicine.

She'd told me once that migraines were like a combination of seasickness, food poisoning, and having a spiked strap tightened around the head, with the spikes on the inside. She couldn't see, she couldn't stand to talk, she could hardly stand to breathe.

And this precious flower who sat before us, eating a hearty meal, had had his nose put out of joint because Marissa had awakened him with her "groaning and grunting," and hadn't been interested in letting him "take her mind off it."

"You're a real prize," I said. "No wonder all the girls are crazy about you. Did you call the ship's doctor for her, at least?"

"I put a tin of pain reliever on the bedside table."

"What a prince." I turned to Jackie. "I ask you: Is this man a prince, or what?"

Jackie didn't want to get into it. "Run along," he said.

I had been about to get up, but now I didn't. "What do you mean, 'Run along'?"

"Unless I miss my guess, you've just remembered something you have to do somewhere that'll keep you busy for a while. Something cold and practical and heartless, probably."

"I don't have a thing to do."

"I'm going to my cabin. You know where it is; feel free to peek down the corridor, to be sure I'm not watching."

"He rambles," I told the steward, who had come to clear our table. I tapped the side of my head.

The steward swept the room with an expression which seemed to say I wasn't telling him anything that surprised him.

~*~

When Jackie left, I counted to 100, then went foraging for supplies.

I found a steward in the lounge, and asked her to bring some things to Marissa's stateroom as soon as she could: a cold compress, a hot compress, a flannel cloth, a jug of ice water, and a package of soda crackers. I had been Marissa's guest before, when one of these had struck, and I remembered the drill.

I went to my cabin and got my book player.

Honey was starting to stir, and I didn't linger, except to

put the magnetic "Do Not Disturb" sign on the corridor wall outside our room.

The steward met me at Marissa's door.

I took the tray from her and slipped in as quickly and quietly as I could.

Marissa moaned in protest when she heard the door.

"Relax," I murmured. "It's Connie. I won't let him in until you tell me to let him in. Now, let's knock this thing."

If she had been suffering for hours, and she hadn't whoopsed yet, I figured she wasn't going to whoops, and she didn't. That meant we only had to fight a holding action on the stomach and put our main forces in against the head.

I alternated hot and cold compresses, wiping her face and arms with the flannel when oily perspiration rose out of them like scum on a puddle. Now and then, I gave her a sip of water. When she could bear to swallow them, I helped her take some aspirin tablets.

By the time Marissa was able to talk, and willing to nibble at the edges of a soda cracker, it was two in the morning, Greenwich time.

"You don't want me to fetch Darryl, do you?" I said.

"No. I'll fetch him myself, when I want him again."

I started a sneer, but canceled it when Marissa went on to say, "He's quite a man; I don't think I'm up to his standard right now." She gave a little laugh that chilled my blood.

"On the worst day you ever had, you beat his best," I said.

"Oh, Connie, you're just being partial."

"I'm partial to anybody compared to that overheated, beady-eyed, bigheaded pea brain. You're too good for him. Honey Clayton's too good for him. A dead sheep's too good for him." Lest she should think I was getting uppity, I added, "But it's your life."

"Honey just doesn't know how to handle him. I do."

"With a whip and a chair and an electrified cattle prod. Come to think of it, he might like that."

"Connie, he isn't—"

"He left you alone, when you needed him. Needed somebody, anyway."

She gave a dismissive twitch of a shoulder. "He just didn't know what to do. I was very rude to him. You know how I am when I feel this way. He really can't be blamed."

But her eyes said otherwise.

I pushed it a little. "Sure, he can. He can't treat Marissa del Hueso like that and get away with it. All bets are off; I move back in here, and he goes back to Honey."

"I like things the way they are."

No, she liked things the way she planned to make them.

"If you see Darry," she said, "tell him I'll be out in an hour or so, and I'll want to dine with him."

"Haven't you suffered enough?"

"Connie," she said, "don't you think it's inappropriate for you always to be subjecting Darryl to your cheap insults? He isn't hurt by them, of course, but it does get tiresome. So use some discretion about it, will you? For me?"

She didn't say, "Or else," but I heard it. She was still the Ace in this pack, and I was still only making as much progress as her status would permit.

I'd deal with that, by and by.

"Okay, Boss," I said.

~*~

I took my book player and went back to Honey's stateroom.

Darryl was just coming out. I could hear Honey inside, crying quietly.

"You do get around," I said.

He grinned, and I almost asked him if he filed his teeth, but I remembered my orders.

"Marissa says she'll be out in an hour or so, and she'll want to dine with you."

"Is that where you've been all this time? I thought perhaps you were.... Of course, I don't suppose you get many offers, these days."

"None I can't refuse," I said, only hoping he remembered that the last offer I'd had had come from him.

"I assume Marissa has recovered, thanks to your gentle ministrations."

"Her migraine is gone."

Darryl smoothed his hair and settled his lapels.

"I'll go wait for her in the lounge. Tell Honey we won't be sharing a table for two after all, will you?"

"Why don't you wait in the kitchen? Maybe you can watch them boil some live lobsters."

The punch he landed knocked me into the wall so hard I dislodged the sign I'd hung there earlier.

It, my book player, and my calculated cynicism clattered to the deck.

For a few seconds, I was too shocked to breathe. Then I knotted my fists, but kept them at my sides. I knew if I could hit as hard as I wanted to hit, I'd kill him.

"That's right," he said. "You know better, don't you? You don't quite dare."

"You don't impress me, hotshot, not in the least. Every dog is allowed one bite, and this was yours. If you ever hit me again, you'd better make it a good one, because it'll be your last."

"I'll do what I like with you. You see if I don't."

He stepped toward me, flicked the tip of my nose, and walked away.

"Jesus, Mary, and Joseph," I prayed, "let him slip and fall on his can."

It was an unworthy prayer, and the answer to it was No.

I picked up my player and went into the stateroom.

Was it possible? Unless he had a social death wish, I thought, he wouldn't try any tickle-and-slap on the Face; but would she stand still while he did his thing on me? Would *I?* I mean, here I was, swelled up with triumph to be on my way to a slave world, after years of contributions to anti-slavery missions and years of signing petitions and performing for benefits. So, after years of sneering at Honey, was it possible that I would follow her act? And what had I just done – not done – in the corridor, and justified to myself?

No. This would never happen. Because, after all, Jackie was right: I didn't need these people.

Nothing bound me to them but my own determination to be one of them. I didn't depend on them for my money or my career. Darryl had no power over me, did he? Did he?

Honey was still in the clothes she'd fallen down in after the party. She had a colorful set of bruises beginning to show on her upper arms.

I made a compress for myself out of a cold washcloth and looked her over with my free eye.

"Is that the only dress you brought?" I said.

She looked back at me – dully, at first; then her pallid lips twisted in a smile.

"So," she said. "You, too. I wondered when it would start."

"Say it again in English."

"What happened to your eye?"

"I ran into a doorknob."

She leaned back on her bed, propped up by a wad of pillows and bedclothes.

"There aren't any doorknobs up here."

"There isn't any 'up' up here, either, Toots."

"He hit you, didn't he?"

"Nobody hit me."

"What did you do?"

At first, I thought she was asking me how I had reacted to being popped, as if she might want to model her own reactions after it. Then I realized she was asking me what I had done to provoke the attack.

"Do you have to do anything that anybody else would hit you for? Think about it. Do you?"

She started to speak, then closed her mouth.

"I was talking about you, not me," she said, after a heart-beat or two.

Her hands were working in the bedclothes, in a regular rhythm, like hands kneading dough, or digging a hole.

"I didn't do anything," I said. "He didn't hit me."

"Where have you been?"

"I didn't know you cared."

"Where has Darry been?"

"How would I know? I've been with Marissa. She was sick and now she's better, and he's meeting her for dinner. I was supposed to tell you that."

"Who told you to?"

"He did."

"When? Where?"

"Just now. Outside, where else? Isn't this where he's been?"

She shook her head. "He just came in, not long before

you did. That's why I thought...."

"Why you thought what? You thought I'd been with him? Can I borrow your barf bucket?"

Honey closed her eyes, turned over, and began to cry; the same quiet, hopeless, cloying, helpless, useless, non-cathartic tears I'd heard as Darryl had left the cabin.

That was *her* problem. Me, I was going to get my knife into Darryl Moran. If Honey profited from it, so much the better, because anything that did her good would twist that knife till the blade broke off inside him. Jackie might think I was playing Little Mem Hero if he wanted to, but I knew why I'd be doing it.

The pismire had hit me. I was going to get him good.

Chapter 5

The first thing I had to do was move out of that cabin. Darryl had access, and I didn't care for that.

Marcus Vadny had chartered the cruiser; all the staterooms were his, except for Jackie's. Jackie wasn't about to let me move in with him for fear I'd try to seduce him into social-climbing, so I had to work on Marcus.

I showered and changed and put something in my eye to reduce the swelling and redness.

Everybody knew Darryl slapped Honey around; I wasn't about to advertise the fact that he'd hit me and I'd taken it.

Honey would tell everybody, but I would continue to deny it. Whether Darryl backed her up or not didn't matter. Hit me or not, boast of it or not, he couldn't put the shame of it onto me.

Let him make something of it, if he wanted to. I'd make him wish he hadn't. If there was one thing I was good at, it was turning humiliation to advantage. God knows, I'd had practice.

When I came out of the bathroom, Honey went in. We didn't speak; we were each alone.

There's no night or day in space, of course, and no "off" time on a cruiser of this class. A full crew was always ready and waiting with everything from coffee and croissants to cocktails and cheese straws. We'd live by our internal clocks until we reached Marner, and adjust then. As for now, some of us were still on party time; our body clocks thought it was 7:30 the night before. Some people had switched to Greenwich time, and their bodies were asleep (or not), so the company was a little thin.

Me, I was hungry again.

Marissa and Darryl were in the dining room.

"There she is," Marissa cried, holding out an arm. "My sweet little nurse." I went to her and returned her hug. Darryl may have liked to see that, or he may not have; I didn't look at him.

"Sit with us," Marissa said.

"Three's a crowd," I said. "I wouldn't dream of intruding." If I sat with Darryl, I'd spit in his plate, and Marissa would probably consider that a cheap insult.

Besides, if everybody knew (and it seemed that they did) I had tended Marissa in her illness, I had to distance myself from her now. Otherwise, I'd turn into her nurse/companion; an honorable calling, but not mine.

So, where to sit?

Jackie was at a full table, facing me. He blinked at me so innocently I had to look away.

Marcus and Rula were sharing a table with Ivor DePere and Hanna Hobbs. I waved, and Marcus raised a hand and motioned me over. Ah, the dear old Egg-on-the-Facers.

"I'm glad you're feeling better," I told Marissa, and went to sit with the Club.

Nobody noticed my shiner: Darryl had hit the eye that was already black, and the mark didn't show. Apparently, he hadn't said anything. Saving it up, maybe, or not sure how Marissa would take it, or smarter than I thought.

The Club and I got to swapping elixir stories, and doctor stories, and most embarrassing moment stories. We ordered mass quantities of food, and traded "tastes" with each other. People stopped by our table to enjoy the company and moved on to make room for others.

When we were finished, we drifted to the lounge and gathered a cloud of lickspittles. Some of the table-hoppers followed us, bringing their satellites with them.

Number of Trucklers Attracted times Degree of Interest Engaged equals Rank. The Egg-on-the-Face Gang Plus Connie were doing pretty well. Word would get around. Even as that thought occurred to me, one of Marissa's household flunkies scampered off to deliver a caste-o-gram.

Honey came in, clean, and in a long-sleeved gown.

"How's the eye?" she said, with a smirk.

"Fine. How's the arms? How's the head?"

A few people chuckled, not knowing nor caring what we were talking about.

"Where's Darry?"

"Never mind *where* is he– *What* is he?"

The message that he was dining with Marissa must finally have sunk in. She looked at the dining room door and back to me.

I nodded.

She scooped up a glass of wine on her way into the dining room. I wondered if Darryl would ignore her or make her sit at the same table with Marissa. I wondered if she would pretend all was merry, or make a scene. I wondered, but I didn't care.

I was getting tired, and I couldn't go back to that cabin.

"Marcus," I said, "do you have any spare staterooms? I know Marissa told you to put me in with Honey, but.... I mean, have mercy."

"There are any number of spare staterooms," he said, "and one is yours for the asking. I'll just have one of the flight attendants move your things." He called a steward over and gave the order.

As if to underscore my evaluation of the Club's (and my) improving status, Marcus said, "And, just for the record, Marissa doesn't 'tell' me what to do. Nor should she you. Frankly, I don't understand why you let her. After all, you are Cornelia Phelan."

"Woman of the Year," said Rula.

"Something of the Year," I said. "But that was last year."

"Nonsense," said the countess. "I have not forgotten last Season, when my luck turned sour at the tables. One appreciates having friends one can count on."

"Did you see that episode of CLUB CALIBAN," said Ivor, "where she did the takeoff on me? It was supposed to be me, wasn't it? Now, say it was, even if it wasn't; I've been telling everybody it was supposed to be me."

"Who else could it have been?" I said.

"I knew it! It was divine! Sheer genius! Did any of you see it?"

"You just know I saw it," Hanna said. "I never do miss Connie's show if I can help it."

Bless me, if there hadn't been a secret ballot. Four in favor of treating Connie as if she were a human being, Marissa and Darryl against, Hurst and Jocelyn probably indifferent, Zizi against Marissa even if she wasn't for me.

Now I was getting somewhere.

Marissa and Darryl made an entrance, with Honey tagging behind. Marissa was deadpan, as usual.

Darryl looked amused, and Honey was happily squiffed.

They joined us, elbowing out some of the lesser lights.

"I've changed my mind," Marissa said. "I don't feel as well as I thought; I need you to change rooms with Darryl tonight, after all."

Now what?

"Trouble in Paradise?"

"Told her," said Honey, attempting to tap her eye with a forefinger.

"Sorry, Boss," I said to Marissa. "I had just washed my mouth, and I couldn't do a thing with it."

"What? What? What?" Everybody wanted to know.

Darryl looked at me and chuckled.

"Nothing important," he said.

"I need you to change rooms with Darryl tonight," Marissa said again. "I don't feel well."

"I think it's a good idea," said Darryl. "I approve." He put an arm around Marissa's shoulder and patted her arm. "Just let me know when you've built yourself back up."

Marissa looked at me as a crime chief might look at his trigger man, but I only smiled at her and nodded.

"Discretion's the word," I said.

Darryl laughed.

"I'll have your things moved in with me at once," Marissa said to me.

"No thanks. I'd rather stay in my own room. Surely you've heard: I've moved to a room of my own."

"A room of your own?"

Marcus rattled the ice in his glass. "Mm-hm," he said.

"I like knowing where I'll sleep from night to night. I'm particular. If you really need looking after, you can pack an overnight case and bunk in with me. Wouldn't that be fun?"

"Does that offer extend to anyone else?" Darryl asked.

"It's only open to people. That leaves you out."

I'd shown I could be discrete if I wanted to be; now I'd show I didn't want to be.

"And as for Marissa having to build herself up after a

night with you," I said, "I have the word of two art patronesses and seven little boys that you're qualified to be headmaster of the Famous Eunuch School. I heard that you couldn't get a rise out of a rabbit in heat. In fact, I was told that that's what's wrong with your reviews: Your sperm has backed up into your brain and made it all squiggly. Is that true?"

Darryl laughed as hard as anyone. Marissa was right – it didn't hurt him. That rap in the eye he'd given me must have released something that had been wound too tight. Or maybe – ugly thought – he considered this (my baiting him, his biding his time and cracking me one) as a form of flirtation.

Discretion might be called for, at that.

The final two days of the trip were sweet. It came to be accepted that I was on the outer fringe of the inner circle.

Darryl and Marissa must have made up; at any rate, I saw them everywhere together, with Honey or without her. Marissa was still alpha female, and Darryl was still her consort, but I was part of a solid core that didn't care.

I avoided them (and, needless to say, Honey) and they made no attempt to seek me out.

When Honey wasn't trailing after Darryl and Marissa like a kid sister on a date, she was hunched over a drink, sullenly refusing to listen to Jackie's advice.

When Jackie wasn't pouring sand down that rat hole, he was socializing; really socializing, the way normal people socialize: skimming over a level sea of talk, no undertow, no hidden reefs.

Must be nice, I thought.

I could have joined him but, if there were others around, I'd still be onstage; if we could ever be alone, the conversation would have come around to Honey, Honey, Honey.

He lifted a glass to me now and then, or saluted, or winked, or smiled, but we didn't speak, except in passing.

I called up an orientation video, "Welcome to Marner," on my room's tiny holobox. It was very upbeat, of course, which struck me as distinctly screwy, slavery being the outstanding characteristic of the society.

There is no pollution on this lovely, unspoiled planet (the video said), *because there is no local motor-driven or beast-powered transport. Travel is done by means of litters, sedan chairs, palanquins, and coaches.*

The tape displayed a hologram of all these vehicles, plus a kind of huge wheelbarrow, with load wells on each side of the central wheel; all borne, pushed, or pulled by Marneri people.

I'd seen Marneri before, of course; not personally, but on holovision specials. They looked humanoid, with long bodies and limbs, and foreheads that sloped back sharply from their muzzles.

They made me think of cats, somehow, though they didn't have tails or whiskers, and their ears were round and set on the sides of their heads. I guess it was the fur: its colors, variety, and patterns were very catlike.

Marneri didn't wear clothes, since only the females had reproductive organs, only open to the outside during childbirth. Even their milk-producing organs were on the inside, the nipples flush with the skin when they weren't needed, hidden by the fur. You could always tell male from female, though; females went sort of in at the waist, with wide shoulders and hips, and the males were more sort of tubular.

All citizens belong to the Empress (the tape said); *therefore, all citizens – slave, indentured, or freehold – belong to her, and are held in trust from her. Contract holders are responsible to the Empress for their dependents' safety. Tourists who dislike the thought of slavery–*

(I raised my hand in the empty room)

–should realize from this that slaves on Marner are treated with the utmost civility, on pain of punishment and even death.

"Yeah," I said. "I'm sure."

Status is easily observed: indentured servants wear plain collars, often in the household colors of their employers–

("employers"–I liked that)

–slaves are given elaborate neckpieces, sometimes quite valuable; freehold necks go bare.

Happy, smiling examples of people in each state stepped out of the crowd of clean and jolly natives, craning their necks to show off their beautiful status symbols. Except the poor old freehold, of course; he didn't have anything to show but liberty. One could have wept.

I turned it off.

Then we were orbiting Marner, then boarding the shuttle, then disembarking in the VIP lounge of the Muimmea Hilton.

As I left the shuttle, Darryl came up behind me, put an arm around my waist, and said, "Remember what I promised you in the corridor that night? I meant it."

"I remember. Do you remember what I promised you? I meant that, too. Stay out of my way, and I won't get in yours."

"I want you in my way. I'll get you in my way."

~*~

The penthouse floor had been reserved for a private party. That meant us. We were provided with drinks and a buffet in the VIP lounge while flunkies arranged room assignments and our luggage was unloaded.

And where did that leave me? I didn't have a flunky, and I wasn't a flunky, so where did that leave me?

I needn't have worried. The desk clerk was a Terran, a holovision addict, and a big fan of mine.

When he spotted me in the crowd on his closed-circuit screen, he came up from the ground floor, asked for my autograph, and gave me the suite with the best view.

I doubt any of the moochers who came to Marner with us enjoyed their free rides as much as I enjoyed paying for mine.

The Hilton was in the center of Muimmea, the capital of Wellki. Beyond the city, to the north and south, were beaches of shining black sand; to the east was one of Wellki's major ports, a gray blister on the skin of an indigo sea. To the west was my view – range after range of high, tooth-like mountains, fuzzy with greenery. A broad, quiet river ran through a pass between two of those mountains.

We'd be staying in Muimmea for a couple of days, to reset our biorhythms or what have you. Meanwhile, nobody wanted to go anywhere or, to see anything. A little partying, a little shopping....

What else is there to do? That was the general attitude.

I thought that that was for the little blue birdies, so I called Jackie on the house phone and invited him to go gawking with me.

I wasn't altogether certain he would come, but he did.

We stepped out into ... well ... another world, wasn't it?

The buildings looked kind of cartoony: There were no angles, edges, or points to them; they were rounded and curved. Even the windows and doors were rounded – some windows were circles, some doors were ovals.

The streets here were wide and paved. People had set up booths along the walls of buildings, and stood nearby, shouting wares and prices. Other people carried their goods on poles across their shoulders. You had to look out for them, or get clobbered as they passed; especially the hot-food vendors, with huge boxes of raw ingredients on one side and burning braziers on the other.

As far as I could tell, everyone I saw was in reasonable health and good spirits.

Most of the people we saw were Mocskans; longer-limbed and shorter-haired than most other Marneri. They liked ornaments. They wore necklaces, anklets, bracelets, earrings, and baubles clipped to their fur or stuck on with Velcro. Some of them had packs strapped to their chests, backs, or waists, or carried purses.

After we'd been walking a while we stopped at a booth to look at some jewelry.

"Notice anything?" Jackie asked me.

I made a great show of looking around, clutched his sleeve, and whispered, "Gee, Toto, I don't think we're in Kansas anymore."

"Seriously. –Nobody's staring at you."

Because he looked at the booth's owner as he spoke, the Mocskan said, "Sepplasas?" – "Please?" in Tudolinguo, the Terran Union's common language.

"I was talking to her," Jackie said, also in Tudolinguo. "I was saying that nobody's staring at her."

The man sneered, showing long but blunted lower canines. "This is Muimmea. We've seen shavetails before. Where do you think you are, up in the hills somewhere?"

"What's a shave-tail?" I asked.

He looked at me more closely, then squinted. That didn't seem to help, so he put on some rimless spectacles. "Terran, by the Mother Ruler of the Western Paradise! Terran, by your poor, flat face– No offense, lady."

"No offense."

"Can I.... " He reached out a furry hand but stopped short of touching me.

"Go ahead." You travel faster than light and go to another solar system, and what do you get? The same old same old.

He rested his pads on my arm, gently, with his claws retracted. His pads scratched a little as he moved his hand from one patch of my color to another, maybe a sign of age, I didn't know.

"Are there a lot of you like this?" he asked.

"Just me."

"Just you. Well, lady, shave-tails are Marneri who keep their fur cut close, and wear clothes. They usually run around with Terrans, but not always. Peculiar-looking– No offense."

"No offense."

"But, like I say, we see plenty of them here. So that's why nobody stares at you – nobody looks too close at anybody in the city, and you look like a shave-tail if you don't look at you too close–"

"No offense," I said.

Jackie and I went back to looking at the jewelry. I bought him a case for his cigarettes and he bought me a bauble to clip in what little hair success had left me.

The booth's owner pulled himself away from trying to signal somebody across the road and took our credits.

"Tell you what," he said. "Because you're you, and because I'm ashamed of my bad manners, this is on me," and he gave me an amulet. "For luck."

We thanked him and walked on.

Jackie started to chuckle.

"What?" I asked.

"Shave-tail."

"You wouldn't tell."

"Ah, I've got something on you! Now you must do my bidding! What shall I bid?"

"Jackie, if you tell any of those piranha, I'll–"

"You'll what?"

"I'll wish you hadn't," I said, feebly.

I threw a dirty look back toward our vendor. He was pointing at us, talking to another Mocskan, who carried a shield and one knife that I could see.

"Let's go back to the hotel," I said.

"I was just kidding. I wouldn't tell."

"If I didn't know that, you'd never make it back."

Jackie put an arm around my shoulders. "You frighten me. Anyway, we're already on our way back. You have no sense of direction– No offense."

As we came near to a large building of yellow stone, a Mocskan man came out, leading a Mocskan woman on a collar and leash. The woman was taller than he was, taller than I am, but maybe not as tall as Honey. Her fur was French vanilla and caramel and fudge, swirled and rippled. Her chin was up and her eyes were half-closed. Her collar looked to be of a supple and soft material, with bright stones dangling from it–a slave, and probably a high-priced one. The chain was so fine it was almost invisible: a token.

The man signaled for a double-sedan chair, and put the woman in first. The bearers moved off just ahead of us.

I was so interested in watching the Mocskan woman's

progress in front of me, I forgot to look behind. It wasn't until we saw the man lead his slave out of the chair and into the Hilton that I remembered the armed Mocskan and turned around.

He was practically breathing down my neck.

I pushed Jackie into the hotel and was through the door and in front of him before he could say,

"What's the shoving?"

The proud slave's owner closed the door of the elevator in our faces, and we had to take the next one. I saw the armed man go to the check-in desk as the doors slid shut and I pressed the "P" button.

"What?" Jackie asked.

"We were being followed. That friendly and colorful native we were talking to put him onto us. Onto me, maybe. He followed us to the hotel. He went to the desk, maybe to ask where he could reach us. Or me."

"Why would he?"

"I don't know."

"You're too full of yourself, Connie. It comes with being a star, I guess."

"The old man was talking to him."

"You're talking to me. Are we conspiring against somebody?"

"No. I keep trying, but you won't cooperate. —But this man followed us here."

"Why us? Is that likely? Maybe he was following that slave. Isn't that more likely?"

Well, of course he had been following the slave. Maybe he had been asking the jewelry seller for directions to the building she'd come out of. He'd got there just in time, and he'd followed her. It had just happened to be where we were going, too.

"You're right. I've been in the business too long –it's got me chasing my own tail."

"Shave–"

"Don't say it."

The elevator door opened into a lobby, where a doorkeeper made sure unwanted visitors didn't get any farther. A double door led to a corridor of rooms. This double door was open now, and the sounds of a party came out to us from the Hospitality Suite.

"I'm going to my room," Jackie said.

"Come to mine. I've got a dynamite view, and a pocketful of credits that says I can beat you at Crazy Eights."

"Crazy Eights. Life in the fast lane. Okay."

They were excited about something in the Hospitality Suite.

"I wonder what that's all about," I said.

"Nothing."

"Let's go see what's up."

"I don't care what's up."

"I don't care, either, but I can't afford not to know."

"Oh, naturally. Of course, you–"

"What if it's Honey? What if she's in there losing it again, with neither of us to bail her out?"

The weary disappointment on his round, white face made me–even me–ashamed of trying to jerk him around.

"All right," I said. "I only thought of that because I hoped it would get me what I wanted. But that doesn't mean Honey *isn't* acting out."

He sighed and took a long time extracting and lighting a cigarette.

"You aren't hopeless," he said. "But you are difficult."

The Mocskan slave-owner we had followed into the hotel came out of the Hospitality Suite and across the lobby and went into the elevator – alone. He gave me a sharp glance, hesitated, then let the doors slide shut.

"Now do you care what's up?" I asked.

He didn't answer, but he followed me through the door.

No one noticed us come in. All eyes were turned toward the far corner of the room, where Honey stood, clinging to Darryl's arm in an attempt at possessiveness. He glanced up with the tight little smile he kept just for her, and jingled the chain he held in his free hand.

The slave woman looked at Darryl pretty much the way he was looking at Honey.

I saw Marissa and went over to her. "What's going on here?" I asked.

"Darryl's bought a slave – through a broker, I understand. Irregular, but permitted. Her name's Tiph. What do you think?"

I thought it was disgusting. I thought it was foul, vile, base, odious, depraved, and stinky. But I wanted to check out everybody else before I said so.

Marissa was charmed. The others were hanging back, waiting for the collective unconscious to gel up.

"Come on," Darryl called, "don't be shy. Come and see her. She doesn't bite. At least, I don't think so. If she does, I'll have her gassed. You don't bite, do you Tiph?"

He was speaking English. I wondered if Tiph knew English. I knew Darryl didn't know Tudolinguo, the cluck.

"I don't bite," Tiph said, in English, "unless the Master tells me I should bite."

Everyone laughed a bit uncertainly and went to meet the slave.

Chapter 6

I should have seen this coming, as soon as I'd heard Darryl wanted us to go to Marner. Silly me, I'd thought frolicking about on a slave planet would be repellent enough, even for Darryl, without this.

I went against the traffic, back to Jackie.

"Did you hear?"

Jackie nodded. "I heard."

"Why? What does he think he's going to get out of this?"

"What any of you get out of anything is a mystery to me."

"Any of *them* , you mean."

"Ohh." Jackie raised his eyebrows. "All of a sudden, you don't want to be one of the cool kids?"

This was no place for a flaming row. I changed the subject.

"That fuzz-faced quisling who brought her here was a 'broker.' I wonder if the man I thought was following us is some kind of policeman; I wonder if some law is being violated, here."

"I wouldn't think so. Darryl wouldn't do anything out-and-out illegal. He's too smart for that, don't you think?"

"Anything's possible. But I don't think he's too smart to be lied to. What if this guy – this broker – saw a way to make a fast buck on a hick? What if that man I thought was following us is a fake policeman? What if that broker sold this woman to Darryl, and now this cop–maybe fake, maybe bent–is going to come in? The cop accuses Darryl of making an illegal transaction and takes Tiph away with him. He gives her back to the broker, the broker splits the money with the cop, and Darryl is left standing there scratching his head and wondering what happened."

Jackie laughed. "The creative mind in action."

"No?"

Jackie shook his head. "How did Darryl arrange to buy this woman? Somebody at the hotel had to be involved, didn't they? This is not some flophouse, where customers have to look out or get sandbagged; it's got TUT ratings to worry about; a reputation to worry about. If one of the staff helped Darryl buy a slave, it's either legal or winked at."

"Marissa said it's irregular but permitted. Still...."

I was remembering the orientation video.

"Still what?"

"I wonder if Darryl knows he holds that woman in trust from the Empress? That he's responsible for her safety? Seems like pain and punishment and death come into it somewhere."

Darryl wanted me in his way, did he? Maybe I'd just make like the Blue Fairy, and give him his wish. Maybe I could get in his way, but good, with technicalities, loopholes, and lawyers behind me.

"Want to come do a little research?"

"I don't think so," Jackie said. He was looking across the room at Honey.

Darryl had pried Honey's fingers from around his arm and she stood there, at his side, drinking her lunch.

The other Socialites moved up, glanced at Tiph, and listened to Darryl tell them how he had picked her out of a brochure the brokerage kept in the hotel's Local Services file. Then they went back to the party as if nothing new had been added.

Darryl had, perhaps, miscalculated the effect of his purchase, though who knew what effect he had fantasized? The Socialites were shocked but amused, or shocked but impressed by Darryl's gall, or were affecting disinterest. Nobody felt in a position to snub him, since Marissa was passing among the crowd with expressions of childish delight. But no one seemed moved to chuck him on the arm and tell him what a jolly scamp he was.

Darryl had invited them to come and see his slave, and they had come, and then what? What were they supposed to do? Run their hands over her and look at her teeth? Give her an order? So, they did what they always did about something they didn't know what to do about: they pretended it wasn't important.

"Fetch me a drink, Tiph," Darryl said, as if he had decided the best way to show her off was to put her through some paces.

"As the Master wishes."

"Go with her, Honey." Darryl handed over Tiph's chain. "Show her what I like."

Honey gave Darryl a long, wide-eyed look, as if her mind had jumped to the same question as mine: What all was Darryl going to order Tiph to do, and what all that he liked was he going to order Honey to demonstrate? That didn't bear thinking about.

Honey drained her glass.

Jackie crossed the back of the room to wait for Honey at the bar. I sort of drifted in that direction, too.

Honey held her head high, and even managed a smile, but if Jackie thought he was going to talk sense to her now, or get any sense out of her, he was almost as buggy as she was.

No, I didn't do him credit; he didn't want to talk to her, he only wanted her to know that he was there.

She didn't notice.

Me, I was going to see if there were any laws I could report Darryl for breaking. If there were, I would. If this town was straight, I might just be able to make things hot for Mama's Little Man. If the town was crooked, maybe I could pay somebody to act honest. I had more money than Darryl and Marissa put together; if it came to a graft war, it was over before it started.

Tiph walked to Honey's right, almost even with her, which is not how she'd walked with the broker. She had walked to his rear, except when he was putting her in and out of the sedan. I had a feeling that Honey was being insulted, and that it didn't matter to Tiph if Tiph was the only one in the room who knew it.

She gave me the twice over as she and Honey passed; down to my feet and back to my face. Her golden eyes were dusky with contempt – nothing personal, just a touch of all-purpose arrogance to show class. She wasn't even really looking at me; her eyes had that slightly unfocused look people get when they think they already know what they'd see if they were paying attention.

She thought I was a shave-tail.

"Look again," I said, holding out a hand and turning it over, showing my thin palms, bare knuckles, and useless nails. I showed her my profile – my poor, flat face – and smiled. All the time, I was thinking about the civic hot-foot I hoped to give her Master, and the smile came from the heart.

I couldn't have startled her more if I'd jumped on a chair and done my impression of The Mad Conductor.

Tiph's eyes widened and lost their smokiness. She

went past, following Honey, but she looked back over her shoulder at me, just before I turned and left the room.

As I came out of the elevator on the ground floor, I glanced around for the armed man. I didn't see him, but I did see the slave broker who'd brought Tiph to Darryl, sitting on his haunches next to the check-in desk. He held a piece of paper in his hand, and looked from it to me and back.

The clerk whispered something and grinned at me as if he were my agent.

The broker came over to me, holding out the paper. It was a page torn out of a holovision guide.

He was a stocky man, well-muscled; the color of goldenrod, with brown markings on his hands and the edges of his ears.

"You're Cornelia Phelan?" he asked in Tudolinguo. "This one? The one on the holovision?" He showed me the picture, a publicity still of me from last season's CLUB CALIBAN.

"Yes."

"This is Budhi," said the desk clerk, also in Tudolinguo. "He's a certified slave broker. I can't think where he's seen you; very few of these people have holovisions, and then it's only for status. They can't see the images, you know, it's just so much movement to them. Maybe reruns, translated onto flatfilm, on a local station?"

The broker gave him a quick smile and a nod, then turned back to me. "You're on your way out? I could show you around."

The amulet's working. Is this good luck, or what?

"Actually, I think you may be able to help me. I want to know as much as I can learn in a hurry about owning slaves here in Wellki."

"You can–" the desk clerk began, but Budhi interrupted.

"You want a slave? I just sold a very nice slave to Mem Moran, right in this very hotel just now."

"I know."

"Then you know I only deal with quality merchandise. You want to come to the Exchange with me and pick one out yourself? You get a much wider choice when you come in yourself. There's a lot of turnover in Muimmea, and the best buys don't make it into the brochures."

"No, I don't want to buy a slave. I just want to know about it. For my own personal information."

"On–" said the clerk, but Budhi broke in again.

"Sure, sure. You want to go to the Exchange. Everything you need to know is there. I'll take you, myself. It'll be an honor."

"Let's go."

"Take good care of her." The clerk wagged a finger at Budhi.

"I will."

We were out on the sidewalk and down the street before I remembered I'd wanted to ask the clerk about the armed man.

I looked behind me – and there he was, about 200 feet back.

"We're being followed."

"By who?"

"A man, a Mocskan, about my size, gray, with black stripes, armed."

"Armed? Nobody goes armed in the city."

"Look for yourself. I mean, I know I'm new around here, but a blade is a blade is a blade."

He glanced back, then said, "If you're worried, let's go faster."

So we went faster.

I could feel the armed man behind us. I could feel him. I looked around, and he was coming faster, too. I felt that sudden chill you get when all your blood rushes to man the battle stations.

"He's still there," I said.

Budhi took my arm and stopped me, saying, "Here we are."

I turned to face the man with the weapons, but he had stopped, too – watching.

I took in the Exchange's entrance with a glance: Yellow-brick, set back slightly from the sidewalk, with two landscaped rectangles on either side of a cobble-stone walk. The facade was windowless, without an overhang or rain gutter.

"You can walk on in, if you want to," said Budhi.

I turned the oversized knob on the oak-yellow door and pushed. Budhi and I stepped in and I closed the heavy door behind us.

Safe. Surely the man wouldn't follow us into an official building; they would have security guards, I supposed. A no-weapons policy; a nice little shiv-check desk with numbered tags, so you could retrieve your daggers and such as you left.

But we weren't in the building, yet: The facade had masked a courtyard, paved with brick cobbles, hung with baskets of trailing plants. Across from us, the real front of the building looked onto the courtyard through eight-foot windows, beneath a carved relief of a crowned woman (the Empress?) holding a double-handful of leashes above her head; the leashes were attached to carvings of smiling people, who danced down the walls.

I heard Budhi shout, "Claim!" Then his hand clamped on my wrist.

I tried to shake him off, then to twist out of his grasp.

"What are you doing?"

"I claim you, in the name of the Empress. You don't have any papers, do you? And you walked in here of your own free will, didn't you?"

"I've got my passport, and I'm walking out."

"No."

The broker threw an arm around my neck. I stomped at his instep, but he spread his legs and tightened his choke hold. I pulled at the hair on his arm, taking out fistfuls of it. My luck, he was shedding.

"Stop it!" he said.

I punched backwards over my shoulder with my free fist, and felt it connect smack on the beezer.

He sneezed blood all over the back of my head, but he didn't let go.

I reached up and grabbed his arm, then dropped – dead weight, and quite a bit of it, on that one point. Budhi flipped over, as nice as you please. It had been years since I'd done any street fighting; it was gratifying to know I hadn't lost the touch.

Budhi was fast, though. He tucked and rolled when he fell and, before I could get to my knees, he was up. He knocked me flat again, and knelt on the small of my back.

As I kicked and twisted and tried to heave myself up or push myself forward, he wrapped something around my wrists, and pulled it tight.

He slapped my head, and I felt a line of needles rake my scalp. He held his hand down near my eyes, so I could see my blood and hair on his claws. "See what you made me do?" he said. "Now, are you going to be still, or do you want me to get rough?"

I whimpered and moaned, "Oh, don't hurt me, don't hurt me!"

He pulled in his claws and got up. When both his hands were occupied with his chestpack, I groaned and turned on my side, facing him.

I drew up my legs, as if my stomach hurt (which it did, come to that), and kicked. I caught him in the right knee.

He fell back on his bottom with a yowl of pain.

I scrabbled to my feet and ran.

My hands were tied, and the door to the street was closed and blocked; blocked by the gray man with the black stripes and the knife.

Budhi howled something I didn't understand. I turned my head enough to keep both of the men in view. Budhi sat where I had left him, both hands on his hurt knee, blood seeping from his nose and flecking the hair of his face and chest. Beyond him, people clustered at the windows and crowded out of the doorway, not involved, but curious.

"I'm leaving," I said. "Stand aside."

The man blocking my way drew back his lips in a smile, showing canines as sharp as broken glass. "I've been trying to catch up to you," he said casually, as if I weren't fighting for my life.

Budhi got to his feet. "Is this who you meant? Following us? Why didn't you say it was a Shar?"

"Do you have any claim on this woman?" the gray man asked.

"She came in here with me of her own free will. She doesn't have any papers. I claim her, yes."

"And how do you know she doesn't have any papers? Did she tell you so?"

"Another one of the Terran tourists told me. He gave me her picture and paid me to enslave her."

"A what?" I said. "Do what? Whoa! Wait a minute!"

"Let him speak," said the "Shar." He turned me around and guided me closer to Budhi. Wounded, bound, trapped, and needing to know more, I went.

The people from the Exchange seemed satisfied that all was proceeding properly, and milled back through the door and away from the windows. Good of them to be concerned.

Budhi said, "I was supposed to bring her and her papers back to him at the Hilton."

"Who?" I asked. "Who told you to do this? Who paid you?" But, of course, I knew.

"Mem Moran. The same Terran who bought Tiph."

Now there was a happy thought: Slave of the Sleaze God. Not that Darryl would have had any pleasure out of me; it would have been something like the little Spartan boy who hid a fox inside his tunic and then found out why his best friends would have advised against it. The idea was probably to shame me – whether anyone else knew about it, or not; whether he could actually have me acting like a slave or not. The dream was probably me in chains at his feet, like Honey only more so. The expectation was probably me on the next ship out, broken in spirit and degraded in soul. Control freak is the clinical term, I believe.

"Slavery," I said, in as level a voice as I could manage, "is illegal, where we come from."

"Well, of course. That's the point. Off-worlders can only hold a contract for a year, anyway – unless he applied for citizenship, and contracts are void for off-worlders as of lift-off. It was just a joke."

He must have seen my differing opinion in my eyes, because he went on to say, "Besides, if you don't like the way he treats you, you can always file a complaint. And, if he tries to sell you, you can petition for review. So ... how about it?"

"What do you mean, 'How about it?'"

"You don't want to do a working man out of a commission, do you?"

"I'd like to do you out of about half-a-dozen of your teeth, Fluff. I'm dripping blood, here."

"It'll clean up. Besides, half of it's mine." He had acquired a red Fu Manchu mustache that was oozing into a Van Dyke beard.

"Die," I said.

"Shar, I'm losing money. Is that right?"

The gray man drew his broad, pointed knife and cut my bonds. "Do you have any credits on you?" he asked me.

"What if I do? I'm sure not giving anything to him. Why should I pay him for trying to shanghai me? —When I get hold of Moran, I'll...."

I'd what? If I rushed in, all ripped up and raving, my already tottery footing might crumble. Right now, although I was starting to be recognized as a real person, I wasn't real enough to let them know I took what happened to me seriously. So. Back to the research that had almost done me in. Assuming "almost" was the appropriate word.

"This deal is off now, right?" I said. "Joke's over? The Shar here stepped in, and I'm no longer up for grabs. Have I got that right?"

"Well...." said Budhi.

"Let's say it's negotiable," said the Shar.

"Yeah, well, I'll tell you what, Budhi. Mem Moran isn't a man I'd like to be owned by. He isn't a man I'd like the Empress to know I sold somebody to."

The broker hitched up his chest pack and flicked a glance around. "No?"

"No. I bet he doesn't know the first thing about the do's and don't's of slave-owning."

"He will, if he reads his manual."

"His manual?"

"Sure. Slave laws are very strict. You have to include a manual; it's only fair."

"A manual. Think you could get me a copy?"

"No. They're supposed to come with somebody. I'm accountable for every one I carry."

"If I might make a suggestion," the gray man said, "why not register her freehold?"

"What's that mean? I thought that just meant not a slave and not indentured."

"In your case, it means you buy yourself. You register as self-owned, pay the broker his commission, and you never have to worry about being forcibly enslaved. All Marneri are registered freehold at birth, and they stay that way, unless they sell themselves to somebody else, or cancel their papers."

"Why would they cancel their papers?" I took an embroidered linen handkerchief – Jackie had called it a "fashion accent"– out of my pocketbelt and daubed at the blood running down my cheek. "Cheap thrills?"

"Cheap thrills, or as the penalty for crimes against the Laws of Property, or as part of renouncing all their worldly goods."

"Renouncing– Oh, like Religious." Chatting away. We might have been waiting for a bus.

"Religious?"

"Nuns and monks. Never mind. I get that part. What I

don't get is why the hotel didn't tell us all of this. This is gross negligence. Don't they lose a lot of guests this way? I ought to sue."

"Didn't you look at that booklet they put next to the visiphone?" said the broker. "Or the video loop they run on Channel 2?"

"...No...."

"Don't blame the hotel, then. Besides, Terrans are generally pretty safe. There's no market for Terrans. Terrans are troublemakers." I grinned as he sopped under his nose with the fur on the back of his hand. "Nobody wants to buy a Terran unless the Terran wants to be sold. Except, like this time, when there's a special order for a particular item."

"Item." Meaning me. "Yeah. But, about Mem Moran—"

"I guess you want to turn the joke around and buy him."

My stomach heaved at the very idea. "I don't buy people. I wouldn't even buy Moran; not even to chop him up for dog meat."

"I was going to say you couldn't, anyway. He registered freehold when he first asked me if I could get somebody for him. I said sure, if they weren't registered and he asked me what that meant and I told him ... well ... what the Shar just told you."

"Oh, he did, did he?"

"So let her register freehold," the gray man said to the slaver. "Then you can give her a copy of the manual, since it'll come with a slave."

Budhi considered for a moment, while I braced myself for fight or flight. I didn't like his toothy smile, when he finally nodded.

"Let's talk price," he said.

I went for him.

The Shar caught me by the upper arms, and held me only as tightly as he had to.

Budhi jumped back at my lunge. When he saw the Shar had me, he began again.

"After all, you ought to be worth more to yourself than you would have been to Mem Moran. You Terrans talk about 'freedom' like it's better than life, or something. Can you really put a price on that?"

"Your sister dates shave-tails," I said.

Budhi's jaw dropped, then he wrinkled his nose and wheezed.

"Is he choking?" I asked the Shar. "I hope?"

"Laughing." To Budhi, he said. "Maybe you should settle on selling her for what your other buyer was willing to pay. You would get the same commission."

"But she hit me, and kicked me. I was injured–"

"I'll give you injured." I struggled against the Shar's gray hands.

"I don't know how much longer I can hold her."

He could have held me till Kingdom come; there was no doubt of that in my mind.

There was in Budhi's, though. He reached into his pack and pulled out a book and a triplicate form.

"Now," I said, when our business was concluded and I had my pink sheet safely tucked away. "Let's talk."

"About what?"

"About you."

"Me?"

"I could make a lot of trouble for you, Budhi-boy, if I wanted to. Not about trying to enslave me; I understand about unregistered people being fair game, and I understand that you were just trying to help a tourist out with a joke."

"That's right, Mem. He paid me in advance–" I could see him realize Darryl would probably want his money back, and I could see it hit him hard.

"Even so, you got a little carried away. Got a little rough with me–"

"Now, that was your fault – You can't file on that! I had a right to claim you, and you threw the first punch. I had to defend myself."

"Were you defending yourself when you subdivided my scalp?"

"I only biffed you. I'm not used to Terrans; who knew they were so thin-skinned? I wasn't going to hurt you, even for the extra money."

"What extra money?"

"I turned it down." Budhi looked virtuous. "Mem Moran offered me extra if I would hurt you, but I said, 'We don't treat women that way on Marner, and we don't mishandle slaves.'"

So that was another one I owed Darryl. He was building up quite an account with me.

"Uhh..." Budhi seemed to be working up the courage to say something. "Would you mind – since it happened, anyway.... Maybe I could collect from him on that? And not get in trouble with–" He wiggled a thumb toward the yellow brick building behind us.

"I would say, 'Soak him good.' But, you know, Darryl's leaving town, and that desk clerk will still be here. He's a fan of mine, and I don't think he's going to let anybody who slashed my head squat in his lobby looking for custom, do you?"

Budhi sat on the cobbles and began picking at the fur between his fingers.

"Now, tell me this," I went on. "Am I the only one Mem Moran paid you to enslave?"

"No. That is, yes. I mean, you're the only one he paid me in advance. But there's another woman he wants me to do for him; he said he'll call for me, or bring her to the lobby or to the Exchange, and I won't have any trouble with that one. He said he'd pay me for that one then."

Just what I thought. No, he wouldn't have any trouble with Honey.

"Okay, Budhi. You go on and file my papers; I'll wait for you out here. Come back to the hotel with me, and bring a whole raft of those forms and manuals. I want you to do me a favor. I'll trade you: You do me one, and I'll do you three."

"What's the deal?"

"I'm going to take you back to that party, where you delivered Tiph. Tell them about registering freehold, and register anybody who wants to. But – this is the favor – tell them that freehold is the only way you can register them. That you can't enslave or indenture them to anyone else."

"But that isn't true."

"If it were true," I said, patiently, "it wouldn't be a favor to me for you to say it, now would it?"

He shook his head. "And what do you do for me?"

"One: you get the commissions on all those freeholds, right?"

"How many?"

"I don't know. It depends on how good a show we put on. One, I can guarantee. I'm going to make sure of one." *Jackie* . "I'm going to make sure of two." *Honey* "Probably more. Maybe as many as fifty."

"Fifty!"

"More or less. I'm not sure how many hem-kissers we

brought with us this trip but, if the big dogs do it, the little dogs will do it, too, so it might be that many. The second thing is: Even though I'm paying you to register me freehold, if Darryl Moran makes you give him back his money, I'll reimburse you."

The Shar nodded in approval.

"All right," Budhi said. "What's the third thing?"

"I'll tell that desk clerk that I fell in front of a runaway wheelbarrow and you accidentally scratched me, snatching me to safety."

Budhi sprang to his feet. "By the Mother, it's a deal! I'll be right back. Fifty!"

He trotted off.

"Now you," I said.

The armed man sank to his haunches and smiled up at me.

I sat beside him, and realized that I had been aching to sit for some time.

Odd, but I wasn't frightened of him anymore. It wasn't because he didn't make a show of his convex shield, his twenty-inch skewer, and the knife he'd used to cut me loose. He didn't, but it's the people who don't seem aware of their weapons who can use them without thinking about it.

"Thanks for your help," I said.

"That's what I do. Thanks for your thanks."

"Are you some kind of Police?"

He laughed, shaking his head from side to side, wheezing the way Budhi had when he had laughed.

"Why were you following Budhi? Or was it me, after all?"

"It's you. My Uncle Shahtsi called me over to his booth this morning and showed you to me." He held up his shield and shook it. "You're just what I've been looking for."

Chapter 7

"Get that out of my face," I said.

"I'm sorry." Almost meekly, the Shar put the shield, face up, on the cobbles between us. Then he said, "We've never seen anyone like you before."

I scoffed at that. "I got a different impression."

He knew what I meant, but waved it away. "Nobody who really looks at you would think.... You don't really look like a shave-tail; it's just that you don't look like anything else we've ever seen."

"I can believe that."

The Shar turned shining eyes to me. "I followed you to your hotel. The desk clerk told me you used to look like other Terrans, but you changed by drinking an elixir."

"Yeah. So?"

"I'm a goliard– Well, that's obvious."

I laughed. "Okay. I should have brought along that issue of National Geographic. I should have watched that orientation film. I don't know what you're talking about. And excuse me but, if I don't need to know, I don't want to know. I have enough trouble with my own culture, without a crash course in somebody else's."

"It's very simple," he said, evidently having decided that I needed to know. I had to wait for Budhi, anyway, so I listened.

"There's the Yol – the Way – the flow of nature, of relationships, of events, of history, of the universe. We call it the Yol. Those who follow the Yol are Yolan. I'm Yolan.

Some Yolan live in Yolanbayts – Yolan communities. They meditate and make up elixirs and explore the byways of the Yol. They provide schooling for the young, instruction in following the Yol, mediation of disputes.... I was a Shar: 'one who brings separate parts together to divide equally.' That's what this symbol means."

He pointed to a circle in the center of his shield. The circle was divided into various-sized sections, some smooth and some scored; I supposed that, for the symbol to mean what he said it did, the smooth and the scored came out even.

"Now," he continued, "a Yolan who leaves the Yolanbayt to go looking for revelry and luxury is a goliard." He put his paw-like hand on his chest. "I'm a goliard. My name is Tosun. Some call me Tosun Shar. You can call me Tosun, though."

"Why should I call you anything? What do we have to do with each other? And why are you following me?"

"That's simple, too. The Yol flows through all things, so all things are holy. But, if you worship everything, you can end up worshiping nothing. In the Yolanbayt, we have focal objects. Goliards find their own objects: it could be a body of water, a stone, a tree.... But goliards usually attach themselves to people – wealthy people, who can afford the extravagance, and worship the Yol through those people. Not the people, you understand, but the Yol that flows through them."

"I understand," I said. "But it still doesn't have anything to do with me."

"I choose you for my object."

"Oh, no, you don't." The last thing I needed was some self-indulgent young drop-out sponging off me; one more banana to juggle, when I had all the bananas I could handle as it was.

"I choose you," he said again. "You're all the colors of the people. This patch is gray, like me," he said, touching a patch of my hair, "and this one is black, like my stripes. This one," he touched my arm, "is like Budhi, and this one is like my uncle. This one is.... Well, you see? You're all the colors of all the people. And you're the only one like you anywhere. And you got that way through drinking an elixir. Do you understand?"

"I don't care. I've got my own problems. I wish you luck with yours."

"I don't have any problems," he said, smiling. "But thank you."

"Yeah, well, thanks for your thanks," I said.

Budhi came back and I rose to meet him. He looked pretty grisly, with blood caking in the fur around his mouth and speckled across his upper parts. I wondered if I looked better or worse.

"I got the forms," he said, "but I can't carry that many manuals with me. I can mark on the papers that they didn't get a manual, and they can claim one at any Registry in Wellki."

"Let's go, then. We both need to clean up." I started back to the hotel. Budhi walked at my left side. The Shar came up on my right.

"Go away," I said. "Get lost. Take a hike."

"I thought he was with you," Budhi said.

"So does he, but he isn't."

Tosun dropped back but, when I looked over my shoulder, I saw he was not too far behind, grinning like a press agent.

The desk clerk gasped when he saw us. He skirted the desk and advanced on Budhi with a spate of Marneri he hadn't picked up from the guidebook.

I stopped him, and told him about the wheelbarrow.

He began to croon over our injuries, praising Budhi for a hero. Talk about casting against type.

"Just get me to my room so nobody sees me," I said. "Budhi too. I, uh, feel safer with him around."

"Of course you do. Of course you do. You can go up in the service elevator. Oh, dear. Shall I call the hotel doctor?"

"No, just let me get to my room."

All this time, I was keeping an eye on the door. It didn't open, and I saw no gray brother pressing his face against the glass. But he was out there. I knew he was out there.

"One more thing," I said. "There's a ... a Yolan –Tosun Shar – following me."

"Goliard," said Budhi.

The desk clerk beamed. "I'm not surprised. Not surprised at all."

"Well, I don't want him following me."

"Then he won't. Not into this hotel, anyway. That, I can promise you."

The clerk took us through a door to a bank of rugged-looking elevators, and gave us directions to my suite's service entrance.

Once I was safe in my room, I had a strong urge to fall down. But I had a score to settle, first; I'd collapse later. I cleaned up, changed clothes, and doctored myself. Again, my coloring disguised the worst of my hurts, now that the blood was washed away. The scrape on my cheek went nicely with the patch of reddish-brown just under my left eye. The scratches on my head (which weren't very deep) I covered with a wisp of a hat.

When I came out into the sitting room and tossed a cold damp cloth to Budhi, he waved a booklet at me.

"This could have saved you a lot of trouble," he said.

"It could have saved somebody else a lot of trouble, too." I patted my hat tenderly. "How's the nose?"

"Mine? A little sore, but not too bad. That was a good punch. You'd have got away, if it hadn't been for the Shar."

"No–The door was shut."

"You'd have managed," Budhi said gloomily, sponging at the fur on his chest and arms.

"Leave that. Just clean your face enough to be comfortable. It won't do me any harm for you to look worse than I do – get me?"

Budhi nodded.

"This might just turn out to have been worth it," I said.

"Mem Moran?"

"Mm-hmm." I made a last check in the sitting room mirror.

"I wouldn't be him for plenty." Budhi went into the bathroom, holding the cloth over his lower face. I heard the sound of running water, and the squish of a cloth being wrung out more than once.

He came out, pressing his cheeks and chin with a hand towel.

"This is the best I can do without grooming," he said.

The fur around his mouth was clean, but slicked-down wet; it had obviously just been washed.

Dried blood still flecked his arms and chest.

"Perfect." I smiled grimly. "Let's go see who's in the Hospitality Suite. –Do you have any of those doo-dahs like

Tiph has? The collar and chain?"

"I think...." He rummaged in his chestpack. "Ahah!" He pulled out a paper packet. He tore it open and shook it out into my hands: a long, fine, golden chain with a loop on one end and a leather-like collar on the other that fastened with Velcro. The collar was a dull green and sparkled with yellow stones.

"That's extra," Budhi said.

We stopped outside the suite.

"Peek in," I said. "Is he in there?"

"Yes."

I put on the collar and gave the end of the chain to Budhi.

"You're about to make a delivery."

"But–"

"I know, but I want to see the look on Mem Moran's face when you do it."

"You're the Mistress."

Budhi pushed open the door and led me in.

It looked like just about everybody was there. The hotel had set up a buffet lunch, and the toadies were hopping from the table to their own special patrons with plates of goodies.

Marissa and Darryl sat together on a sofa. Tiph stood behind the Master, the end of her chain in his hand. Honey stood by his side. Jackie stood by hers.

My skin prickled when I imagined myself in that picture. If that Shar hadn't been there....

Darryl must feel pretty sure of himself, I thought. Even the Society might be outraged at his putting a brand on two of the party. Or maybe he felt sure of somebody else. Maybe Marissa was in on this with him. Maybe they all were.

No, that was paranoid. Marissa, maybe, but that crew couldn't build a sand castle together without two or three of them getting careless with beach balls.

Darryl was probably in it alone, counting on a boost from Marissa.

None of the Socialites looked to see who was coming through the door; Made-You-Look was part of the whole game. One of the reasons you supported toadies was so they could look for you.

I heard some chokes, some gasps, some startled near-laughter.

And the thud of a glass hitting plush carpet.

Jackie, of course, always looked up when people came in. Now he stared at me; so pale, his already white face was faintly blue.

I shook my head slightly, hoping he saw and knew what I meant, wishing I could have warned him, wishing that warning him had occurred to me.

"We're on," I said.

I would have liked to play this scene straight but, as usual, I would have to act the fool. I would have to make a show of pretending I believed the story I was going to tell, and let them read the truth between the lines. That way, if nobody important was scandalized, I wouldn't lose face; if somebody important was, their backlash would do me more good than my own.

Budhi led me toward the sofa.

The chattering Society grew silent, and turned to watch us as we passed.

Darryl stood up and came toward us, leading Tiph.

"I told you to deliver her to my room," Darryl said, in

an undertone. He smiled with his wine-colored lips, but his eyes looked like razor blades. "We want some time alone, before we make a public appearance together. Take her away."

"It's all right, Darryl," I said, real loud. "You're too modest. I must say, I misjudged you, and I'll be the first to admit it."

I faced the room. "Folks! Your attention, please!" I hadn't had to ask, but it's these little niceties that sell or scrap a show.

"Now, we all know that slavery is legal on Marner, but what we don't all know is that any people who aren't registered freehold can be forced into slavery. Even tourists. Even Terrans."

All right, there's no market for us. You only swear to tell the *whole* truth in court.

I went on, "Darryl found out about this forced slavery stuff from Budhi, here, and he gave Budhi a job. Darryl told Budhi to find me, and offer to show me around, and take care of me. He even paid him in advance. And Budhi earned that advance."

I held up my pink slip in one hand and waggled the slack of my chain with the other. Marissa stood and glared down at Darryl over the crags of her million-credit cheekbones.

"Completely open with each other?" she said.

Sounded like he had counted on Marissa's support without bargaining for it. *Oh, Darryl.*

"I was going to surprise you," Darryl said. "I planned for us to bring her in together. As a joke."

There was a soft rumble of protest, while I smiled and nodded; like I didn't hear what the dumb, stupid, idiot was saying.

Honey was too sozzled to grasp what was going on.

Jackie leaned forward over the back of the sofa, hope in every rounded line of him. I decided to wrap it up.

"I am now registered as a slave...." I said. Darryl hesitated, then stuck out his hand for the end of my leash. Budhi, a natural showman, handed it to me, as I finished, "To myself."

There was a gasp, a pause, and Zizi began to laugh. She handed her drink to a lapdog and applauded.

"That's right," I said, "let's hear it for Mem Moran! He found out about registering freehold, and he did that – Darryl did. Then he sent Budhi to take me to the Slave Exchange, where everything would be nice and legal, and register me. I ... uh ... persuaded Budhi to pause and reflect, and Budhi told me everything. I tell you, Darryl's a true friend. Just imagine–what if some creep had got ahold of me? Some jerk. Some worm. Some maggot."

I had to stop; they couldn't hear me over their laughter.

Tiph's eyes were nearly shut, her mouth open, her tongue showing. According to the National Geographic, that meant she was enjoying the proceedings greatly.

She didn't enjoy it, though, when Darryl, trying to bayonet me with his glare, began tightening her chain. She closed her mouth and the hair on the top of her head began to bristle. With a low, throaty growl, she braced herself. The delicate chain snapped off in Darryl's hand.

Darryl turned on her.

For a moment, they faced each other. Then Darryl said, with cool smoothness, "You didn't mean to do that, did you?"

Honey shuddered, but Tiph seemed to relax. I believe she took the question as a peace offering.

She sank to the floor at his feet and raised her palms. "The Master needs no chain."

"The Master likes chains," I said. I unfastened my collar and put it in one of Tiph's upraised hands. "Here, you can have mine."

I turned away from the charming tableau: Devotion, at the Feet of Dreadful Duty.

Jackie was still behind the sofa. When he saw me start toward him, he came to meet me.

"My God," he said, "you scared ten years out of me! What an act! How did you get the broker to go along with it? A bribe, or the power of your personality?"

"His name is Budhi, and it wasn't an act. Darryl paid him to enslave me. Darryl has similar plans for someone else, and I can just guess who." I nodded toward Honey, who turned her glass around and around, looking at Tiph.

The Mocskan woman fastened my collar above the one she'd come with. She handed the end of the leash to Darryl. He took up the slack, gave a playful tug, and then she stood.

"Get Honey another drink and get her to register freehold," I said. "If she doesn't have the credits, I'll pay and make her a present of herself, but she is not going into Darryl's inventory. And don't give me any of that 20th Century slobber about my better side winning out – I just want to stick it to Darryl. Right?"

"Absolutely."

"Budhi, write 'Not for Resale' or something on the bottom of the form."

"That isn't official."

"Do I care? It only has to *look* official, see?"

Jackie eased the broker and Honey away in a flow of chat.

Zizi and Marissa, trailing freeloaders like crumbs, both got to me at the same time. The glitter in their eyes told me that their blood was up. Somebody was going to get a great big bite taken out of him – or her – before this fever passed. Better shake my bells, or it might be me.

"Look," I said, opening my belt's biggest pocket. "I got an owner's manual and everything. This is going to be fun. Every morning I can get up early and bring myself hot chocolate in bed. If I don't move fast enough, I can shout and slap my face. Maybe I can get a little whip–"

"Is it true?" Zizi asked. "Did Darryl pay that cat-man to make you his slave? Darryl's?"

"Oh, Zizi! Not even Darryl would be that low. I told you, he paid Budhi to take care of me, and Budhi misunderstood. You can't possibly believe Darryl meant for him to... Oh, no, I won't hear of such talk."

Marissa looked at Darryl as a hunter might look at a boa that's managed to eat somebody else's baby and get away with it. He was hideous, he was detestable – but you had to admire the beast, somehow. So said her look, anyway.

"Imagine his not telling you about it," I said to her. "He probably just didn't want anybody to know what a softie he is underneath. When I think of all the nasty names I've called him over the years – did I ever call him a goggle-eyed, slab-sided, pie-faced, bugwit?–Well, when I think of all the nasty names I *have* called him, I could just weep. I could. And, just think, if he'd do this wonderful thing for me, as little as he thinks of me, he might have even better plans for people who matter."

They thought about that.

"Connie," Marissa said, "could I speak to you privately for a moment?"

"I don't have any secrets from Zizi. We're completely open with each other."

"And aren't you and I? Wasn't it I who went out of

my way to visit you on the set of your silly show? Wasn't it I who invited you to come with us, when the others only assumed someone else would do it? And aren't you the only one who can help me, when I have one of my horrible headaches?"

"Of course, darling." Trust Marissa to put my nursing her migraines in a list of favors *she's* done for *me* . "Please excuse us, Zizi." We winked at each other, behind Marissa's back. This was playing pretty well.

"You're making this up. Darry wouldn't have done this."

"You heard him – he admitted it."

"He said it was a joke."

"Spare me from such jokes. No, Budhi's a real broker, and he really..." I pantomimed twisting my arm behind my back, then biffing myself on the head, then finally said, "He really took me aside and told me about Darryl's ... concern."

Marissa allowed me a quirk of the left side of her mouth. "Spare me from such ... concern," she said. "In fact, I think I'll do just that, and register myself right now."

"You'll have to move fast if you want to beat the rush."

Zizi was drifting in Budhi's direction, pulling her satellites along with her. She stopped to say a word to Marcus.

Marissa could hop along when she needed to. She cut Zizi out by seconds.

I helped myself to some buffet and found Jackie again.

"Where is she?" I asked. "Honey?"

"I got her a plate of food and told her Darryl wanted her to eat something."

"Oh, well done! Her papers?"

"In her handbag. Now, give, in detail. What happened?"

I made it as short as I could. When I got to Tosun, I couldn't resist saying, "I told you he was following me."

Jackie didn't rise to it. "Go home," he said.

"Do what?"

"Go home. Take the first flight back. Go home." Jackie's warm brown eyes crimped, not just from his cigarette's smoke.

"You're worried. –Do you think I'm in serious danger? From That?" I wiggled a thumb at Darryl.

"It isn't funny. I never would have thought he'd go this far."

"Neither would I. But it's as far as he can go. Like you said, he isn't dumb enough to do anything out-and-out illegal, and he already tried the worst he could do within the law. I'm safe as houses. You just worry about Honey. I'm all right."

"I guess so."

"Sure. I'll tell you what: If you can talk Honey into going home, you and I will go with her. Okay?"

He gave me a lopsided smile. "Not much chance of that, is there?"

"I understand they do have cold days in Hell."

Jackie laughed.

"That's the way," I told him. "What are you so spooky about, anyhow? That isn't my blood in Budhi's fur – it's his."

"It is?"

"Oh, he bounced me around a little, but I'm an old snoot-popper from way back."

"You poked him in the nose?"

"He laid unwelcome hands upon my person. What was a lady to do?"

It did me good to see some of the tightness ease out of Jackie's face. He looked almost benevolently at Budhi, who was busily signing the socialites into bondage to themselves.

"While he's at it..." I said.

Jackie pulled his hand out of his pocket and showed me his pink slip.

"Good boy."

The Socialites were having a high old time, waving their registration forms at one another and giving Darryl the fish eye. His personal space was so empty it was practically a vacuum.

I knew better than to gloat, though. Darryl was far from through.

As I watched, Darryl sent Tiph, her new chain wrapped around her wrist, to carry a note to Marissa.

Marissa read it, looked quickly from Darryl to me and back to Darryl, and smiled. She held out a hand, and Darryl came and kissed it. The note fluttered to the floor.

Somebody's toady picked it up and read it before he handed it back.

Now, I thought, let's just see who he padded off to tell. Then I could follow along and winkle it out of.... Whose toady was he...? Bless my soul, he was between engagements, and he padded off to me.

"I thought you'd like to know," he said, "Darryl just told Marissa he bought you for her. He was going to give you to her and then tell her about freehold registration. Then, when they brought you in together, they'd tell everybody else. He said."

"Oh, no!" I cried. "Darryl was going to give me to Marissa? And I spoiled it? Oh, I could just spit!"

More laughter. More fish eye.

Darryl laughed along this time, and Marissa laughed, too. So Marissa was supporting him after all, convinced that she could swing the Society in his favor. Too bad; I wasn't gunning for Marissa, but if she wanted to put on a black hat and ride into Dodge with the bad guys, she'd just have to pay the price.

"They make a perfect couple," I said to the toady, knowing it would get around, "The Face and The Rear End. What a team."

The gathering broke up, after that. The hotel had a floor or two of duty-free shops, a mild-UV room, a pool, a casino, a fitness center, and so on. Plenty to do, for those who didn't want to do anything.

Me, I wanted to go back to my suite and twitch; it had been a little more morning than I could take in my stride.

The toady acted like going with me, but I shunted him off. Why? —when Number of Trucklers Attracted times Degree of Interest Engaged equals Rank? Maybe because I was a bit of a truckler myself, and I knew better than to twitch in front of a witness.

I told him to keep his ear to the ground and I'd get with him later. Maybe he would, or maybe he'd hint to Darryl and Marissa that I'd tried to get him to spy on them. I'd deal with all that later. Enough, for now.

Honey had chugged off in Darryl's train, so Jackie offered to walk me to my rooms. Lucky for me: as soon as I took his arm, my legs began to tremble.

He put his hand on mine. "Are you okay?"

"About what you'd expect from somebody who's been mugged, enslaved, hit up for a broker's commission on herself and laughed at for it. Why wouldn't I be okay?"

"I had to ask." He patted my hand and helped me down the hall.

After a short silence, I said, "Why do you do it? Why do you put up with me?"

"You know why. I'm not going to tell you, because you'd

just say I was a poor judge of character and I had you all wrong. But you know."

"That isn't fair. If I'm so swell, why don't you team up with me, like I asked you, instead of standing back like you're so superior, trying to make me feel bad when I score off of Honey? How am I supposed to function in this shoot-'em-up, if you keep getting in the line of fire? You'll get in my way once too often, Jackie, and I'll say something or do something we'll both be sorry for."

"If I can take it from Honey, I can take it from you."

"And why do you take it from her?"

He looked into the distance, into the past. "She's been working for me ever since she started modeling. She was about nineteen, I think. She used to be something. My top model." He paused. "I introduced her to Darryl."

"Jackie, people introduce people all the time. Introducing people doesn't make you responsible for what they do to each other."

"Responsibility is what you take."

"That's what I say: Why should you take responsibility for her? She doesn't want you to."

"I'm her friend."

We'd reached my suite. "Just a friend?"

"There's no such thing as 'just' a friend. —You want I should come in? Maybe we could have that game of Crazy Eights we didn't get to before."

"Crazy Eights. Yeah, maybe. Sure, come in."

"I don't mean to act superior," Jackie said, passing me as I swung the door wide. "I don't feel superior. I feel sorry —" He stopped talking, stopped moving.

"What's wrong?" I asked.

"You already have company," Jackie said.

Chapter 8

Tosun Shar, disarmed, sat on my couch in the attitude of a man roused from a first-rate sprawl.

"How did you get in?" I asked. "I told the desk clerk particularly to keep you out. He promised."

Tosun smiled and got up. "Only the Mother Ruler of the Western Paradise never blinks. The sunniest day casts the deepest shadows. And there's more than one way into a hotel."

"I see. Well, there's also more than one way out. Take your pick."

"Who is this?" asked Jackie.

"The man I told you was following me. Tosun Shar, the goliard who wants to worship at my feet. Through my feet, excuse me. –Where's your gear? Your knife and things?"

He motioned to the couch. "Under there. –I don't suppose you'd let me sleep on the floor by your bed?"

"On the floor by my–"

"Well, then. I saw that there's another bedroom, but I'd feel closer to you out here: only one door away instead of two."

Jackie sat down and made himself comfortable.

"I want you to leave," I said to Tosun. "I don't want a goliard. I don't want to be your object. I want you to go away."

"Rahzumiek," he said, making no move to go. "I understand. You're afraid you'll look foolish in front of your friends. People do sometimes laugh at goliards' objects, but they usually end up wishing they had somebody following them, too."

Now, that was a thought. I didn't mind looking foolish, of course, since that was what I did best. I didn't mind being laughed at, and I certainly didn't mind having something everybody else wished they had.

On the other hand, if this guy was my follower, that made me his leader, and leaders are accountable for their troops. I mean, this man wasn't a toady who knew he was trading his honor for some second-hand prestige.

I gave Tosun a good, long look. At about my height, he was short for a Mocskan. He was the color of pussy willows. Black stripes flared out in wedges around his rib cage. His ears were black, his nose was black, his lips were black (we had something in common, there). He wore nothing but his fur. Without his chestpack, weapons, and shield, he looked much younger and thinner than he had before.

He stood there, smiling and offering himself for the taking, and his eyes were so trusting, so open and innocent, I could have hit him with a brick. He might as well have been wearing a sign with "Easy Mark" on it in flashing lights.

"Go away," I said. I sat in a chair near Jackie's and rested my head and my eyes. I could hear Tosun go to the couch and drag his stuff out from under it.

"There's a lot of people in this party she's with?" he asked Jackie. "She said about fifty?"

"About fifty altogether, on this trip. About nine that call the tunes. The rest just dance."

"Is she the head of them?"

"On the contrary."

"Ha, ha," I said, not opening my eyes.

"Is she the richest of them?"

"One of the richest."

"Others of them are rich?"

"Yes."

"Will you describe the richest of them to me?"

"Why?" I asked.

"I told you," Tosun said. "I left the Yolanbayt for revelry and luxury. My object has to be rich."

I opened my eyes. "And that's all? Rich? No other requirements? Not decent, or productive, or kind, or brave? Not thrifty, clean or reverent?"

"No. The Yol also flows through the wicked and shiftless, the cruel and cowardly, profligate, dirty and obscene. So, all things being equal, all I require in an object is affluence. That's all I require of you; you're special, because of your colors and because you take elixirs–"

"I took one. One was plenty."

"Only the wise know plenty when they have it."

Jackie smothered a laugh.

"Just for the sake of conversation," I said, "what does an object do?"

"What the object wishes, so long as the object provides the goliard with food and shelter. And the occasional extravagant gift."

"I see. And what does the goliard do?"

"What the object wishes."

I thought about some of the objects he'd have available in our little group. I thought of the sorts of things they wished from people who were, supposedly, out for themselves; and I thought of Tosun, out only to please his object. I thought of Tiph in Darryl's power. I thought of this boy in Marissa's.

"Look elsewhere," I said. "We'll only be on Marner for three months."

"Three months are three months." He wriggled into his chestpack.

"These people are killers. Not murderers, not of the body, but... Some of them like to hurt people. The rest of them don't mind seeing people get hurt."

"Rahzumiek." Tosun buckled his shield onto his chestpack.

"No, you *don't* understand. You don't know what you're walking into."

Tosun smiled. "I'm walking into whatever the Yol leads me to." He buckled on his belt, and made sure his knife and skewer were firmly seated in their scabbards.

"Wait a minute."

"Will you describe the richest of your friends?"

"No, no, no."

"Introduce me, then?"

"No!"

He smiled again. I was getting pretty tired of his eternal good nature.

"That's all right. I'll find what I'm looking for. I'll wait in the hall until one of your friends comes out."

I tried to catch Jackie's eye, but he was staring into the empty fireplace. Okay, he was asking for it.

"Oh, Tosun."

"Yes, Mem?"

"Jackie's rich."

Jackie shook his head. "I'm wealthy. That's not the same thing. Rich people have money; wealthy people have inventory."

"All you have to do is feed him, and throw him a belt or

a scarf or something once in a while."

"I'm a goliard," Tosun said to me. "Not a pet."

"Besides, everything I make goes back into the business. That's the only way to keep your head above water."

"That's what my Uncle Shahtsi says. You won't do, then."

"Sorry. No."

They both looked at me.

"I won't do, either. No. This Season is everything to me. If I play it right, I'll leave Marner one of the inner circle, with a guaranteed place that can go up or down but never Out. If I play it wrong, I'll leave as a nothing; a bootlicker without a boot to lick. Jackie doesn't understand what that means to me, so I don't expect you to, but it means everything to me. It means everything."

"I understand that this time on Marner is important to you," Tosun said. "Why it is, I don't have to understand. Are you afraid I'll interfere with what you do out of scruples of my own? I promise you, I won't."

"No, that isn't it at all."

"She's afraid," Jackie said, "that you'll get in her way. She's afraid that you'll get caught in the machinery and she'll have to decide whether to stop the line or let you go through the gears. She already has me to worry about, so I guess she thinks you'd be one too many."

"You're one too many," I told Jackie. "And I'm not worried. I know what I'll do if anybody gets in my way. I know." I was so strung out and weary, my voice was shaking. "So take him down there, if you're so interested in helping him find an object. Introduce him, if you want to."

"To Darryl Moran?"

"He won't be the first," I said, and wished I hadn't.

"There's a limit." Jackie stood up. "Come on – what's your name? –Tosun?"

"Where are we going?"

"Maybe knock on a few doors."

"Don't try to bluff me," I said.

"Don't I know the name Darryl Moran?" said Tosun. "Isn't he the one who tried to enslave my gamba?" He gestured to me.

"Whatever a gamba is, I am not your one."

"The object I prefer," Tosun corrected himself.

"If the Yol flows through the wicked," Jackie said, "Darryl's full of it. And he'd love to be your object."

"Go ahead and take him, then. What are you waiting for? Am I supposed to jump up and clutch your lapels and dissolve in a flood of tears? 'Oh, please, please, I didn't mean it, I take it all back, boo-hoo-hoo!' Don't hold your breath. I have troubles of my own. I don't care about his. Or yours."

Tosun sat down at my feet. "She doesn't mean it," he told Jackie. "She's tired. She's sorry for what she said to you, too. She'll apologize later."

"I can speak for myself. I have a mouth."

"Ain't it the truth," said Jackie.

I put my hands on the arms of my chair and looked away. It seemed to take forever to make the movements, and I seemed to see myself making them before I felt them in my body.

"You are tired, aren't you?" said Jackie.

"I'm all right."

"I've never seen you run out of rope before."

"You're going to see me hang myself, if you don't kick this Yolan out of here."

"Kick him yourself," said Jackie. "You have a foot. All you have to do is take it out of your mouth."

I turned my head back to face the men. "All right. I'm sorry. I really am very, very sorry I said the thing about introducing him to Darryl. I really am. But I don't care, and I won't be his gamba."

Jackie lifted me to my feet and put an arm around me. "I'll tuck you in before I leave."

"And then throw the goliard out of the hotel if not the window. Hire guards for all the doors. I'll pay."

"If my object wished me to go," Tosun said, "I'd go."

"What?"

"I do as my object wishes. If you were my object, and you told me to leave, I would leave."

"That's blackmail. And it doesn't make sense." At least, I didn't *think* it made sense. "Okay. If that's what it takes to get rid of you, consider me your object. Now leave."

~*~

When I woke up, it was evening. Purple dusk filled the air outside my windows, and the mountains to the west were wreathed in mist.

Jackie was gone, Tosun was gone; I was alone, and alone was how I liked it.

I felt rotten. I liked that, too. It made me mad, and mean, and ready for anything anybody wanted to try on me.

I moved around the suite, practicing not groaning. Being knocked down and sat on hurts more than your pride; I ached all over. The scratches on my scalp were beginning to sting, too.

A warm shower and a little Neosporin would help all that, but where was the help for that little pink paper?

What Home Remedy was a sure cure for selling yourself into slavery? Even to myself, even to spite Moran, selling myself into slavery.... I resented it. I had had no choice, and I resented that even more.

So what? What could I do about it?

"Do your best, and leave the rest." That's what Aunt Bootsie always told me to do.

Trouble was, Darryl had made it clear he wasn't going to let me leave anything. He had declared all-out war on poor old Connie, with no quarter given or asked. Maybe the best I could do would be to sweeten up The Face, and make Darryl invest his own status in his dirty work.

Dirty work coming to mind, I thought of how close I'd come to wrapping a tentacle around young Tosun the Shar. The work wouldn't have been any less dirty because he was asking for it. Some people won't take "no" for an answer.

Come to think of it, he *hadn't* taken "no" for an answer.

Well, he'd have to do his worshiping from afar, if he did it at all. Maybe I could send to TerraNet Central for an 8 X 10 glossy, and autograph it for him. "To Tosun Shar, the best darned goliard a gal ever had. Love and kisses from your old object, Connie."

I had my shower, and I salved my wounds. Now: What to wear? Something important and serious had happened to me, and I was struggling grimly toward belonging. So, this being the Good Society, and me being me, I needed something almost offensively stupid.

I had just the thing. It was gold brocade, too short, too full; bouffant sleeves, low neck; with a matching hat just big enough to cover the salve slick on my head. Not a Jackie Eastman original; I had bought it at the DAV for half a credit, hat included. I stuck gold and topaz fringes around the rims of my ears, and admired the effect. There was no patch or blotch on me that didn't clash till it shimmered. I coated my blackened lips with gold-flake gloss and went hunting for the party.

I half expected to find Budhi in the upper lobby, selling collars and chains, but I guess the Socialites weren't as dippy as I thought – not quite.

I didn't try to make an entrance this time. I didn't have to. Darryl and Marissa stopped holding court when I came in, anyway, and looked me over and laughed.

I pretended I didn't understand. "What's so funny?"

"I am sorry," said Marissa. "I thought you were joking. Lovely dress."

"Yes," said Darryl. "Reminds me of the toilets at the Palace of Versailles."

"They don't have toilets at the Palace of Versailles. You must have been standing in front of a mirror."

It was that kind of party, all night long. I circulated, being as jolly and harmless as a jelly bean. I hoped Marissa would sidle up to me again for another private conference, but she seemed to be throwing all her weight behind Darryl.

Darryl, on the other hand, wouldn't leave me alone. He would think up a good one and find me in the crowd and toss it out. If it really was a good one, I'd answer it. Usually it was pathetic, and I'd just say, "You got me that time, junior. Ow, it hurts." Drove Darryl nuts.

Marissa didn't take any shots at me after that first one. She just fed lines to Darryl and let him take the flak.

Nice party.

And, all the while, Tiph followed Darryl around at the full extent of her chain. I told them they were a hazard to navigation, but neither one of them seemed to care.

Jackie watched Honey, and Honey watched Tiph. The evening wore on, but the malice in Honey's stare never lessened or wavered. Tiph's chain took a droop as she moved closer and closer to her boss.

Very nice party.

~*~

The next afternoon we went in convoy to the river in ten-passenger omnibuses, each omnibus pulled by a team of twelve Mocskan slaves.

Jackie, the Egg-on-the-Face Club, and I found ourselves loaded with my pal Face and the Moran menagerie.

I slumped in my seat and pretended to doze off.

Since I seemed to be unavailable for twitting, Twitmaster Darryl started in on Jackie.

"I thought you were morally opposed to slavery," he said. "But here you are, riding in a slavedrawn carriage, about to be rowed up the river by slaves to a resort staffed by slaves. Don't you have any principles? Don't you have any backbone?"

"Darryl...." Jackie lit a cigarette, "...when you start wearing women's clothes, I'll start answering your stupid questions. How about it?"

I could have pretended I was snorting in my sleep, but I don't think they would have bought it.

"What about you?" Darryl asked. "The same question applies to you. Doesn't it just make you sick inside?"

I looked at him for a long moment and shook my head. "You make it too easy." Louder, I said, "I never claimed I had any principles, or any backbone. 'When in Rome,' and all that."

We weren't being any fun, so Darryl and Marissa put their heads together and whispered and giggled the rest of the way. So much for me sweetening up The Face.

We disembarked at the riverfront. The quay was cobblestone, made gay by stone flowerpots overflowing with bright-blooming plants. Small-to-moderate-sized ships and boats passed, or bobbed at anchor. A wooden gangplank led from the quay to the deck of a long narrow boat; the arch at the ship's end of the gangplank was hung with a banner saying, "Welcome aboard, Moran party." A canopy shaded the deck, and oars stuck out the sides from below, where the galley slaves sat.

We pulled out of the dock, easing through an undergrowth of smaller craft and other tour boats.

We went slowly until we'd passed between the first range of high, narrow mountains, and plains of scrubby bluish vegetation opened up on either side. Then the splash of the oars changed tempo and we picked up speed.

It was shortly after that when I noticed people drifting toward the stern. Jackie and I drifted, too.

A Mocskan was sitting on a heap of pillows, plucking a little harp with his claws. Jocelyn Demmarie had set up her Lasernova and was improvising with him to the plash of the oar strokes.

He was short for a Mocskan, the color of pussy willows with black stripes like ribs around his sides; his chestpack and weapons were stuffed behind him.

"Look who's here," said Jackie.

Tosun. Now, why had I supposed he could be trusted to do what he said he'd do? People are people, even when they're covered with fuzz.

As soon as he saw me, he stopped playing. Jocelyn looked up and broke off in the middle of a twiddly bit.

"What happened? Keep playing."

"As my gamba wishes."

"You promised you'd go away," I said, more in sorrow than in anger.

"I did go away. I didn't even go away and come right back; I went altogether someplace else and waited."

"This is true." He was still here, calling me his gamba, and I still didn't want him here, calling me his anything, but he had kept his word. I felt much better, somehow.

"You know each other?" said Ivor.

"We've met," I said.

Marissa pretended to try to smother a laugh and said, "The captain says he's some kind of defrocked priest, looking for action."

"That isn't quite how he explained it to me, but I guess it's something like that."

"She's agreed to be my gamba," said Tosun. "My picture, my image, my icon; the object through which I worship the All and the Eternal. And I'm her goliard. At her service, in her service." He came and sat at my feet and raised his palms to me, like Tiph had done to Darryl when she'd snapped her chain.

"Listen carefully," I said, doing American Sign Language on his upraised palms and speaking slowly in Tudolinguo, "'I am not your holy picture. Jump off the boat and drown yourself.'"

He dropped his palms and looked up at me. His lips parted and he started huffing with that wheezy Marneri laughter.

The captain translated for those who didn't speak Tudolinguo.

"Just a minute." Darryl stepped forward. "Don't tell him

that; why waste him? Somebody else might want him, if you don't. You don't have any paper on him, do you?"

Tosun rose and stood by my side.

"That's Darryl Moran," I said. "He wants you to be his goliard. A smart guy would rather jump off the boat and drown himself."

Darryl's fingers twitched. I decided I'd better shovel out some more discretion, or next time he caught me alone he'd punch me again – try to, anyway. I didn't want to drive him to that point; he enjoyed it too much.

Darryl was letting Tiph carry her own chain this afternoon, but she still stayed at his heels. She had been standing beside him, facing away from Honey, and toward – I thought – the Master. But, when Tosun moved, she turned to keep him full in sight. Now she whispered to Darryl, "Let him be your goliard, if he offers, Master. I like the looks of him."

Tosun bobbed his head to Tiph four or five times and smoothed the fur around his muzzle with his pads.

Darryl looked at Tiph as if she'd grown a second nose. "You like the looks of him?" He laughed, and Tiph stepped back, her eyes wide in surprise. "What do I care if you like the looks of him?"

Tosun cocked his head. Tiph bristled, but held her peace. The captain made a noise of disgust and stamped away, and I had the delightful feeling that Darryl had just put his foot in it.

"I like the looks of him, too," Marissa said. "He looks sweet. Would you like to be at my service?"

This wouldn't do. This was just what I had been afraid of. No, I didn't want him but–call me a dog-in-the-manger – I didn't want Darryl or Marissa to have him, either.

"What about Jocelyn?" I said. "Think of the music.

Jocelyn, wouldn't you like an accompanist?"

Jocelyn flickered a glance from me to Marissa to Darryl and back. "I don't want to get into it."

Darryl spread his thin lips as if he were smiling. "Into what?"

"Anything." She began playing softly, looking past all of us at the scenery slipping by.

"I guess it's just between the two of us," Darryl said to Marissa. "What shall we do, bid?"

"Wait till you're asked," said Tosun.

"Spirited youth," said Darryl. "Well, go on and ask."

Tosun turned to me. "I don't want to be released from my service to you, but I'll accept my liberty if you force it on me." When I didn't say anything, he went to his chestpack and pulled something out of it. Something that crackled as he unfolded it. He brought it back to where Darryl and Marissa and I stood and handed it to me.

It was pink. The seller's name was Tosun; the space for the buyer's name was blank.

I remembered Tosun telling me that some Marneri, ones who renounce their worldly goods (like Religious, I had said), cancel their papers. That meant they were anybody's who took them. Tosun was one.

"Budhi could have claimed you as well as me."

Tosun nodded. "If he'd wanted to, although goliards–" he grinned wickedly, "–are in less demand than Terrans. But I wouldn't have stopped him. The Yol–"

"When you're quite through," said Darryl. "Let me see that paper."

"What's to stop me from selling you to somebody else, if I accepted you, just like any other slave?"

"Nothing."

"What's to stop me from buying you and giving you to yourself?"

"My vows. Yolan can't own slaves."

"I have vows of my own. Don't they matter?"

"Only you can say what matters to you. As for me: it's you or them."

Darryl snatched at Tosun's paper. "Let me see that."

"Just a minute. Don't be so grabby."

Where did principles and backbone come into this? Was it principled to own another person?

Was it principled to let Darryl own him? But what was I going to do–run around after Darryl all Season, and dash out with a fistful of credits every time he looked like buying somebody?

No, but....

Tosun watched me, waiting for my decision. He didn't understand. He didn't care. He wasn't afraid.

He wasn't asking me to be afraid for him, either. Why should I–

Darryl grabbed for the paper again.

I whipped out a pen and put my scrawl on the dotted line. To the glee of everyone who'd yawned in my face when I'd moralized on the evils of slavery, I bought a man, and paid for him with a token credit.

Probably worth about thirty pieces of silver.

Now I was really part of the gang. Christians aren't as joyful when a lost lamb returns to the fold as villains are when the lamb turns out to have been a wolf all the time.

Chapter 9

Tosun and I found Captain Margent, and went with him to his cabin to have our transaction notarized and registered.

"Now," Tosun said to me, as the captain shook my hand, "what shall I call you? Mistress?"

I thought I was going to be ill. "No."

"Gamba?"

"That makes me feel like something you make out of tomatoes and okra. Connie's my name; call me Connie."

"I'd like to call you Managlawn."

Captain Margent coughed to cover a wheeze of laughter.

"Managlawn? What's that mean?"

"It sort of means 'many-colored.'"

"Mm-hmm. What else does it sort of mean?"

"Sometimes people – entertainers of a certain kind – tie or fasten lots of colored ribbons to their fur. It's traditional. That form of decoration is called managlawn."

"Entertainers of what certain kind?" I asked, although I had a good idea. When Tosun hesitated, I said, "The tumbling, juggling, dancing, singing, joking, comic acting kind?"

"You know about them?"

"We have them on Earth. We call them clowns."

"'Clowns.'" Tosun wrapped his mouth around the new word, savoring it.

"Their traditional dress is called 'motley.'"

"'Motley.'"

"It means 'many-colored.'"

"Fancy that!" said Captain Margent. "And is Motley a girl's name, too?"

"A what?"

"Managlawn," said Tosun, "is a minor name for the Mother Ruler of the Western Paradise. It was a very popular name for Mocskan females a long time ago, but you don't hear it much now. Still, I like it."

"I had a grandmother named Managlawn," said the captain. "Grand old girl."

"That's me, all right." *Managlawn. Many-colored. Clown.* I liked the sound of it, and the meaning certainly fit. Then, too, Tosun calling me by another name made me feel like it wasn't really me that owned a slave; it was that other person with that other name.

"Okay, you can call me that. But, if anybody asks you what it means, lay off the Mother Ruler stuff."

"It's no shame to talk about her. The Mother Ruler is a fiction, true; only a manifestation of Reality, but everybody talks about her as if she were real. Everybody knows she's only a sort of a mental focal object, but–"

"That's tremendously interesting, and I don't dispute the point. All I'm saying is, if you don't want her – or what she stands for – and me – hooted at by those hyenas, don't mention the connection. Get it?"

"Got it."

"Good. Now go play."

"Will you come listen?"

"Sure, sure."

"No, wait," said Captain Margent. "I'd like a word with you, if you please, Mem."

I nodded. "Go on," I told Tosun. "And don't let them pump you."

"Pump me?"

"Get information about me out of you without you knowing they're doing it."

Tosun shook his head. "Managlawn, my gamba, you don't know me yet."

When we were alone, Captain Margent had trouble coming to the point. He drew his eyebrows into knots, as if speaking were an effort. He ran his claws through the smoky gray fur around his broad face and scratched his pale pink nose.

After a couple of harrumphs, he said, "I'm speaking out of turn, but.... The way you and the Shar go on, I'm hoping you won't report my presumption, and you might be able to drop a hint where I couldn't. —Hasn't your friend with the slave read his owner's manual?"

"He isn't my friend, and I doubt if he has. I haven't read mine, either, to tell you the truth. I plan to, though. I plan to make notes in the margins."

"Good. That's the way to do it. If you're going to take on the responsibility of ownership, you owe it to yourself to know the law and what you face if you break it. My owners at Muimmea Transport are famous for going by the book, and they've never had an action against them, not in two hundred years of operation."

He nodded, more to himself than to me, and continued, "I've carried many an owner in my years on this run, and I know the signs of one that's heading straight for trouble."

When I didn't speak, he said, "I'm talking about your friend."

That was good news. "I told you, he's not my friend. What kind of trouble is he heading for?"

"For one thing, doesn't he know.... Well, not to be

indelicate, but.... Doesn't he know a female when he sees one? Aren't you a female? Same general shape as ours? Mem Moran's slave, for example: she's a female. Same as you?"

"Yes."

"Female meaning the one who bears the young?"

"Potentially, yes."

"Po– Ah, I get your meaning. They can, but they don't have to. Same as here. But, because they can, and because the choice is theirs, aren't your females revered, like ours are? I mean, the only source of people.... They bring us to life, deep in their bodies, and let us grow there, tucked away safe, and feed us with their flesh and blood, and bring us out when we're ready, and guard us with their teeth and claws until we can fend for ourselves."

The captain's pale gray eyes shone; I made a mental note to teach him "'M' Is for the Many Things She Gave Me" before I left the resort.

"Our females," he said, "are our Prime Citizens, the Powers that Be. Naturally. Aren't yours?"

"Our females have the babies. The resemblance ends there. Don't get me wrong; our females don't take any guff. It isn't because we're given our due, though, it's because we've made refusing to take any guff a habit."

"Then Mem Moran isn't used to talking to Terran females the way he talked just now to his slave?"

"Mem Moran talks ugly to anybody he can get away with talking ugly to. Male, female – Mem Moran is an Equal Opportunity lout."

"Well, on Marner he'd better limit his abuse to free males, and treat slaves and female Marneri with respect. Maybe you could drop a word in his ear. He might take the warning from you; I don't think he'd take it from me."

"I don't think he'll take it from me, either, but...."

"Do what you can, will you? I don't like to see anybody run aground if I can steer them clear with a timely word."

"What kind of trouble are we talking about, here? I saw a piece of an orientation film.... Are we talking the Big Walk here? Death?"

The captain began to laugh, then stopped and fixed me with a stare.

"You know your friend better than I do. Is he that bad?"

"I'm asking *you* . I'll read the manual; do you want to hit some highlights for me, or do you just want to drop dark hints?"

Captain Margent held out a palm and tapped it with a forefinger as he itemized his list.

"First, disrespect toward a female is ... barbaric. It just isn't done. Second, contempt toward a slave is also just not done. Neither thing is actionable, but it puts people off. People won't like him."

"He's used to that. What else?"

"If he mistreats her – neglects her welfare, or physically abuses her – she has the right to file a complaint against your friend. He can be fined, or even jailed."

"He isn't my friend. I think stir would look good on him. What else?"

"If the abuse is bad enough, she can beg sanctuary from a protector in the name of the Empress. That's mandatory prison for your friend, though it takes a few weeks to process and he'll probably leave planet before he comes to trial – that's the way aliens usually do things, I'm told. If he abuses her while she's in protective asylum, he's really in trouble. That's an aggravating circumstance, and that carries heavier penalties. If he kills her...."

"No, he won't kill her. It takes either guts or passion to

kill, and Moran is a stranger to both. He might scare her; he might even try hurting her some, but he doesn't put enough stock in people to kill them."

"If he kills a slave, he's a dead man. The Empress doesn't care whether one of the witnesses carries out the sentence, or whether he's saved for public execution. He's dead. Tell your friend that, will you?"

I started to tell the captain, yet again, that Moran was not my friend. Then I realized that he used the term as a way to avoid saying Darryl's name.

"Thanks, Captain, I'll see what I can do."

I knew one thing I could do; I could stand back and watch while Darryl went full speed toward a sand bank. It would do me good, I thought, to see Moran spend vacation in the clink. Kind of hard on poor old Darryl, not to mention Tiph, but hey – I didn't make the world, I just came with a tour group.

On the other hand, if Darryl was going to get into trouble, it would be safer – and a lot more fun – if I tried to light him across the bar and shook my head sadly when he ignored me.

I went back to the impromptu party in the stern. Darryl was there, lounging on cushions with my pal Face. Jackie stood by Tosun and Jocelyn.

I headed their way but got sidetracked by Honey, nearly sober, holding the business end of Tiph's leash. I was always surprised at how tall Honey was. At almost six feet, she was taller than all of us but Marcus and Hurst, and heavier than even they were. Of course, she squinched down some, hoping to get in good with Darryl by making herself shorter than he was, but you can't keep yourself squinched down from five-eleven to five-seven-and-three-quarters all the time.

Now, with the drink not on her and her spine unkinked, she looked a fine figure of a woman. I almost told her so. I opened my mouth to tell her, but she spoke before I could.

"Where's yours?" She twitched Tiph's chain. "Aren't you afraid he'll run away?"

"Afraid he'll run away? I'd pay his passage on the underground railroad if he'd run away."

"Of course you would. You snapped him up fast enough when it looked like Darry might buy him, though. Are you a spoil-sport, or just a hypocrite?"

"I'm a philap ... a phila ... a good-deed-doer."

"You're a meddlesome.... You're like a Jack-in-the-box. Always jumping up in people's faces. Darry's only teasing you when he pays attention to you. He's only pretending, you know."

I was glad to hear it; or would have been, if I'd thought she spoke from assurance rather than hope.

Tiph's cream-colored ears were flattened against the sides of her head, and she looked at Honey the same way she had begun to look at Darryl.

Jackie or no Jackie, enough was enough.

"I'm surprised Darryl trusts you with his trained monkey," I said.

"Darryl knows he can trust me with anything," said Honey.

"I was talking to Tiph."

"That wasn't funny, was it, Tiph?" Honey asked.

"No, Mem Clayton."

"Connie Phelan isn't funny at all, is she?"

"No, Mem Clayton."

"Tell her she isn't funny at all."

Tiph turned to me. "You aren't funny, at all."

"I'm glad to hear it," I said. "Because I'm not trying

to be funny now." I straight-eyed Honey, willing her to listen with her mind, not just her ears. "Tiph came with a manual. Before you start trying to please your flea-brained sweetheart by poking at Tiph with a sharp stick, you'd better read it."

Honey's eyes shifted.

"They aren't treating you right, are they?" I said to Tiph.

Darryl joined us before she could answer.

"Darry! Connie's trying to make trouble, as usual."

"Not trouble between us." He put an arm around Honey's waist and gave her a squeeze. "She couldn't do that, could she, Honeybunch?"

Honey gazed down at her darling with enough adoration to gag a Magi and shook her head.

"This is touching," I said.

"She's jealous," Honey stage-whispered. She giggled as Darryl hugged her again.

"Gosh, who wouldn't be? Just looking at you two kids makes me all misty-eyed. In fact, I feel so darn tender, I'm going to do you two a favor. I don't know why, because it can't possibly profit me, but I am."

Darryl gave me a thin smile. "An altruist. This is a new side of you, Connie."

"I was telling Honey, you'd better read that owner's manual that came with Tiph." I moved closer to the lovebirds, though I felt like a dinosaur edging up to the tar pits on a dare. "She could o-gay to ourt-cay if you don't atch-way out-way. Get me?"

Darryl didn't understand Tudolinguo, but Pig-Latin was about his speed. He wasn't impressed, though. "It's sweet of you to care, but I'm not afraid of someone I own. If I thought I needed to be...."

...It wouldn't be good for the someone. He didn't have to finish that sentence for me to see how it would end. Tiph stood like a stone, pretending she wasn't listening, which was probably wise.

I gave it one last shot, because I'd promised the Captain, and because the only thing worse than a Yahoo is an ignorant Yahoo.

"Call me a meddlesome Jack-in-the-box– No, wait, Honey just did that – Anyway, take it easy on women and slaves, or you could land in deep trouble. That's what I was told, and I thought I'd pass it along to a fellow Terran. We've had our differences – all in fun, of course – but if it's Us against Them, I've gotta side with Us."

Providing, I told myself, Darryl and Honey are Them.

"Women are powerful medicine on Marner," I went on, hearing the hollow ring of words falling on deaf ears. "Slaves have legal rights. Now we all know how you handle women–" Honey giggled again, "–and I'm sure you're a natural-born slave driver, but just be careful. One Terran to two others, okay? It's hard to bill and coo in the calaboose, I would imagine."

"You're a doll." Darryl winked at me.

The music played on, while Honey and I both ground our teeth till they squeaked.

Served me right for not trying to be funny.

The Tammi Resort Lodge snuck up on us. We rounded a bend in the river, and we were there.

It was a strange-looking place. I'd seen pictures, like I said before, but seeing pictures is a far cry from being there, even seeing life-size holograms. This looked like something designed by Roger Dean in the last half of the twentieth century.

Like the buildings in Muimmea, the resort structures were rounded; all the windows were circles and all the doors were ovals. The rooms seemed to grow out of the ground on arches or spiral stems; their roofs were covered with sod and wildflowers. They looked like mushrooms, tree roots, foam, and meringues with sprinkles, all at the same time. All the staircases curved, all the walls curved, all the connecting corridors, stairways, walkways, and paths curved.

Each suite was a separate unit, raised on its own stem, with no unit overlooking any other unit's windows. Each suite contained a sitting room and one, two, or three bath/dressing/bed rooms. Mine had two.

The beds were crazy: in each bath/dressing/bed room was what looked like a bubble, squashed against the ceiling; to get into the bubble, you went up a set of steps through a hole near the bubble's bottom. Inside, there was a mattress, a light, a shelf for books and a water jug, and controls for temperature, music, and scent. Like a uterus, with amenities. Womb service.

The inside walls of the resort were plastered, with pictures or designs painted on. There wasn't any furniture; just lumps, humps, snuggles and plains of soft carpeting. The shower was an oval; even the john was a rounded cube.

"Very nice," said Tosun. "I could get used to this. How long are we going to be here?"

"About ten standard weeks," I said. "Then back to Muimmea for a couple of days, then we go home. And you? Back to the whatsit?"

"The Yolanbayt?" Tosun unloaded his weapons in the sitting room. Since there was no couch to shove them under, he tucked them into a nook made into the wall. "I doubt it. I guess I'll find another gamba. Maybe I'll ingratiate myself with the management here, and take up residence. Maybe I'll go off into the caves inland and spend some time with the Omata. They don't follow the Yol, but they have a superstitious respect for Yolan. Especially Shar Yolan."

"What's the Omata?"

"That's the name of a people, like I'm a Mocskan. Omata means 'man-eat.'"

"Translate that a little more clearly, please."

"They eat people."

Clear enough. "Cannibals? You mean they eat people like you, or people like me– Terrans?"

"They eat anybody they can get. Not very often, though; you have to volunteer to be eaten, and not many people care to do that anymore."

"You surprise me. –Are you making this up?"

Of course he wasn't making it up.

"Ask the Manager – she'll tell you. This resort is almost in the exact center of the Omata reservation. In fact, 'tammi' is the Omata word for river. Also for noodle, which makes sense."

I could hardly wait to tell. Either Darryl knew, and I could torpedo his surprise; or he didn't know, and I could drop a live grenade in his lap at dinner. I could hardly wait.

~*~

The dining room was held, by a web of gently arched corridors, suspended over the river. The tables were long, and curved in random ways, so that a diner at one table might be tucked into a bend in another table.

Hanna Hobbs was on my left, Ivor DePere on my right. Tosun was across from me, and Jackie was at my back.

"Isn't this enchanting?" asked Hanna.

"I'll tell you after I see a menu," I said. "Good thing we have a translator here. I don't want to order something with a fancy Marneri name and then find out I've been eating Roast Leg of Insurance Salesman."

"What are you babbling about now?" Darryl asked from two tables over.

"I'm saying I may go vegetarian until we get back to Muimmea. Didn't you know?" I made my voice loud enough for everyone to hear me. "We're in the middle of cannibal country here. So help me. Ask Tosun."

Darryl's smile became fixed. He hadn't known. He had probably sold the Society on Tammi Resort because it had offered him the biggest kickback.

"How colorful," he said.

"Ordinarily you wouldn't have to worry," I told him. "They're man-eaters. Unfortunately, Tosun tells me they aren't that particular."

"But they are," Tosun said. "They have a highly-developed cuisine, with a different style of preparation and a different set of recipes for children, young men, young women, old men, and old women. They even have separate sets of cookware and dishes for each, so the flavors don't—"

"Oh, my God!" somebody said, and somebody else laughed helplessly.

"But Tosun tells me they only eat volunteers," I said. "So don't let's anybody volunteer, okay?"

The headservitor, a Mocskan, caught the drift of our talk. She deployed slaves (with free wine) to assure us that the hotel served no two-legged flesh in the main dining room.

Still, we all amused ourselves by appealing to Tosun for

translations and contents of Marneri dishes. The inevitable jokes about "filet of sole," "rump roast," and "ladyfingers," notwithstanding, it was a pleasant meal for me.

Darryl tried to get somebody to pay attention to him – I mean, he had a slave, too, and he'd had his first – but nobody would.

After dinner, we drifted up a staircase to a party room. Its floor was even with the dining room's roof; in fact, it wrapped part way around and let onto it. Like all the other mushroom caps, this one was a miniature meadow. A railing of something transparent turned it into a belvedere, very pleasant on such a clear and balmy evening as this one.

Tosun produced his clawharp and followed me around, playing softly. I decided this gamba stuff wasn't so bad, after all. I started wondering what sort of extravagant gift my goliard would appreciate.

What a swell time I was having. What swell people these were. I couldn't figure out why I was having such a good time. Then I realized that Darryl and Marissa hadn't come up with us. They had returned to their suite, with Honey and Tiph and an assortment of running-dog flunkies, for a party they could pretend was ultra-exclusive. I didn't see Jackie, so I assumed he had gone along, in his capacity as human safety net.

Well, that explained it, but it was too good to last.

By the time they showed up, though, the party was on cruise control and nobody was in the mood for drama – high, low, or otherwise.

I would have ignored the lot of them, but Jon Hister, the dog who was running for the office of my flunky, found me on the belvedere and insisted on making a report.

"Wait'll I tell you," he said.

"If it's about Moran and his Harem from the Black Lagoon, I don't want to hear it."

"It's a secret."

Since he put it that way, I did want to hear it. Knowledge is power. So all right – trivial knowledge is petty power, but there it is, all the same.

"Give."

"I went with them to their suite. I thought you'd want me to."

"'Well done, thou good and faithful servant.'"

"Huh? Anyway, Honey's handbag fell off one of those ledges cut in the walls. Everything spilled out. I put it all back, but I looked at her pink slip while I had it. You'll never guess what she's done."

"I don't want to guess what she's done." I could, though.

"She sold herself to Darryl."

"But I told Budhi to write something on the paper...."

"I wouldn't know about that, but I saw the signatures."

"When was it dated?"

"Today. The place of transfer was Tammi Resort. They must have done it as soon as they got off the boat."

"How much did he give for her?"

"Two credits. Just a token payment, of course. –Twice what you gave for yours."

"Yeah, but mine was worth it. Thanks. See what else you can pick up."

"Right."

When Jon had ratted off, Tosun stopped playing. "Mhrr," he said.

"Did you just growl at me?"

"I said, 'Mhrr.' It means 'peace ... be at ease ... set your mind at rest.'"

"I get the picture. What do you want to say it to *me* for? I'm all right."

"You're upset."

"I'm just mad, is all. I went to a lot of trouble to save a scrap of that yellow-headed clotheshorse's self-respect, and now she's gone and flushed it down the toilet."

"You did what came your way to do. What passes beyond you is beyond you."

"Yeah. I just hate to waste an effort. It isn't thrifty."

Of course, this wasn't necessarily bad, from my point of view. Surely I could find a way to use this. What Jackie would say, or do, or think, or feel when he found out, I hated to suppose.

"Connie!" It was the countess. "Darryl is selling Tiph. He's going to auction her off to the highest bidder." The countess looked like she wanted somebody to tell her whether or not to be shocked. "He says the auction starts in fifteen minutes, to give us all time to freshen our drinks. Are you coming?"

"You bet!"

"Are you bidding?"

"Sure! Some fun, eh?"

I must not have sounded convincing, because the countess retreated, still looking like she wanted somebody to cue her in.

"This isn't how it's done," Tosun said, vague and bewildered.

"Amateurs," I said.

"Barbarous."

"It's a lucky break for Tiph, however it's done."

I got some soda water, and stood at the back of the crowd that was forming around Moran. I was all fixed for slaves, but I might as well put my bid in, just to show everybody I was a team player.

Sometimes, I wondered if it was worth it.

"Managlawn, will you really buy her?"

"Buy her? I never said I would buy her."

"You could afford to outbid everybody else, couldn't you?"

"I could afford the money, yes. But I told you, I don't buy people. Same as you."

"Somebody's going to. If it were you...."

I could set her free. That would throw them a curve. Not to mention reinforce the moral statement I'd compromised by buying Tosun.

It wasn't my place to make a moral statement, I told myself, even assuming anybody would bother to listen to one.

Darryl grinned at me as he climbed onto the bar, and I sneered in reply.

"What am I bid, Mems?" he began abruptly. "What am I bid, for this glorious creature, this prize, this jewel?"

He stuck his hand down, and Honey climbed up beside him, her pink slip in her hand, an uncertain smile on her face.

So much for my inside tip.

The crowd went dead silent. This was a bit much, even for them. I mean, a Marneri was one thing, they didn't much mind that, but Honey was practically human.

I heard Rula say, "No, he just said his slave; I assumed he meant Tiph."

Honey laughed, but her face was cherry red, white around the mouth and eyes; I didn't like the look of it, and not just from an aesthetic point of view.

"It's all right," Honey said. "Like Darry says, we're all friends. It's just for fun."

"Just a mock auction?" Hanna asked. "Like in college, for charity?"

"No, it's for real," Darryl said, "but just among friends. Honey knows it's just for laughs, don't you Honey?"

"Sure," Honey said, but she didn't look sure.

Darryl caressed Honey's neck. "Do you think she would have sold herself to me, once she was registered freehold–" he gave me a filthy look–"if she didn't know she was safe doing it?"

Everybody knew the answer to that.

"No bidders?" Darryl said. Honey's hand tightened into a fist around her registration paper. "I'll start the bidding low. Five credits."

I hoped Darryl noticed his auction wasn't generating much good cheer. We were all checking out each other's reaction, and nothing we saw indicated that it would be unfashionable to be appalled.

Even Marissa's olive skin had drained to the color of spicy mustard. Her hands trembled so that tiny waves glinted in her drink. Maybe she had a heart, after all.

Jackie didn't look appalled. He looked weary and sad ... sadder than Honey looked ... as sad as Honey ought to have been.

"Nothing?" said Darryl. "Shall I lower the price?"

"Five credits." It was Jackie, of course.

"Five's awfully low, even for a joke," Darryl said. "I have five, will someone offer ten? Ten credits? Cheap, at the price."

"Ten," I said. If the woman was going to be humiliated on the block, the least I could do for her was bid her up. Too bad, if that took some of the fun out of the "joke" for Darryl.

"Twenty," Jackie said.

"Fifty."

"Seventy," said Zizi.

"One hundred," said Marcus, and Rula gave him a private little round of applause.

I heard Ivor call Darryl a very naughty name, and I heard Hurst say, "Hear, hear."

The bids went up and up. I dropped out, once it got going—God forbid I should win.

Honey relaxed a little; lost some of her unnatural color.

Darryl held up his hands, frowning. I sincerely doubted this was going any of the ways he'd wanted it to.

"Stop the bidding," he said. "This was supposed to be a joke; I believe you people are taking it seriously. No sale. Sorry, folks."

Darryl hopped off the bar, and left Honey to clamber down after him or stay where she was.

"Darry?" she said.

He turned and took her hand, holding it at an awkward angle. Once down, Honey pulled her hand away and rubbed her wrist. Darryl made a sour face and walked off. Honey followed, apologizing for hurting his feelings.

"You see?" Jackie said, watching them. "How can she let him treat her like that?"

"You tell me," I said. "She's your friend."

"I've asked," he said, "but she doesn't make sense. She says he needs her. —Connie, I can't stand seeing what he's doing to her! What can I do?"

"Don't look," I said.

"Cut it out. This is me you're talking to. Are you telling me it doesn't bother you, his owning Honey, like any piece of property?"

"Just between you and me and the lamp-post," I said,

"it bothers me, his owning Tiph. Honey, he's owned for some time now. And none of it is any of my business. Or yours."

"You tried to help her."

"Because I knew it would needle Darryl. And look how much good it did her. I wash my hands of it."

Jackie made a sound of disgust – "Pah!" or "Bagh!" or something of that nature – and walked away.

I went to my bubble and read my manual. I made notes in the margins.

One little problem: The manual was in Marneri and Tudolinguo, and Darryl didn't read either one.

Chapter 10

Late the next morning I was awakened by something flopping onto my stomach. A square of cloth, tied into a bundle, full of warm rolls.

Tosun's head poked up through the hole in my sleeping bubble. "Breakfast in bed," he said. "Will you come down for tea, or do you want me to toss the pot up next?"

I shied the bundle of rolls at him. He impaled it on the claws of one hand.

"I'm coming down," I said. "Stand aside."

While I showered and dressed, I thought about what Captain Margent had said about Darryl's abuse of the slave laws. I also thought about what I could do to get through Darryl's vanity to his brain. He was headed for a good dose of trouble, but he didn't deserve the fun he was having getting there.

It obviously wasn't going to do any good to talk to him about it. He'd all but said he'd turn the dogs loose on any slave who brought an action against him. That wasn't the spirit I'd been looking to encourage.

Maybe he thought I'd been kidding. Maybe, if he saw it in black and white, in a language he could read, it would make a difference. I could key a translation of the laws Darryl was most likely to break, have the resort's Registrar verify that it was accurate, and send it to Darryl "from a wellwisher."

Maybe, if he didn't know it came from me, he'd believe it.

It wouldn't take long. It wouldn't be much trouble. It

wouldn't be like I was putting myself out, or wasting time better spent doing something else.

I started out of the bedroom, then jumped back.

Tosun was leaping and whirling all around the sitting room; his right forearm was covered by his convex shield, his right hand gripped his knife, his left hand held his 12-inch skewer. He was silent and, though he came within a hair's breadth of the breakfast things, he didn't even wobble them.

"What in Jehoshaphat are you doing?" I said.

He stopped in the middle of a twirl, interrupted but not startled. Not even out of breath.

"Practicing."

"For what? Lord'a'mercy, child, I haven't seen such shines since I left Hell Alley."

"A Yolan has to keep in shape. Not 'for' anything. Dexterity, balance, strength – these qualities of mind make one wise. Being follows action, so dexterity, balance, and strength of the body are the buds from which the spiritual qualities flower."

"Yeah? Well, my Aunt Bootsie would have told you to do your roughhousing outside."

Tosun gave a sharp-toothed grin. "My Uncle Shahtsi would tell me I should go get some fresh air and sunshine."

"Why don't you? –Take some free time after breakfast. I've got business."

When I told him what it was, he nodded. "Good idea. Make sure the Registrar notes your name as the one who gave Mem Moran warning. It'll be kept confidential unless it comes to court. If it comes to court, you'll want it on record that you made the effort."

~*~

The Registrar was a weedy-looking female, white with black patches and a pink-and-black nose.

Her claws were gilded, so she kept pressing them out into view. It made her look threatening in spite of her weediness. The name plate on her desk said, "Emtis Bulfa."

"I remember Mem Moran," she said, when I told her what I wanted. "Clearly." She flexed her claws.

"This will be confidential unless called in evidence, right?" I asked.

"Absolutely." Claws.

I tapped the notarized print-out. "Can you see that this gets delivered to Mem Moran right away? Anonymously?"

"Yes." Claws. "You understand I can't issue an official warning in the absence of physical evidence?"

"That's okay. I'm hoping he'll take the hint and there won't be any 'physical evidence.'"

"I understand. I believe you Terrans say, 'A word to the wise is sufficient.'" Claws.

"Yeah, but Darryl Moran takes a three-page authorized document. –Nice nail job."

She seemed pleased I'd noticed.

I had to pay for the notarization and the register of warning. While my credit book was still warm, I decided to hit the Resort gift shop, maybe pick up something for Tosun.

I bought him a set of six egg-shaped objects, carved and polished from six kinds of semiprecious stone, each a different weight and color, but each the same size and shape of a Terran chicken egg.

There were a couple of racks of status collars, too, plain and fancy. I bought one for Tosun: silk ribbons, in all the colors of the people. The ribbons were tied in an open-weave pattern, and fastened with gold rings encrusted with gem chips.

Very pretty. If I had to be a slave, I might wear a collar like that myself. In fact....

I bought one for myself. After all, I was a slave; why should us poor old freeholds go barenecked?

And how everybody would laugh to see us in matching collars. Think about it, no; laugh about it, yes.

I met Tosun in the lobby and took him to lunch on a plaza with a view of the river. There were Socialites at a couple of the other tables, but nobody I needed to chum up to, so we sat alone.

Over lunch, I gave Tosun his goliard gift. "I thought maybe you could learn to juggle," I said.

"Oh, lovely. These are wonderful. Let me see...." He picked up a couple, hefted them, shifted them, and began to juggle them. He took another, then another, then he was juggling all six.

When he added a wine glass, I said, "Show-off."

He laughed and put everything back. "They're lovely," he said again. "I've always wanted something like this. Thank you."

"I guess you won't thank me for this," I said, and brought out the slave collar.

When I had looked at the thing in the gift shop, when I had seen it wrapped in tissue and put in a little paper sack, even when I had passed it across our table, the collar had been just a silly thought.

Now, coiled on Tosun's palm, it was real, and it wasn't silly, and I felt ashamed.

I put out a hand and tried to take it back, but Tosun slipped it out of the tissue before my grip could tighten.

He held the collar up, turned it, looked at it. "But it's beautiful," he said. "It looks like you."

"It looks like everybody," I said. "Everybody with jewels in their navels. I got one for myself."

That excused me to myself, a little bit.

Tosun looked pleased. "Did you really?"

"Should I wear it?"

"By all means. Humility is a virtue."

"Humility? –Nobody but you would accuse me of that."

Tosun fastened his collar. The ends of the soft ribbons hung down his gray chest. He looked very dashing.

"I hope it looks as good on me as it does on you," I said.

"Really? Do you think Tiph will like it?"

"Ahh. So that's the way of it. Let the boy off the Yolanbayt, and see what happens?"

"Only if the boy is lucky. She spoke for me, didn't you hear? She said she liked my looks. Don't you know what that means?"

"No, but I'm sure you'll tell me, unless I get up and run."

"It means that she might want to know me better. She might want to ask me to be her...." he said a word I didn't know, and seemed to struggle for a translation: "...her intimate. She might want to generate kits. In response to me!"

It's awfully hard not to laugh out loud at young love, but I managed, somehow.

"We'd both have to belong to one person," Tosun said, "or have written guarantees that we wouldn't be parted once we married. Even if it is the female who generates them, kits need both parents. Males are important, too."

"Yes, dear, I'm sure they are; no home should be without one. Unfortunately for you, I don't see Moran and me doing anything together except fight to the death. But, like I said, we'll only be on Marner a couple of months, and then you and Tiph will be free again."

He wasn't cheered by the prospect. "Unless he sells her away from me."

"Just don't tell him any of this. He'd never think of it on his own."

"Tiph will tell him."

The words held the knell of unwelcome truth. Darryl owned Tiph; Tiph wanted Tosun; Tiph would tell.

"Why would Tiph do a goofy thing like that?" I asked, hoping Tosun would say I had heard him wrong.

"It's the natural thing for her to do. She asked him to buy me on the boat. Since he didn't, she'll ask him to propose a match to you."

"No, she won't."

"That's the way it's done."

"What does that have to do with anything? You said the auction last night wasn't the way it's done, but that didn't stop Darryl from doing it that way. Tiph's not stupid; it doesn't take long to get the measure of that man. Caring about something is a weapon he can use against you; Tiph won't be giving him any ammunition."

I hoped.

"But suppose he sells her away, just to be doing it? For some reason I can't even imagine? I don't mind waiting for his contract to lapse when he leaves the planet, but...."

"Who could he sell her to, except one of us? The resort Management? The Omata? —or would she have to volunteer?"

"Only to be eaten. He could sell her to the Omata, although I don't think they'd buy her: She's obviously not a worker. The Management is more like it, or one of you."

"So if he sells to one of us, keep waiting. If he sells to the Management, I'll buy her and free you both. Not a problem. As long as Darryl doesn't suspect I have any personal interest in his household – which I don't – everything will ease itself out."

"With no effort, water wears a path through rock."

"Ain't it the truth. If you're finished eating, let's go."

"Go where?"

"I don't know, yet. I want to find Zizi or Ivor or one of that crowd and boost my interest with them. Want to come?"

"I'm at your service, Managlawn. But.... Don't you ever take time off?"

"From what?"

"From ... whatever it is you do with these people."

"Sure, I do. I have to, or my mind would snap. Matter of fact, the day you latched onto me I was out walking with Jackie Eastman."

"I like him," said Tosun.

I smiled. "You can't help but like Jackie. He's a nice person."

"Why don't we go boost our interest with him?"

"Because he isn't one of Them. Boosting my interest with Jackie wouldn't get me anywhere."

"No?"

"No."

"It seems to me," Tosun began, but I gave him a look I learned from my Aunt Bootsie and he stopped speaking.

We cruised the resort for an hour or so, looking for one of the upper Them, but no luck. Everybody was elsewhere, it seemed, or otherwise occupied. Even Jackie.

"Looks like it's just you and me," I said. "What's to do?"

"How about an excursion? A little one. A quiet one."

Tosun and I spent the afternoon poling a reed boat through a backwater. Tosun pointed out plants and critters and various items of nature, and I wondered why I never did this back home.

We tied up under a shade tree and Tosun played me to sleep on his clawharp.

When I woke up, the shadows were long, and there was a scent of spicy herbs in the air. Tosun was chewing on something, a green stem sticking out of the side of his mouth.

"Peasants' Pleasure," he said, holding up a handful of stalks. "Can you smell it?"

"Yes. Smells good. I wonder if it's safe for Terrans."

"Sure. It isn't a stimulant or anything. Want some?"

It tasted bright and rich, like raw gingersnap dough.

"Nice here," Tosun said.

"Sure is. I can almost understand why people would want to live in the country."

I dabbled my hand in the water and wished I could stay here, like this, for a long, long time. I was almost forty, I'd been fighting to get out of the Alley all my life, and I was tired of it. Maybe Jackie was right. Maybe fighting to get out was what was keeping me in.

So what was I going to do, give up? When I was this close? Darryl was being such a pain in the rear it was a wonder any of us could sit down, but other than that everything was going great. I was going to go home one of The Precious Few, the tenth member of the Inner Circle of the Good Society.

True, that would mean moving in the same circle as Darryl and Marissa, but that was a price I was willing to pay.

If that happened – and it would – maybe I wouldn't sign up for another season of CLUB CALIBAN.

Maybe I'd get TerraNet to do it as a mini-series, instead, or a set of movie-length specials. Maybe I'd retire altogether, join the leisure class, and run with the Society all year round.

Suddenly, I hurt so much inside I grunted.

"What's wrong?" Tosun asked.

I spit out the herb I'd been chewing. "This stuff's giving me gas. Let's go back."

Tosun and I had dinner in our suite so we could make an entrance after the party began.

I had just the dress to set off the collar. One of Jackie's, it was a plaid of my colors, tight silk in the bodice and pleated crepe in the skirt.

In poking through my jewelry box, I came across the amulet Tosun's Uncle Shahtsi had given me. I hadn't looked very closely at it at the time, but now I saw that it was the figure of a Marneri woman holding a kit, worked in Marneri gold, inside a filigree sphere. A flash of memory/recognition surprised me into a laugh.

"Silent Night," I said. When I was a kid, sitting in St. Philemon's with Aunt Bootsie, every time I'd sung that hymn, this was what I'd seen: Mary and the baby Jesus inside a golden circle. The circle was the "round" in "'Round yon virgin, mother and child."

The old memory pleased me – terribly, frighteningly. This was no time for cheap sentiment to kick in. I almost put the charm back in my box, but tied it to my collar, instead.

Tosun gave a start when he saw it. "Where did you get that?"

"A present from your Uncle Shahtsi. Why?"

"That's Managlawn," he said. "The Mother Ruler in her incarnation as the Mother of All the People."

"Fancy that," I said, for lack of anything better.

"I told you she wasn't very popular anymore. Trust Uncle Shahtsi to push off cold merchandise on a tourist."

"Well, I like her. I'm taking her as my patron saint; my totem. Maybe your Uncle Shahtsi has another one collecting dust that he'll give you."

"I can only hope," said Tosun.

As soon as we walked into the party, Marcus complimented Tosun's collar. His own neckwear tended toward soft cloth and jeweled fastenings, and I offered to give him mine when I was through with it.

That was the first anyone had noticed mine, and it got as big a laugh as I'd hoped.

The laugh seemed to release a tension; to relieve a strain. Well, that was what I did; that was one of the reasons I was invited to these functions.

When I made it to the Inner Circle, and became one of the Powers, we'd have to look for a new Court Jester: There was always a lot of friction when the whole Society got together, a lot of jockeying for position, a lot of intrigue; it made for a certain amount of nervous energy. Now, for instance, there was a strong current at large, just waiting to send four million volts through somebody.

Jackie came over, lighting one cigarette from the butt of another. "Evening, Connie. Tosun. Can you feel it?"

"What's up?" I asked.

"Honey's in long sleeves and high necks again."

"What's that mean?" Tosun asked.

"It means Darryl didn't like it that we stood up for Honey at the auction," I said. "He got mad at us, and he took it out on her."

"Is that acceptable, where you come from?"

"Not where I come from, no. The Socialites usually overlook what Darryl does to Honey; I guess this time they take it as a criticism of their attitude last night."

"And," said Jackie.

"And?"

"Come take a look at Tiph."

"At Tiph..." said Tosun.

"Maybe you better wait here," I said. "I don't want you doing something rash."

"Rash? Me?" Tosun's clear black eyes didn't have the look of youth in flame. I had expected him to rush to the suite and come back brandishing his weapons. But I had forgotten: defending the helpless was a female thing. Tosun confirmed that by saying, "If anything needs to be done, Managlawn, you'll do it."

"I'm not doing anything. I don't even want to look at her." I didn't. I wished I'd never seen her in the first place. What was Tiph to me?

"She doesn't mean that," said Tosun.

"I know it," said Jackie, taking my elbow.

Tiph was sitting at Darryl's feet. Darryl had her chain wrapped around his fist, shortened too far for her comfort. Only a few days ago, Tiph would have snapped that chain and showed her teeth. Now, she knew better.

"I wonder if he's been hurting her," I said, "or if he's just been making her watch him hurt Honey."

"Look at her fur," Tosun said. "Where it's palest."

I did. The light wasn't great but, when you looked, the blued skin under some of the cream coloring was obvious.

"She'd better file a complaint," I said.

"How?" asked Jackie. "You think he would let her do that, supposing he knew she could?"

"He knows," I said. "Didn't you say Darryl isn't dumb enough to break the law? Looks like he is."

Honey was standing next to Darryl's chair. She was back

on the bottle; her face was puffy and her eyes were dull.

Tiph saw us come up. She looked – not at Tosun – at me. "Sepplasas," she said. Tudolinguo for please.

Darryl gave me one of his very best smiles. I smiled back, of course. He stood up, dragging Tiph to her feet, and put his hand on my back.

"Connie and I have something to discuss," he said. "Alone."

He slipped Tiph's chain off his hand, and gave the end of it to Honey. Honey looked at Darryl with his arm half around me, at the chain in her hand, and at Tiph. Her mouth hardened and her eyes brightened, and Tiph's chain began to tinkle – whether the trembling came from Honey or from Tiph, I didn't know.

Tiph was nothing to me. I didn't care what happened to Tiph. I didn't need to get involved. It would all work itself out, somehow. Pigs fly.

"You're not leaving Tiph with her," I said, loud enough for Jackie and Tosun to hear. "You know Honey: Her mind might wander. Tiph might escape."

Darryl chuckled and stroked Tiph's head: The Fearless Darryllo Tames a Tigress. "Tiph would never try to leave me, would you, Pet?"

Tiph didn't answer.

"Okay, but if she turns up missing, don't forget who warned you. Jackie, you and Tosun are my witnesses."

Tosun looked lost, but Jackie nodded, his gaze avoiding mine.

"I won't forget," said Darryl. "Now come with me." He took my arm as if he were a little gentleman and I were a little lady.

"Tosun," I said, "fetch me a drink. Do it fast and do it

right, and find me, wherever I am, as soon as it's done."

"Now?" Tosun said.

"Now. I hope I don't have to tell you twice. Jackie, show him how to fix it."

"I know just what you mean," Jackie said.

"And don't be long," I said to Tosun.

"No, Mistress."

"I knew you had it in you," Darryl said, leading me through the party room. "You just needed the chance to let it out."

"When you're right," I said, "you're right."

We stepped out onto the belvedere. I propped myself against a wall, facing the room so that Darryl would have to face away from it. He tried to lead me to the railing, but I didn't trust either of us that close to a deadly drop.

We listened to Jocelyn play a song or two. When he figured the mood was set, Darryl spoke.

"I wanted to thank you," he said. "For the information."

"What information?" I said.

"The translation. Did you really mean for me not to know you sent it?"

"I don't know what you're talking about."

"None of the others ever picked up their manuals," he said. He raised my hand and kissed it, his lips warm and soft and moist against my knuckles.

I pulled my hand away and wiped it on my rump. "You are out of your mind."

"We're alike, you and I. We both took our training in the streets. We learned young to go for the throat, and give or ask no mercy."

"We are not alike."

"Who else has had the nerve to do what we've done?

Who else has a slave, I ask you? Who else has done anything but giggle about it, like kids with a dirty book? Who else admits that we're a collection of rivals, not a group of friends?" He put out an arm and leaned against the wall, not quite pinning me in place. "Come on, Connie. Let's throw in together, for this Season, anyway."

I must have been doing better than I had thought. Darryl was an Olympic social climber. When it came to elbowing for place, he made me look shy and retiring. And now he wanted to combine households with me.

That would put me In for sure, but there are some depths too low even for me.

"What about Marissa?" I asked.

"Marissa doesn't count."

"Dropped you?"

"I hardly think so." He gave me another of his very best smiles. "Ask her yourself; here she is."

He raised a hand, and Marissa came over. She must have been waiting for his signal. And here I'd been thinking she was a real person. She looked more gorgeous than usual, too: her color bright, her thick black hair brushed and oiled to a high gloss. I wondered if Honey and Tiph had been loaned to her as handmaids. Under the circumstances, they could do worse.

"Marissa, wouldn't you like Connie to join us?"

"If you would, Darry."

"You'd never say that," Darryl said to me. He began, slowly, to bend his elbow, closing in on me.

I could smell him: expensive cologne and body heat.

"You're a match for me. Let's strike some fire off each other."

Tosun came to the door. "Your drink, Mem."

Darryl turned on him with a curse.

"That's my slave you're talking to," I said. "Watch your mouth."

I moved out of Darryl's range and said, "Thanks, Tosun. Just in time. Where's Jackie?"

"In there." Tosun's black lips parted in a smile he couldn't squelch. "He helped me fix it."

I started in, but Darryl caught my arm.

"Think about what I said?"

"I'll store the memory in a bottle. It'll be better than Ipecac."

He chuckled. I should have left it at that but discretion, as we know, was never my strong point.

"Let me put it to you another way. No."

His grip tightened. "Why not? Marissa, me, you – think of it! The three of us, together. Not only would we have some lovely times, but we'd own this group. We could do anything, and not have to worry about their quibbling opinions of us. They wouldn't dare have any opinions, if they didn't match ours. They would do what we did, say what we said, think what we thought. If anybody didn't like it – out they'd go. As for this tin pot planet's laws, we can ignore them. We can afford to. How about it?"

How about it? Status, power, king of the mountain in a bulletproof vest. Wasn't that what I wanted? Yes, of course, without a doubt. But not with Darryl.

"Take your hand off my arm," I said, "before I take it off for you."

He smiled and squeezed tighter.

With my free hand, I pinched his nose and twisted it until he yelped and let me go.

"Thank you," I said.

He was laughing when Tosun and I went in. Some people

just can't take a hint.

Tosun led me to a door on the far side of the party room. Near the door was a curtained alcove, where I glimpsed Honey and Jackie sitting on a divan. Half of Tiph's leash hung from Honey's hand.

"This door leads down to one of the main landings," Tosun said. "Nobody saw her slip out. Nobody knows she's gone, yet."

"You didn't take her down, then?"

"I told her the way. I thought this would be better."

"Maybe you're right. Good work."

"I didn't do anything."

"Well, *I* certainly didn't do anything. Let's go pin a medal on Jackie."

"Hadn't we better go after Tiph? She'll be getting nervous alone."

"But she isn't alone, is she? Isn't she with the resort Registrar – what's her name – Emtis Bulfa?"

"I told Tiph to notify her, but the Registrar won't come until you're there."

"Why not? What do I have to do with it? I'm not in this, you understand? Tiph's got her chance to bring an action against Darryl, or whatever it is abused slaves do around here, but that's between the two of them, not the three of us. Clear? And what do you mean, until I'm there? Where's 'there'? Where is Tiph, anyway?"

"In our suite, of course. Sanctuary."

Of course.

Chapter 11

Tosun and I left the party unnoticed.

"I'm not having this," I said. "She'll have to go somewhere else. I'm not getting into this. 'Sanctuary'– Do I look like a cathedral to you?"

Tosun followed me, in silence.

"Don't you have anything to say?"

"No."

"Did you tell her she could take sanctuary with me?"

"We assumed it. Didn't you?"

"No. Why would I? I remember about sanctuary and protectors, but I don't remember volunteering."

"Managlawn–"

"I'm not doing this."

I didn't see Tiph when we stepped into the suite.

"Find her and get her out of here."

"Yes, Mistress. –Tiph! It's us!"

Tiph uncurled from behind one of the sitting room's larger bumps, and knelt before me, putting her head on my feet and her hands on my ankles.

"Don't do that," I said. "Get off your knees."

"Shall I stand?"

"Stand, sit, squat or sprawl, it's all the same to me."

"You aren't going to send me back, are you? Please don't. Please don't!"

"Tosun, I really could use a drink–maybe we all could – and I don't think I could manage, without christening the carpet. Would you mind?"

"Yes, Mistress."

"Oh, stop it, with the 'Mistress.' And make mine soda water."

Tiph stood until I settled into a carpet shape that suited me for sitting, then she sat on a lower one, as near me as she could get.

"Drink up," I told Tiph, when Tosun had handed her a glass. "Then go find that Registrar and make your complaint. Tosun can go with you, if you're afraid to go alone."

"But...."

"No buts. I almost took a kiss from Romeo Moran while you made your getaway. That's above and beyond. Now I'm giving you an escort to the Registrar, and then I'm done with you."

"Please!"

"She doesn't understand," Tosun told her.

"I threw myself on your mercy," Tiph said. "I begged sanctuary. At the party. When Tosun told me you'd ordered him to liberate me, I thought–"

"I didn't offer to take you in. I didn't." I turned to Tosun. "I didn't, now did I?"

"But who else would help me?"

"Help you how else? What more do you expect me to do? Take you with me to see the Wizard? –When the case comes up, I'll testify that Darryl Moran is unfit to own anything more sensitive than a credit book, if that'll do you any good. But, until you take him to court, I'm just a bystander."

"But where will I go in the meantime? I belong to him. I could make a complaint, but I'd have to stay with him, don't you see? Do you really believe I'd be safe with him? After making a complaint?"

I knew she wouldn't.

"You know what he's like; you can claim my contract in the name of the Empress, and bring suit, along with me, as a friend of the Empress. In the meantime, I would belong to you." She didn't look at Tosun, but I'll bet we both thought of him.

I nearly weakened, but said, "I don't want you. No offense, but one slave is one too many."

"She didn't want me, either," Tosun said. "Remember? She only took me to keep me away from your Master. The thought of him as my owner overcame her scruples. It was more than she could bear."

"I get the message, Tosun," I said. "But, look: Why pick on me? Jackie didn't want the expense of a goliard, but surely he'd shelter Tiph. I can go back to the party–"

"Don't leave me, Mistress!"

"Can you people not pronounce the name 'Connie'?"

"Call her Managlawn," said Tosun.

"Please don't leave me." Tiph started sagging toward a kneeling position again.

"Tosun would protect you– Oh, all right. I'll call the front desk and have Jackie paged."

Tiph nodded, glumly. "This isn't the way it was supposed to be. I'm a luxury slave. I invested a lot of time and money to learn the ways and cultivate the manners. Not to mention having myself declawed – that's why my price was so high. When the Mem paid it, with no haggling, I thought it had all been worth it. Instead, I'm beaten, humiliated, refused refuge.... I wish I had it all to do over again."

Regret. Empty regret. The words came to me out of nowhere, sounding hollow in my mind.

"Never say that. Take what you've got and work with it. You can't make a silk purse out of sow's ear, but you can certainly talk some boob into thinking a sow's ear is just what he's always wanted. Believe me, I should know."

There was a knock at the door. Tiph jerked.

"If it's him," she whispered, "and you don't grant me Sanctuary, he can take me back." She huddled down, as if she could hide behind herself. "He'll kill me, and the others will swear he didn't."

"Oh, for–" That was a little strong, I thought, even for a guy who fancied himself as a street fighter.

Still, I didn't doubt that he'd make things most unpleasant for her, if he got her back.

"Connie? You in there?" It was Darryl, all right. Maybe he'd go away. "Connie!" Oh, he was angry, and enjoying it to the hilt. "I've got the Manager with me, and she has her passkey."

"I would prefer not to use it," said a woman's voice.

"Why can't you just ask for a date, like a normal person?" I moved closer to the door, so I wouldn't have to shout.

"Don't flatter yourself. Tiph's run off, and I'm searching the Resort."

"So?"

"Let me in!"

"Just a minute. I don't have to jump when you say 'frog.'"

If what he'd said was true, if he was searching the whole Resort, he didn't suspect me of having anything to do with Tiph's escape. If he didn't expect to find her here, maybe he wouldn't look very hard.

"He'll kill me," Tiph said. She stood and dropped her hands to her sides.

At that, I was angrier than I'd ever been before. I reached her side in three steps, and nearly slapped her, myself. "If that's what you think, you're crazier than he is."

"Wait and see."

"He isn't going to kill you, because he isn't going to take you. Darryl Moran never saw the day he could take anything or anybody away from me. And I'll find somebody to protect you. I promise."

"Trust her," said Tosun.

"I do," Tiph whispered. "Thank you."

"Now, keep quiet and go in that room there and hide in my bed bubble. Don't make a peep."

I finished my soda water and put the glass on the bar.

Then I opened the door to Darryl.

The Manager, Tabba Inson, was a sleek looking taffy-colored female. She stood outside the door until I invited her in. She was obviously there only to carry the key, and had no intention of helping Darryl search.

"Why did you leave the party?" Darryl asked.

"You overwhelmed me. Have a drink? Tosun and I were just sharing a jug."

"So I see." Darryl's eyes shifted to the bar. "You two and who else? There's another glass over there."

"I confess. You got me. I dirtied two glasses when I could have done with one. Don't tell the dishwasher, please? –Do you want one, or don't you?"

"No, thanks."

He walked around the floor-bumps, craning his neck in a caricature of searching. When he got tired of that, he waved a hand at one of the suite doors. "What's in there?"

"Tosun's room."

"And in there?"

"In there is something you've never seen, never in your life – something you'll never see, however long you live."

"What's that?"

"My bed." Really, he made it much too easy.

He only smiled.

"You told me not to leave Tiph with Honey. I should have listened. Tiph broke her chain. When I get her back, I'm having a leash made out of metal and plastic cord, something she can't snap. Maybe I'll get more than one."

"This is going to be a very long Season."

"Long for some," said Darryl.

That was nightmare talk. I thought it was long past time somebody woke up.

"Tell me: What are you going to do when the Season is over? When we're off Marner, and you're nobody's Master; when you're back to being just plain Mem Moran?"

"Worried about me, sweetheart?"

"Just wondering what you could possibly do for an encore."

Darryl laughed. "Now that may be difficult. But I'm sure, together, we could think of something."

"What about a suicide pact? You first."

"Ah, Connie, Connie."

"If you tell me I'm worthy of you, I'll slay you. I have had it with your smarmy compliments. Do you think I don't see through you? Do you think I'm going to fall for your crummy, cheap, soft-soapery? I have an over-active power drive, myself; do you think I don't recognize it in somebody else?"

"But that's why we–"

"Baloney. You don't want to share power, with me or anybody else. You want to put me in your trophy case. One more freak in Darryl Moran's freak collection."

"I'm sorry you feel that way. You misjudge me, Connie."

"Prove it."

"How?"

"Do something human."

Darryl knotted his fists, but kept his temper in check. "I'm going to search your rooms. That's my right."

"Is it?" I asked Tabba Inson.

"I'm afraid it is."

"Go with him, Tosun, will you? He's liable to hook something if he isn't watched."

"The slave's room first, I think," said Darryl.

"Suit yourself."

When Darryl came out, I said, "Was she there?"

"Now yours."

"Time's wasting. While you're playing cops and robbers up here, she could be out and away."

"I doubt she feels much like traveling today," he said blandly, and went into my room.

I stood in the doorway and watched him ruffle through my closet. When he stepped onto the stairway that led into my bed bubble, I went over and pushed him back down.

"Ah-ah-ah." I waggled a finger. "Not for bad little boys."

"I only want to look."

"That's what they all say." I sat on the steps, blocking them.

"Move." He had his mind set on it, now, but it wasn't going to happen. His mind against mine – no contest.

I shook my head and lounged back onto my elbows.

Darryl backhanded me, hard enough to knock me off the steps.

I fell hard, and I got up mad.

He started up again.

I made a frog: a fist, with my index finger's knuckle sticking a little out. I punched that knuckle into the back of the knee bearing Darryl's weight.

He fell harder than I had, and he had farther to go. He got up with mayhem in his eye, and more than a little joy. He swung at me.

I ducked, and he hit the side of one of the steps.

"I can't believe it!" I said. "He fell for the old duck-and-make-him-hit-something-hard-behind-you trick. What a mutt!"

While Darryl rubbed his numbed fingers I said, "On the cruiser, on the way here, when you popped me in the eye, I told you the next time you hit me would be your last. I was counting that smack as your last."

He shoved me aside and started up the steps again.

I grabbed his belt and pulled him off. He stumbled back, into Tosun's arms.

"Careful," Tosun said. He held Darryl off-balance, making it seem as if he was trying to set him back on his feet.

Darryl fought against Tosun's hold.

"Be still. You're going to make me drop you."

"...Sepplasas...." Tiph barely breathed it, but I heard.

I stumbled on the steps, shouting for Mem Inson.

She was already there, watching our slapstick act.

"If somebody wants to take sanctuary with somebody, how is that done?" I asked.

"I knew it!" Darryl struggled harder.

Tabba Inson spoke as if Darryl weren't flopping at her elbow like a fish in a net. "The suppliant asks and you agree. A Registrar fills out papers, you pay a fee, and the owner transfers the suppliant to you. In such a case, the owner has no choice."

"I knew she was here!"

"You didn't know it," I said. "You wouldn't know your hind end from a hole in the ground with the aid of computer graphics."

"Let me go!"

"Let him go, Tosun."

Tosun released Darryl's body, which hit the floor with a solid whump.

Darryl stood and brushed himself off. He straightened his clothes and smoothed his hair as if he'd just gotten up from a refreshing nap.

Mem Inson called out something in Marneri.

Tiph poked her head out of the bed bubble and replied. Then, to me, Tiph said, "I beg sanctuary, in the name of the Empress. This man has abused me. Please, Mem Phelan."

I reached out and took the hand she offered me. "What do I say?"

Tosun answered. "Tell Mem Moran you claim Tiph in the name of the Empress."

"I claim Tiph in the name of the Empress."

Tabba Inson held out a hand to Darryl. "I'll have her registration, please."

Tosun moved toward the sitting room. "I'll call the Registrar."

"Get out," I said to Darryl.

Impressive, but it wasn't that easy, of course.

"The Mem must order things as she pleases," Tabba Inson said, "but the Registrar will require Mem Moran. Proof and testimony against an owner should be offered in the offender's presence, when possible."

"In that case, Darryl, sit back down and put your feet up. Have a drink."

I had expected Darryl to be furious. That showed how little I understood him. He had told me and told me: He thought we'd make a good team. As long as I gave as good as I got, as long as I never showed him any weakness, he'd be the happiest of men – but he'd always be hunting for that weakness.

When he found it, he'd take me to pieces and look for another brick wall to run his head against until one of them cracked.

He was right about the Society, too. He and I could rule with iron fists, kept that way by continually slugging at each other. Punch and Judy in the flesh. What a life.

The weedy-looking Registrar with the fancy claws wasn't long in coming.

Tiph showed her bruises and detailed the physical and verbal abuse she'd been taking. Mem Inson bore witness that Darryl had knocked me off my own bed-ladder without provocation, and that Tiph had asked for and been granted asylum.

Darryl made himself at home while the Registrar completed the paperwork.

"What a workout! I'm exhausted!" He stretched, lounging in a long, knee-high cavity in the carpeting. "Suppose I stay here when the bureaucrats are finished with me? Have my things moved in? Tiph and your boy can stay in my rooms with Honey; that can be our slave quarters, hmmm?"

"No."

Darryl shrugged.

"I notice you left Marissa out of the arrangements," I said.

"So I did. You drive all thoughts of other women out of my mind, my dear."

"Good thing I ate light at supper."

The Registrar finished her documents. She handed one to me and one to Darryl. "You'll be notified when the case comes up, if you're still on planet. It's always the same with you aliens. You lumber in and make a hash of everything, then lift off without notifying anybody, leave litigation on the books, property unclaimed–"

"We're not interested," Darryl said.

"Forgive him," I said. "He's morally deficient. If either of us leaves before the case comes up, I'll file notice."

"It's in the manual. There's no excuse for not doing it."

"No excuse at all," I agreed.

"The necessary forms are available in all Registry offices."

"That's good to know. I'll take care of it."

"They're free of charge."

"I will do it."

"Sure you will," she muttered.

"Will there be anything else?" Mem Inson asked Darryl.

He cocked an eyebrow at me. "How about it, Connie? Shall I have my things moved in here?"

"If you like."

Darryl sat up.

I turned to Mem Inson. "And have my things moved to a larger suite. My household is expanding. Tell you what, let's make it a self-contained family unit with cooking facilities – got anything like that?"

"Yes, Mem." She looked delighted. Maybe it was because the family units carry a higher charge. Maybe it tickled her to see that Darryl didn't like the change. He sometimes had that effect on people. I can't think why.

"Can I be moved right away?" I asked.

"Management never sleeps."

"Never mind moving me, then," Darryl said, his wine-colored lips drawn into a pout.

Mem Inson gave me a good-for-you smile, and left.

Emtis Bulfa started after her, then hesitated, and spoke to Darryl. "Forgive me, if I state the obvious, but this is vitally important."

"What is it?" Darryl said, his mind on other things.

"Don't listen to her," I said. "She might tell you something you need to know."

He gave her what passed for his attention.

"Mem Phelan has claimed the slave, Tiph, in the name of the Empress. Interference with the slave, Tiph, is an Imperial crime, enforceable by extradition from anywhere in the Terran Union. Do you understand, Mem? There are some things you aliens can't do and then run home and brag about."

"I understand, I understand. I've had my fun out of Tiph, anyway. The Empress is welcome to her."

"Yes, Mem." The Registrar looked at Tiph, at Tosun, and at me, nodded, and left.

As for Tiph, her golden eyes were not only sparkling again, they were glittering.

"Shall I make him leave, Mistr–Managlawn? My pads are harmless, but I still have my teeth."

"I'm going." Darryl looked at me from under his lashes and grinned boyishly. "The Season's only started. So far, I've never enjoyed one more. I'm going back to the party now– What a story this'll make! Coming, Connie?"

"I'll be along later. I wouldn't want to steal your thunder."

The sap actually bought it, and left looking pleased. What a chump. It was almost a shame to take advantage of him – almost.

He'd go back to the party and turn this series of random pratfalls into an uproarious story, and he'd never realize that, goofy as I was, I won the fight. He must have made it on the streets on meanness: it couldn't have been brains.

When the door closed behind Moran, Tiph sank to the floor.

"She'd better not be getting ready to kneel," I said. "If she kneels at me again, I just might forget I'm a friend of the Empress."

Tiph cast a worried glance at Tosun, who shook his

head and murmured a few words in Marneri.

Tiph smiled up at me with a sickening look of confidence.

"I won't kneel, if you don't like it, Managlawn."

"Oh, you won't?"

"No, Managlawn."

"I don't like owning slaves, either, but that doesn't seem to bother anybody, does it?"

Tiph looked to Tosun again for an explanation.

"Sorry," he said. "I don't understand it, either. It's against some principle of her religion."

"Oh, yes, I remember. Terran missionaries used to come to the Exchange all the time—"

"I am not a missionary. I'm about as far from a missionary as I can conceivably be. Slavery is... inhuman. It's wrong. Can't you people see it's wrong?"

Tiph and Tosun looked at each other.

"No," they said, in unison.

Well, what did I expect? If the good old missionaries hadn't made any impression, *I* sure wasn't going to. I'd put money into those missions, too. Waste of good money.

"The thing is:" Tiph said, "we aren't human. How can I say this, without sounding patronizing? We don't seem to be the same sort of people you are."

"People are not property, no matter what 'sort of people' they are."

"They are, if they choose to be."

"Like I chose to be sandbagged in a back street?"

"That was irregular."

"...Irregular...."

"Slavery is a career choice. Money down, in lieu of salary. We retain our citizenship rights. We can't be separated from our mates or our kits. Our kits are born freehold. We have a union. Room, board, full medical benefits, a certain percent of labor value accrued towards buying ourselves freehold...."

"What are you – a recruiter?"

"It isn't the worst sort of life."

She had me there, but I only admitted, "For a Marneri."

"And with a Marneri. Off-worlders – tourists, I should say – come to Marner for a holiday, and the ones who can afford it often do indulge in short-term purchases. They seldom know how to deal with what they've done, and their confusion leads them into error. Usually it's merely irritating. Sometimes it's worse. Sometimes it's much, much worse." She reached up and removed her collar, possibly thinking of how close she had come to being one of the much, much worse, herself.

"Maybe something should be done about that."

Tosun opened his mouth to speak.

"By someone else."

Tosun opened his mouth again, but closed it without saying anything.

"Good," I said. "Now, I'm going back to the party."

Not that I felt particularly festive. I had to go back, to test the waters and see which way the wind was blowing and which way the cat would jump and so on.

Tiph stood up, rising to her full, sleek height for the first time in days.

"Are you?" she said. "And may I come, too?"

"Do you want to? Wouldn't you rather huddle here with Tosun, to recover?"

Tiph, her golden eyes dangerously narrow, shook her head slowly. "People only huddle from danger. I'm safe with you. Let him see me unafraid."

I looked at Tosun, who nodded at me.

"Good for you. Just don't push him. That's my job."

Tiph wore my slave collar to the party and I wore a tan neckerchief with my Managlawn amulet tied onto it at the knot. I'd wanted to go down and get another collar for myself but, unlike the Registry and Management, the gift shop wasn't on 24-hour call.

The three of us were almost cheered into the room. I found myself up to my armpits in applepolishers and second-string Socialites. The Egg-On-The-Face Club rallied around me. Even Hurst and Jocelyn took enough interest in the power shift to catch my eye and smile and nod.

Zizi invited me to tour the Omata cave-dwellings with her, and gloated about it to Marissa when I agreed.

This was more like it. In fact, this was just like it. A little more of this kind of stuff, and nothing would be able to shake me loose.

Darryl flashed a big smile when he saw me, and signaled me to join his group.

"Come tell them how it was," he said.

"I'm saving it for the autobiography."

"Come talk to me." He gave me what, I supposed, was meant to be a seductive look.

"No can do. My lawyer will call your lawyer."

He laughed, and the Socialites loved it all.

Marissa stuck to Darryl like a leech. She had it bad, that one. I'd warned her. She'd been so sure she could handle him.

"Good work, Connie!" Jackie Eastman gave me a one-armed squeeze. "Darryl's been telling how you out-maneuvered him. He doesn't seem to be angry; he seems to think it was all in good fun. –That's quite a relief."

I blew a raspberry.

"It's a relief to me, is that all right?"

"Sure, sure. Be my guest."

"Tiph ... er ... I don't know that congratulations are exactly in order, here, but...."

"My thanks are in order. I'll never forget your kindness."

Jackie blushed. Even his scalp turned rose-pink. "I didn't do anything."

"There goes your medal," I said.

"My medal? Oh, my medal." He laughed.

"Did you ever think you'd see the day when I'd own slaves and you'd be proud?"

He shook his head. "These people make you crazy. They're an alternate universe. But never mind them. –Now for Honey."

"'Now for Honey' nothing." I may look stupid, but I was quick enough to make this connection. "If you think I'm going to let Darryl slobber on my hand and then slap me upside the head for the sake of Honey, you've got another think coming. Tiph didn't know what she was getting into when she sold herself to That Man. Honey did."

"But this is our chance! He's given it to us, himself!"

"What's all this 'us' stuff? I only have to do one good deed a day to get my merit badge."

"Darryl's gotten more attention out of losing Tiph than he got out of buying her. He'd sell Honey in a minute, if he thought it would make a good story."

"He might. He might."

"So.... Why don't you see if you can buy her?"

"I gave at the office. Why don't you buy her yourself?"

"He'd never sell her to me; he knows I respect her. He knows you don't; that's why he might sell her to you."

"I set her free, and she sells herself back to Darryl.

Nice racket."

"Don't set her free. Keep her out of Darryl's hands while we're on Marner. Talk some sense into her: without him knocking it back out, maybe some of it will stick."

My collar was getting tight. Probably the vein that had started throbbing in my neck. I loosened the knot, and said, "Trust me on this: Darryl would not sell Honey Clayton to me, even if I wanted to buy her, which I don't. I am not a clearing house for second-hand people."

Jackie stared at me for a minute. "You're right, of course. He wouldn't sell her to you." He ran a hand over the top of his head. "I feel so helpless. And I am helpless."

He lit a cigarette. "You should have seen her when she started work. Thick hair, clear skin, a real body – not one of these toothpick women – a brown paper bag would have looked like dynamite on her. That's been twenty years, and it seems like yesterday."

"Jackie," I said, "young and pretty, she'll never be again."

Nor would I, but let's not let that bother us.

"No, he's taken that."

"He didn't take it. She gave it to him."

"I can't just abandon her. She's worked for me, off and on, for twenty years. She used to talk to me. She used to tell me everything. We have history."

Before my better judgment could kick in, I said, "There's one thing.... What did Darryl say to her, when he found out she let Tiph get away?"

"Nothing. Nothing I heard. He stood there, looking at us, and looking at Tiph's chain there on the floor. I acted surprised, and said, 'Where's Tiph? I thought she was on the other side of the curtain, waiting to tell you Honey was sneaking drinks.' He laughed and left. When he got back, he told us what happened with you. Then he took Honey's arm and walked outside with her. He didn't seem angry with her at all."

"He might have been saving it till he had her alone. Anyway, if he hasn't said anything yet, she'll be expecting him to land on her with both feet after the party."

"What if she is?"

"You could offer to claim her, like I did Tiph."

"I could offer to claim her?"

"What do you think? I've got a monopoly? Why not you?"

"All right, all right. But you come along, and tell me what to do."

"Tiph, Tosun, you come too, please. We wouldn't want to do it wrong."

We found Honey alone on the belvedere, sitting on the grass, her knees drawn up to her chin, her arms around her legs.

"Are you all right?" Jackie asked.

Honey looked up at him and laughed. "Of course!"

Jackie sat down next to her. "I want to talk to you. You know about Tiph?"

"Yes!" Honey lifted her chin, with a sneer toward me. "She only did it because she thought it would turn Darry against me."

"Hello," I said. "This is your wake-up call. I–"

"It didn't work."

Jackie had a go at it. "Honey–"

"It didn't work! I was afraid..." She fingered her neck through the high collar of her dress. "I thought he'd be mad, but he wasn't. He said it wasn't my fault. He...."

The countess came up in a swirl of skirts, literally looking down her nose at Honey.

"I'll tell you what he did," she said. "He held her, bent

backwards over the balcony, and told her the only reason he didn't let her drop was because he loved her. And she wept for joy. In my country, we know what to think of such a woman."

She spat on the ground.

I thought that was pretty good, coming from one of us. "Take it easy. What did you do while he was holding her there? What have any of us been doing, except Jackie? I haven't noticed any of us giving the poor gink any support. Why shouldn't she weep for joy that Darryl didn't drop her? There sure wasn't anybody there to catch her if he did."

Rula stalked off.

I shouldn't have let go like that – I hoped I hadn't set myself back too far by it. Rula's status wasn't all that sturdy just now, though, in spite of Marcus' patronage; maybe I was strong enough to take a higher hand. If not, I'd just have to crawl a little to make up for it. I'd deal with that later.

"Honey," Jackie said. "Listen. You don't have to be Darryl's slave. You don't have to let him hurt you anymore. You can give your paper to me, and Darryl won't be able to touch you. He couldn't hurt you, at least as long as we're on Marner. Wouldn't that be nice?"

"Don't talk to me as if I were an idiot. I'm not an idiot. Or a child. Connie's using you, can't you see that? She wants you to take me away from Darryl so she can have him for herself."

"Honey," I said, "sewage is free; why do I need Darryl?"

"I don't believe you! I don't trust you!" She struggled to her feet and staggered off.

Chapter 12

Our new rooms were a lot like our old ones: same carpet lumps for furniture, same bubbles for beds. The sitting room was twice as large, though, with a kitchen and dining area one step up from it.

The kitchen actually held a table and chairs – the exotic touch, I supposed. There was one large bathroom to serve the four small dressing/bed rooms. The master bedroom had its own Necessaries, two closets, and a double-sized bed bubble.

I woke to the sounds of quiet activity from the kitchen and the purring murmur of conversation in Mocskan.

I sang in the shower and whistled while I dressed and bustled out with a cheery, "Good morning!"

Tiph started to kneel to me, but Tosun caught her arm and held her up.

"Good morning, Managlawn," she said.

"You're in a good mood," said Tosun.

"And why not? Everything's going my way – so far. Why shouldn't I enjoy it while I can?"

"While you can?" said Tiph. "What do you expect to go wrong?"

"Nothing ever goes wrong," I said. "It just goes for you or against you. If it goes against you, you have to get with it, or wait for it to come your way again. Right now, everything's going my way, so I'm in a good mood."

"You have definitely got to spend some time in a Yolanbayt," Tosun told me. "You could lecture."

"Tempting. Tempting. Speaking of which, what's for breakfast?"

"Lunch. Breakfast is what you eat in the morning."

"Nice of you to let me sleep. What happened to breakfast in bed? You didn't cut me any slack yesterday."

"Yesterday I was lonely. Today, I wasn't."

Apparently, Tiph still liked the looks of him.

Tosun was cooking, of course, Tiph being a luxury model and all. He gave us fresh melon and citrus fruits; a clear, strong, soup; fish quick-fried in peppery oil; and hot green tea. For dessert he fried up thin, crispy, pancakes and drizzled them with molasses.

"Where'd you learn to cook like this, young'un?"

"In the Yolanbayt. My parents placed me there when I was a kit, and I asked to stay when I was old enough to decide for myself. I rose through the ranks of domestic work. Kitchen service makes up several grades, in itself. Then come several grades of student, and so on."

"How far did you get?"

It was Tiph who answered. "Servant, Student, Master, Sage, Shar. A Shar can administer the Yolanbayt for life, but most of them only lead for seven years."

Tosun licked molasses off the fur on his hand and said, "Six was plenty."

"After that, they turn the post over to another sage and serve the children just entering the Yolanbayt. Or they go out into the world as goliards."

I stared stupidly at Tosun. "So you aren't a kid. You've been around a while."

"Longer than you, my gamba."

"You're not a dropout, either."

Tosun laughed. "Oh, but I am. It takes a lot of spiritual

concentration to hold the position of Shar. But the petty squabbles that need settling, the papers that need signing– The never-ending details distract your attention like ... ten thousand tiny copper bells ringing in your ears. So I gave up my post and came out to refresh myself – and to find the Yol in someone else and follow it, through them, back to the source."

"Through me?"

"Through anyone. It was just good fortune Uncle Shahtsi put me onto you."

Surprised isn't the word for what I felt, although that was part of it. So was shame, at not having learned more, sooner, about a man who'd made himself my slave.

"So, what should I call you? Shar?"

"What's wrong with calling me Tosun?"

"It doesn't seem ... respectful. I feel like I ought to be treating you with more respect."

"You treat me with respect. You just don't think you do. Still, let's see... You can call me Chichibaba, if you want to."

Tiph shook her head and wheezed with laughter.

"Chichibaba," I said. "What's that mean?"

"Grandfather," said Tosun.

~*~

We met Zizi in the lobby. Tosun carried his pack and weapons, and I was dressed for hard travel.

Jackie had decided to give the trip a miss. I asked Tiph if she'd rather stay at the resort with Jackie, but she insisted on sticking with me – or, possibly, with Tosun.

Spencer Stedman, Zizi's cookbook author, came along, and Zizi's own particular spongers, and a handful of hardy freelance dogsbodies.

The rest of the Good Society preferred to view their Omata in the touristy "village" some of the more enterprising young cannibals had set up on the floodplain, a mile or so from the resort. We were going to trek to the Omata caves, back in the rocky hills to the north.

A dozen shaggy, stubby-legged, short-bodied creatures were corralled not far from the resort's rear entrance.

Two Omata stood near the corral. They were shorter and stockier than Mocskans, with thicker, coarser, longer fur. Their muzzles were narrower and more pronounced. Gold wire as fine as thread was woven and braided into the fur on their chests. They introduced themselves as Nikki (a reddish-orange male) and Lotte (a tortoiseshell female).

Our little beasts (aazzis, Tosun called them) moved fast, once they got going. We were across the floodplain and at the base of the hills in less than an hour. Then we stretched out into a line and started up, Lotte in the lead, Nikki in the rear.

After another hour of this, we came out onto a broad, wide shelf, like a plaza, with cliffs on three sides and a canyon on the other. The cliffs were perforated by doorways and windows: the Omata cave dwellings. The rock around some of the doors and windows, and some whole sections of the cliff, were stained colors other than the rock's natural yellow-rose. Some of the windows had boxes of flowers in them, and earthenware pots of plants sat everywhere there was an outcropping to hold them.

"It's beautiful!" I said.

"We're not barbarians," Nikki said, riding past me without a glance. "We were reading and writing and calculating accurate almanacs when the Mocskans were hitting each other over the heads with aazzi bones."

Lotte heard him and laughed. "Follow me, Masters and Mistresses," she said, "Shar, slave and shave-tail."

My fellow Terrans didn't catch anything after "Masters and Mistresses," but Tiph said, "Shavetail? Oh, don't tell me there's one of those around."

I rubbed my bare arm. "Shave-tail."

Tiph raised a hand to her mouth, as if she could take what she'd said earlier and push it back in.

"Don't worry about it," I said.

Lotte pointed out the homes of the Chief Shaman and the elders, and took us into one of the dwellings. The walls and ceilings were whitewashed, and the floors were covered by thick, spongy mats woven out of reeds and herbs. The mats rustled and sent up a different mixture of scents with every step. A woman was rolling a grainy-looking pastry onto a stone hearth, and offered us some of the cracker-like bread an earlier batch had baked into. She had baskets of the stuff made up, and Lotte told us that the woman would probably let us buy some to take back with us if we wanted to.

Tosun poked me with his elbow. "Buy some."

"It's a set-up," I said. "This isn't anybody's home."

"Of course not. Would you want a lot of tourists and aliens trooping through your home? But the cakks are real, and they're great with cheese or sugared fruit. Come to think of it, you'd better give me some credits and I'll buy them. They might not serve you."

"Why not? Oh, yeah. They think I'm one of those."

"Shall I tell them that you aren't?" said Tosun.

And hand the insult to the Socialites?

I shook my head. "No big deal." I gave him the credits and watched Lotte make sure everybody was satisfied. Me, she ignored. It was just like the dear old school days.

The funny thing was, it didn't make me mad. It was tiresome, and it seemed awfully silly of her, but it didn't make me want to foam at the mouth and chew the furniture, the way it had when I was young. Sign of age, I supposed.

I thought about it on the trip back. I thought about how odd it had felt to be a nobody again, and how weird it was that it hadn't hurt. Probably, I reflected, because I knew it was temporary. At the resort, I'd be back where I belonged, with only two or three faces to step on before I got to the top of the heap. Not surprising that I didn't care what a couple of ridge-runners thought about me, really.

"You've been awfully quiet," Tosun said, when we bunched up back on the floodplain. "What've you been thinking about?"

"Nothing."

"Ahh. The proper meditation of the wise."

"Will you stop it? —Where are we going now?"

The others, not satisfied with the real thing, had turned their aazzis toward the fake Omata "village" on the plain.

"What's the attraction here?" I asked.

"This is where they send their export goods," said Tosun. "More cakks—but not as fresh as the ones we got today – woven linen, jewelry, and – oh, Managlawn! – the noodles!"

The Omata here didn't care whether I was a shave-tail or a bandicoot, just so I was a customer. I bought myself a jar of perfumed wax– "for rubbing into the fur" or, in my case, hair. I bought Tiph some bangles for her ears and arms, and a box of solid gold false claws set with opals. I bought Tosun several vials of foul-looking stuff the shopkeeper said were rare ingredients for Yolan elixirs.

I ripped off a page of credits for Tosun, and he disappeared into one of the shops. He didn't come out until the rest of us were remounted and ready to leave. When he did come out, it was with two bags each as big as his chestpack.

"What all have you got?" I asked.

"Plenty. Some of it will keep, but some of it we need to eat tonight. Is that all right? To eat in the room?"

"The way you cook? You bet."

"There's enough fresh stuff just for us. With some of the other things, we could have guests. Would you like that? Would that help any of your plans?"

"I only have one plan. Everything else is a distraction. But, yes, I think it might help my plan."

"Then you wouldn't like to ask Mem Eastman."

"No."

"Not Mem Moran, I hope," said Tiph.

"Only if I was on a hunger strike. No, I think I'll invite my pal Face. Marissa del Hueso. I was supposed to be her guest this Season, but things kind of got out of hand. Now she's in with Darryl, but I'm thinking she might be pried loose with a little effort. If it just gets around that she came to our place for dinner, I'll rack up a point or two. Showing everybody that she hasn't turned into a Honey Clayton clone wouldn't be bad for her status, either. Great idea. Thanks, Chichibaba."

"It wasn't my idea, Managlawn."

"Well, it wasn't mine."

Tiph laughed and shook her head. "Yolan."

I left a message at the desk for Marissa.

Back in our rooms, we washed off the dust and the smell of aazzi. I rubbed a little perfumed wax into my hair,

Tiph put on her pretties, and Tosun stashed his elixir fixings in his chestpack.

I wondered if Marissa would show. I wondered if she'd at least call, or if she'd just ignore me and laugh in public about my invitation.

I made us all drinks and settled back with Tiph to watch Tosun cook. *Marissa's loss if she doesn't come* . We were having sprouts and fresh vegetables, stir-fried with some kind of chopped up stuff that looked like dried paste and smelled like heaven. We were having birds, about the size of small chickens, boiled, stuffed with dried mushrooms and onions, wrapped in fat, and roasted until they were crisp. We were having roots, cut into slices, fried, added to the bird broth with vinegar, wine and spice. And three kinds of noodles.

When I was freshening our drinks, there was a knock.

Marissa had come, after all.

I opened the door and drew her in. "Marissa, darling! I've hardly seen you lately. Seems like years. I was hoping you could dump the chump, but I was afraid he'd cry and kick his heels if you went somewhere without him–"

"Oh, Connie, please shut up!"

I did.

"I'm glad you asked me, it's glorious being away from him, but I'd have had to come, whether I wanted to or not."

"What? Marissa...."

"Darryl made me come. He wanted me to come, so I had to."

"You didn't have to. He doesn't own...."

Marissa lifted her jawbone and dared me to make something of it. When I didn't, she took a deep, shuddery breath, closed her eyes, and said, "It was after dinner the first night here. I didn't know he'd asked Honey to sell herself to him. I thought it was something special, just between us." Two spots of color made her famous "strong" cheekbones look like the tail-lights of a hovercar. "Then, at the party, when he auctioned Honey instead of," she flicked a hand at Tiph, "instead of her, I knew it wasn't special. Not if he'd done the same to Honey ... maybe said the same things, made the same promises...."

"I'm curious. How does it feel, to be dumber than dirt?"

Marissa's eyes flashed. "I suppose I deserved that. You told me not to try to deal with him. You have every right to crow."

I certainly did, but I didn't feel cocky, somehow.

"You can't imagine how I felt, seeing Honey ... knowing it might have been me, instead."

"Gee, that must have been awful. Lucky for me I didn't know about you then. I was too busy imagining what Honey must have felt like, standing up there, to think about how sick you were, safe on the floor."

Marissa took my hand. "You couldn't have known."

I let my hand stay where it was for three seconds, then pulled it away. "So he bought your registration. So what? So he says go and you go? Marissa— You're acting like a slave."

"Connie, I've just told you—"

"Yeah, yeah, Darryl conned you into signing yourself over to him; that, I believe. But that's just names on paper. You're acting like it's real. Like he could play The King and the Slave Girl with you and get away with it."

Marissa didn't say anything.

I had a wonderful idea. "Marissa," I said, "has Darryl mistreated you?"

Tiph gave a short, throaty laugh. Marissa ignored her.

"Certainly not. He treats me like a queen. Honey – and

Tiph, when he had her – were told to obey me as they would him. He didn't even tell them that I had signed myself over."

"Pretty nasty trick to play on them," I said, and Marissa shrugged. "If he treats you like a queen, why is it so glorious to be away from him? Why don't you just tell him to take your registration papers and put them in a safe, dark place? Seems to me like Budhi told me slaves could protest a sale they didn't like."

She shook her head.

"You know, if he abuses you, you can claim sanctuary."

"He doesn't abuse me. It's just... He's sweet, and charming, and treats me beautifully, but there's something else with it, now. He never says or does anything, but he never lets me forget ... what I did. It's insupportable."

"I feel real sorry for you. Tiph feels real sorry for you, too, don't you, Tiph?"

"As a matter of fact," Tiph said, her lips drawn back in distaste, "I do."

"Why don't you tell on him?" I asked. "This wouldn't go over too well with the others. He'd have lost a lot of status over what he did to Honey, if it hadn't been for you acting like you approved. –Or, look: threaten to tell, unless he signs you back over as quick as he can."

Marissa shook her head. "Tell? Let everybody know I sold myself to Darryl? That might be the end of him, but it wouldn't do me much good, either. But I suppose you'd like that."

I didn't say anything. The whole discussion left me cold, not to say chilled, but I didn't expect Marissa to believe that.

"Besides," she said, "it'll only be for a little while. And Darryl won't abuse me – he wouldn't dare. This Season won't last forever, you know."

"But the memory will, won't it? Darryl will always know that you were stu– trusting enough to make yourself his slave. Just like Honey." Darryl did have a hold on her, then: the threat of public ridicule, which she might or might not be able to deflect.

Okay, but something still smelled like a wet dog at a tea party. Maybe if I nudged it with the tip of my parasol it would roll over for me.

"He's got you good," I said. "If he told, you'd look awful silly, wouldn't you? And he will tell, you know. Sooner or later, when he needs a boost."

"No, he won't. He swore he wouldn't, if..."

Mm-hmm. "If what?"

"Can't we speak privately?"

"We are private, aren't we? Slaves don't count, do they? –Oops! no offense."

"Oh, Connie, stop teasing!"

Tosun pulled out a chair and motioned Marissa to sit in it. He gave her a napkin for her damp eyes and another for her frosty drink. She didn't thank him.

"If you're quite comfortable now," I said, "Darryl swore he wouldn't tell if what?"

"He wants..." Marissa cast an eye at Tiph. "He wants to trade. You tear up Tiph's warrant, or subpoena, or whatever it is, and he'll give you..."

"Honey?"

"No, Mistress! I beg you!"

"Sh-sh. I won't."

Marissa laughed. "I wouldn't, either. Honey, indeed. That's hardly a compelling offer. He'll give you ... Me."

Marissa lowered her eyes modestly, to give me time to

realize my luck. "You two would merge households, and he would sign me over to you. I wouldn't mind that. As you said, it isn't as if we have to take it seriously. And I've always thought of you as a friend, Connie. Sometimes I think you're the only friend I have."

Touching. And nearly irresistible. Of course, I would give Marissa back to herself. She ought to be everlastingly grateful, and the two of us could tag-team Darryl right out of the Inner Circle. If the two of us swore he'd never owned her, it wouldn't matter what proof he might produce; a strong enough lie beats solid reality any day – at least, it did with our crowd.

There had to be a catch.

"And what's to keep me from leaking your secret?" I asked.

"Your silence is part of the deal."

"Suppose I don't accept the deal?"

Marissa smiled. "Why wouldn't you? Because of her?" Meaning Tiph. "You could keep her. He doesn't want her. He just wants the charge against him dropped."

"Dropping the charge isn't up to me. That's between Darryl, Tiph, and the Empress. In fact, I don't think it can be done."

"It can," Tiph said. "I've known many cases settled out of court."

"I wouldn't ask you to – you've got your rights. Besides, he's got it coming. Three to five in the salt mines might make a man of him. Nothing else has."

"He might do more, if you agree," Marissa said. "You seem so concerned about Honey."

"Honey? Me? Jackie's the one whose heart bleeds for her. He's the heavyset fellow, about my height, smokes tobacco."

Marissa fingered her glass, but refrained from beaning me with it. "As a favor to Jackie," she said, "suppose you could persuade Darry to sign Honey over to you? Or to Jackie? Darryl would tell her to do whatever you wanted, and she would. What do you say? All he asks is for you to get Tiph to drop the charges against him, and agree to move in with him for the rest of the Season. —And he wants paper on it."

"Paper what? What are you talking about?"

"Darry isn't stupid, you know. He wouldn't make all these concessions with nothing to hold you to your part of the bargain. I don't think he trusts you, Connie."

"Really?" We had a companionable little chuckle over that. "What does he want, some kind of a contract? He doesn't want me to marry him, does he?"

She looked me over and wrinkled her famous nose. "This would be strictly business. Darry would get the charges against him dropped and whatever he hopes to gain from your proximity. I would get your silence, and freedom from his disgusting superior attitude. You'd get Honey, me, and the status of having Darry's and my ... friendship."

Status? Marissa, dealing in status like a huckster with a load of hot watches? Life with Darryl was coarsening her spirit.

Maybe.

"It strikes me," I said, "that you don't get much out of this deal. It also strikes me that Darryl wouldn't be willing to give up so much if he didn't expect to get more."

Marissa looked innocent. "I've told you all I know. Are you going to give me an answer, or aren't you?"

"This is a big decision. Wouldn't he settle for the usual casual agreement?" (Which I could casually dishonor.)

"Darry wants paper."

This was starting to irritate me. "What do I care what 'Darry' wants?"

"You care. You don't fool me. You care."

Then I got it. I'd have laughed, if it hadn't been so pitiful. That whole household was fogged in by Darryl's ego. They breathed that smog; they were blinded by it; they couldn't believe somebody else might have infrared goggles and a gas mask.

Darryl, Honey, and Marissa – they all thought I was secretly as crazy about Darryl as they were.

Darryl and Marissa – I knew it as well as if I'd heard them murmuring on their pillow – had plans for me: I would bind myself to Darryl with a Terra-legal contract. Darryl would charm me into setting Marissa free. Then, with me shackled by the contract and this love they all thought I secretly bore, they'd turn on me – goodbye, Connie. The old school set-down.

Did Darryl really think I'd fall for his game, or was that just the sucker-bait he'd dangled in front of Marissa, to get her to act as a shill for him?

I sat back and tried to look thoughtful. If I didn't look thoughtful, I hoped I looked shifty. Anything but what I felt, which was enraged. "Gee, I don't know."

"How can you hesitate? What more could you want? What's the matter, don't you think you can manage Darryl?"

"I know another woman, not a hundred miles from here, who thought she could, and couldn't."

"Yes, but you've learned from my example," Marissa said, humbly.

"I learned from Honey's example."

"You won't do it?"

"I didn't say that. It sounds good–almost too good. Still, with you on my side...."

"Of course I'm on your side, Connie. What else could I be?"

"I'll think about it. It might be worth the risk."

"Darry wants an answer tonight."

Darry, nothing; Marissa wanted an answer. Marissa wanted this show on the road. Marissa wanted to be freehold again, and she wanted to show me who was the ring-tailed leader of this merry band of pleasure-seekers.

While Marissa sipped her drink and tried not to glare at me, I did think about it. I thought about wading into the middle of that septic tank of Darryl's and flushing it out. I thought about taking over Honey's title, and Marissa's, and holding them for the Season, with all of them helpless to do anything about it. Marissa would never forgive me, but I might be able to make that a matter of little importance by the time we left the planet. I thought about working some kind of scam to get Darryl's papers, too, and selling him to Muimmea Transport as a galley slave.

I must have smiled at that, because Marissa said, "You'll do it?"

"Tell Darryl I'm seriously considering it. Tell him I'm afraid he's too smart for me; I'm afraid he'll get the better of me, somehow."

That was sweet to Marissa's ears, and it would be sweet to Darryl's. It was true, too, except that "smart" wasn't the word I used to myself. "Twisted" was the word I used.

"So I hesitate," I said. "Still, I can't help thinking how much better off you'd be with me than with him. Us being such good friends, and everything."

Tiph surprised me by saying, "That's something to consider." Then she went on, "Think what you could do for her. You could have her declawed, to increase her value."

"You've got a mean streak," I said in Tudolinguo, watching Marissa tuck her nails into her palms.

To Marissa, I said, "You go on back, now, and tell Darryl I need some time."

"I don't want to go back to him without an answer. I'm afraid."

"But you said he wouldn't dare abuse you. And, if he does, you can always come to me for sanctuary."

She protested. She did everything but hang onto the door jamb, but I got her out, and I didn't give her the satisfaction of taking back a firm answer.

Things were very quiet after she left.

Then Tiph said, softly, "I'll drop the charges, if you say so, Managlawn. So long as you protect me from him."

"You put entirely too much faith in me. You shouldn't put that much faith in anybody, not even yourself."

"Should I congratulate you, then?" Tosun asked. "Are you clearing away the distractions, and prospering your plan?"

"If I didn't know how old and wise you are, Grandpa, I'd think you were stupid."

"She means," he told Tiph, "she isn't going to do it."

"The Season is young, yet. I can wait. I don't have to jump into the snake pit to get what I want."

"In fact, you'd better not–unless what you want is snakebite."

Chapter 13

I remembered that remark when we walked into the party that evening, and saw Darryl in his glory. He had an arm around Honey and another around Marissa. When he saw us come in, he whispered to Marissa and let her go. He smacked her on the rear as she came, and she turned and simpered at him.

"I saw that," I said. "Let's take him to court."

"Oh, Connie, can't you ever be serious?"

"Yes, I can. The trouble is, when I'm serious, people just think I'm failing to be funny. What do I have to do, say 'Mother May I?'"

And she laughed.

"I'm glad to see he isn't mad at you," I said. "Gosh, I was worried."

"Of course he isn't mad at me. He understood. He likes it that you're making him wait. He says it's like waiting for Christmas."

"Christmas. Here comes Santa Claus, with three little dolls for Darryl, is that it? You can be Barbie, and I'll be Chatty Cathy. Honey can be from Snow White and the Seven Dwarves: Let me see....Was there a Boozy?"

"I know what you mean. She gets worse every day. She's never sober. First she's happy, then she cries; then she hangs all over Darry; then she sits in a corner and sulks–"

"She's just no fun at all, is she?"

"No, she isn't."

"What's he need her for, anyway, when he has you?"

"That's a very good question. I'll be glad when you join us, so you can take her off Darry's hands and send her away with Jackie. You are going to do it, aren't you? Please say yes."

"Let's see how the Season goes. Maybe you and I can think of a way to get what we want without giving anything for it, eh?"

"Ahh...." Marissa seemed to like that. "Did you have anything in particular in mind?"

"Not yet. I'll let you know as soon as I come up with something."

That should buy me some time. Marissa would tell Darryl I had something up my sleeve, and they'd both settle down to wait for me to tell Marissa all about it. It would be fun to see them watching for moves I wasn't going to bother making. Of course, it was possible I actually would come up with something. In that case, the last person I'd let in on the plot would be Marissa, and wouldn't Darryl be cross if he thought his Trojan Horse had rolled back on him?

"Don't make me wait too long, will you?" Marissa asked.

"Trust me."

She started back to Darryl, who waved her off. She didn't like that, but she went. Give her the rest of the Season, I thought, and Darryl would have her looking like Honey Clayton's understudy. If, by chance, I needed to work with my pal Face, I'd better do it before Moran finished pulling all her brains out and playing Silly Putty with them.

I circulated, chumming up to Zizi and the rest of them, tossing out jokes and passing out compliments. I felt like a politician wrapping up a campaign, except that babies are much nicer than what I was kissing.

It was all paying off, too. Tosun and Jocelyn started improvising again, and Tiph danced. Suzanne Lizabette, the prima ballerina who'd come as one of Ivor's guests, joined her, while someone else got it all on holotape.

I told Spencer Stedman, Zizi's cookbook author, about the dishes Tosun had made for us. I invited him to spend a few days looking over Tosun's shoulder, taking notes for his next book. With all this class, and wise cracks, too, Darryl's steamy little peepshow wasn't getting much play.

I looked around for Jackie, and saw him on the belvedere, inhaling a cigarette.

I went out to him. I didn't say anything at first, just stood there, looking up at the stars.

"Congratulations, Society Pet," he said. "Looks like you've made it."

"Not yet."

"Not ever, then. I told you. You'll never be Up enough, or In enough, or It enough."

"Yes, I will."

"When?"

I didn't have an answer, so I evaded. "I'll know when."

"Is there any use, my staying? I hate this, you know."

"I know. But stick around. It won't be much longer."

"I wish..." He looked past me. I didn't have to turn around to know who those big brown eyes were misting for.

"If wishes were horses, beggars would ride," I said. "My Aunt Bootsie used to say that. She also used to say there's no use beating a dead one. Horse."

"I suppose not."

"Oh, don't! And don't think you're going to leave her

on my conscience, either. Stick around. It won't be much longer, believe me."

"I didn't want to take her home in a box."

"More like a bottle. But I didn't mean like that."

"What, then? Is she going to do it? Leave him?" He didn't think so, even when he asked.

"I doubt it. The woman must be made of steel. I can't believe anybody can take what she's taken and still keep coming back for more. She's tough. Not bright, but tough."

"What did you mean, it won't be much longer?"

"Things are shaking. Power is shifting. You never know what might happen. Darryl wants me to move in with him. Among other things, he offered me Honey's pink slip and marching orders. He wants a Terra-legal contract with me."

"You aren't going to do it, are you? My God, Connie, you can't do that!"

"Not even to get Honey away from Darryl? I could give her to you and you could take her away from all this. That's what you want, isn't it?"

"Yes, but not if it means leaving you in it. A contract, for God's sake!"

"Contracts were made to be broken. Meanwhile, you and Honey could be home, sweet home."

"No, you were right about that. It wouldn't do any good to take her home. The next ship out, she'd be back, begging Darryl to say he didn't mean it. She has to leave him on her own, or not at all. –But you mustn't do this, even if it would work. You mustn't put yourself at the mercy of that man, because he hasn't got any. Don't even think about it."

"I wasn't, really, but I would have – thought about it, I mean – if it had been worth it to you."

He paused, with his cigarette almost to his lips. "I don't get it."

"Get what?"

"The joke."

"I didn't make one. I meant it. Mother May I?"

Jackie dropped his cigarette and ground it out.

"What you think means a lot to me," I said. "It always has. That's why I get so mad at you when you tell me things I don't want to hear."

"I knew that. I didn't know you knew it. And I sure didn't think I'd ever hear you admit it."

"Neither did I. I guess I always thought, if I didn't admit a weakness, it was the same as not having one. It doesn't work that way. And it doesn't seem to matter anymore. I have a weakness for you, Jackie. How about that?"

"I have a weakness for you, too. I love you, that's my problem." He put his arms around me.

I put mine around him, and rested my head on his shoulder. I didn't say I loved him; I was saving that. But I thought it.

I closed my eyes and sighed deeply. I felt safe. For what seemed like the first time in my life, I felt safe. I didn't have to prove anything or keep on my guard or put up my dukes – I was safe. I knew it was an illusion, that nothing could make me safe but myself, but I relaxed against Jackie and enjoyed the moment while it lasted.

A bark of laughter and a smothered giggle came from the doorway. Jackie and I held each other tighter for a second, then moved apart.

"We aren't disturbing you, are we?" said Darryl. He still had an arm around Honey.

"No more than usual. Say, you're not going to dangle

her over the balcony again, are you? The people downstairs are starting to complain."

"I told him about last night," Honey said. "About how you two tried to talk me into leaving him. He told me what was behind it, that you wanted to move in with him, and you were hoping to use me as bait."

"Sure. Worms are the bait of choice for barracuda."

Darryl laughed, and Honey shrugged off his arm.

"Honey," I said, "believe me: I don't want Darryl. It beats me what you want with him. He's dangerous. He's deadly. If he were a household product, he'd have a skull and crossbones on his label. I mean, there are the remains of a fine woman about you, but look at yourself tonight; just look at yourself—"

Honey slapped me, hard; harder than Darryl had when I'd blocked the bedroom stairs. The sharp, solid sound of it rang over the roof and through the party room. I wouldn't have thought she had the strength.

She held her hand to her breast, as if she'd hurt herself on my face. Maybe she had; my cheek certainly felt like half of a two-car collision.

Darryl's eyes shone, and his entire face was flushed. "Hit her back."

"What?" I said.

"Hit her back. She asked for it."

Honey just stood there, willing to suffer whatever blows he directed toward her, even if they came from me. Her eyes looked at me, but they were empty, waiting for me to fill them for her.

"I don't take orders," I said. "I never will."

The buzz of voices started up again, muted and angry. Angry with Darryl, but more angry with Honey. This was too much, she'd gone too far. She'd lost control, she'd struck the current favorite, and in public, and it just wasn't done, and what was Darryl thinking of, inflicting her on decent people?

"Honey," Darryl said, "I think you'd better go back to the room. Dear."

"Maybe you'd better go with her, Jackie," I said.

"Are you sure?"

"Somebody ought to. She needs somebody to talk to. Do you know what I mean?"

Jackie nodded, and took Honey away.

I went past Darryl into the party room. I half hoped he'd grab my arm, the way he had before. This time, I wouldn't have tweaked his nose, I'd have ripped it off. "Hit her back"–I'd make him think, "Hit her back."

Tiph brought me soda water disguised as a drink. Tosun brought me a cloth napkin full of ice chips to hold to my face.

Darryl followed me, but he didn't have the nerve to touch me. "Connie, I'm so sorry. That woman drives me crazy; I haven't been myself since I started seeing her. I don't know what came over me. The woman is so sick, it's infectious. I'm so terribly sorry."

"You toad."

"I thought buying her pink slip would give me some control over her," he told the crowd, "but apparently not. She's too much for me, and I'm man enough to admit it."

"Poor Darry," Marissa said, "I've seen what she's put you through. Nobody could have done any better."

Like I said, in our group, reality is for people with no imagination.

"If she's such a trial to you," I said, "maybe you'd be better off without her."

"I can't seem to get rid of her. I never should have let her talk me into taking over her papers."

Rather than foam at the mouth, I said, "Sign her over to Jackie. She can protest the sale, but she'll have to stay with him until the local law sorts it out. That should keep her out of your way for the rest of the Season."

"Oh, no – Jackie's a friend. I couldn't do a thing like that to a friend." He didn't get much of a laugh, but he got one.

"I'll tell you what: I'll free my slave, if you'll free yours."

I heard Marissa catch her breath.

"No," Darryl said, "I don't think so."

"Not even if I can get Tiph to drop the charges? And, listen: I'll free Tiph, and you can lease Honey to her for the rest of the Season. Wouldn't that be funny?"

Darryl pursed his lips and looked at me from under his lashes. "Let's say I'm seriously considering it."

In other words, Honey was starting to look like a liability. As Jackie had put it on the cruise out, he had used her up and was ready to toss her over his shoulder. Jackie might make the catch after all and, after all, I'd help him hold the net.

"Please yourself," I said. "You always do. Just don't try to fob her off on me. I don't like being slapped. Some people don't."

"You never know what you'll like until you give it a good, long try."

Marissa looked at him like she was Little Red Riding Hood, and she'd just noticed what big teeth he had.

"Remember," I said to her, "my door is always open – to you."

Tosun and Jocelyn began playing again, but Tiph stayed with me, getting me fresh drinks and ice chips.

"Look, Tiph," I said, "this is very nice. I like it. But I don't require it. Go back to dancing, if you want to."

"Thank you, Managlawn, but I don't feel like dancing."

"No, I don't, either. I never thought, when I was climbing into the lap of luxury, that it would turn out to be full of spikes. Did you?"

Tiph shook her head.

Jackie didn't come back to the party. When we got to our suite, I called his room.

"What's the word? Did you talk to her?"

"I talked. She cried."

"Did you talk her into leaving him?"

"I wish I could say yes, but no."

"Well, behold, I bring you tidings of great joy. After you left, Darryl started making noises about dropping her."

"You're kidding."

"This time, not. Sleep well, my dear old chum. Things are looking up."

I woke with the feeling that something was wrong– No, not wrong. Changed. Then I remembered – I'd told Jackie he was important to me. Said it, right out loud. I'd be getting a heart tattoo next.

I should have felt like kicking myself, but I didn't. I felt smarter and stronger; even the prospect of tap-dancing around, hoping Darryl would toss Honey into my hat, couldn't squelch me.

My left cheekbone was sore to the touch; it matched the right one, where Darryl had backhanded me. What with the slaps, and the mouse Darryl had given me on the cruiser, and Budhi, and all, this had turned out to be a pretty knock-about vacation. And none of that could squelch me, either.

Tiph and Tosun had waited until I got up to have breakfast.

Tosun had made a kind of spangled white mush out of hot honey-water and cracked grain. Now, he sprinkled it with a ground spice that tasted like cinnamon and licorice, and served it with cream and cakks.

It made me think of oatmeal, and other warm echoes of my later childhood.

"Sticks to your ribs," I said.

Tiph toyed with her food, then finally said, "Managlawn, did you mean what you said last night, about sending me away with Mem Clayton?"

"When did I say that?"

"To Mem Moran, at the party last night."

"Did I? I've got to start keeping a diary."

Tiph shared a look with Tosun, and seemed to relax.

"Why?" I asked.

"Nothing. I should have known better."

"Oh, really? I guess Tosun told you it was some kind of crafty trick to fool the enemy."

"He told me you promised to keep us together, if I wanted it."

So I had. To my shame, I had completely forgotten. I tried to resist, but I snuck a look at Tosun.

He knew. I could tell that he knew.

"Mhrr," he said, and winked awkwardly, probably having had Jackie show him how.

"Ah, yes. Indeed, I did. –Do you? Or is it impolite for me to ask?"

"I want what you want, Managlawn."

"Don't do this slave stuff with me, Tiph. As far as I'm concerned, you two are employees."

"It isn't because you hold my paper, Managlawn. It's because.... You took a blow for me. You took responsibility for me, when you could have left me trapped. If you want me to take Mem Clayton away and keep her for a month or two.... A month or two of my life isn't too much for that."

"To tell you the truth, Darryl's so contrary, I don't think I ever considered he might accept that offer. But, if he does, Tosun can go with you. It'd be a poor way to start married life, but you wouldn't have to deal with her; just keep her away from us–away from Darryl, anyway. Maybe she could clear her head and start thinking again. The poor stumblebum's so punch-drunk she doesn't have the sense to protect herself anymore – if she ever did have it."

We were all quiet for a minute while the Kid from Hell Alley told me I was a sucker to think about anybody but myself, especially during the Season; and I told the Kid from Hell Alley to take a break.

"If he doesn't accept," Tiph said, "–if we stay here with you–you wouldn't object to my taking Tosun as my spouse?"

"Why would I object? It's between you two. I told Tosun, I'll only be on Marner for a couple more months; when I leave, I'll sign you both over to yourselves and pay you lump sum salaries. Tosun can worship the Yol through you a whole lot better than he can through me."

"If you agree, and if Tosun accepts, I propose we have the Registrar marry us as soon as this matter of Mem Clayton is settled. As for kits, I think they'll have to wait. I don't think I want to generate in this atmosphere."

I certainly couldn't quarrel with that; although a pang surprised me, at the thought of Tiph's and Tosun's babies coming when I was gone.

The phone rang. Marissa, perhaps? Honey? Jackie?

I moved out of range of the visual as Tosun pressed the "receive" button and said, "Cornelia Phelan's rooms."

It was Jon Hister, my spy in Darryl's camp. He wanted to speak to me, of course.

I turned a thumb down and made a face.

"I'm sorry, she can't come to the phone right now. May I take a message?"

I lounged in my chair and put my feet up in another. This wasn't half bad, a social secretary to screen the geeks. I'd have to look into this, when I got back to Earth. Of course, the only geeks I knew were supposed to be my friends, but....

Jon insisted.

I sighed and went to the phone.

"Marissa needs you," Jon said. "She's sick; she says she has a migraine and you know what to do for her."

"And where's Darry darling? Sitting by her couch, holding her hand, I don't think?"

"He took Honey and left. He told me to stay with Marissa. He said if she didn't feel any better in an hour, she could send for you. She didn't feel any better, so she told me to call."

"You mean he left and she waited?"

"One hour on the dot." Jon looked pleased to have some juicy details for me. "I believe she's afraid of him. He told me, in front of her, to tell him when he got back how long she waited. I said I would, but I honestly expected her to call as soon as the door closed behind him. I even asked her if I should go on and call, but she just told me to mind my own business and went back to bed."

"When did this start – Marissa playing I-Hear-And-Obey?"

Jon waved a hand in an "abracadabra" manner. "Overnight. I could hardly believe it."

"Anything else?"

"No. Except that Darryl was in a good mood this morning."

"I don't like the sound of that. Any idea what he's up to?"

"Not the slightest."

"Tell Marissa I'll be along."

When Jon clicked off, Tosun said, "Shall I set the phone on automatic?"

"Yes, thanks."

"Standard message, or do you want to record something?"

"Standard."

He tapped some keys and said, "Done."

"Very professional, Grandfather. Where did you learn correct office procedure?"

"We do have phones in the Yolanbayt, you know. Executive Secretary to the Shar was one of my posts."

"You're a very handy guy to have around. Speaking of which: I hate to ask, but will you come to Marissa's suite with me? I'm not afraid of her, but Darryl might come back while I'm still there, and I'm all out of cheeks."

"Of course, we'll come," said Tiph.

"You don't–"

"You would be foolish to go there alone. I'll wear my new nails. Then let him lay a hand on any of us, and he can draw back what's left."

I had become accustomed to other women either flinching or swooning–or both–when Mr. Trouble came around. It refreshed me to see a companion spirit in Tiph.

"I'll bring my pack," said Tosun. "I have elixirs to dull her pain and make her sleep, if those would help you."

"Great! I wasn't looking forward to spending the best part of the day stroking Marissa's brow, but I want to know what's going on."

Jon let us into the suite.

Tiph pointed to a hollow in the carpeting near the wall. "That's where I was told to sleep. I!"

"Could have been worse. Think of where Honey had to sleep. And Marissa. Makes a pocket in the floor look like Paradise, doesn't it?"

Tiph's lips twitched; not quite willing to smile.

"Would you bring me two damp cloths," I asked her, "one warm and one cold, and a glass of lukewarm water?"

"Yes, Managlawn."

"Tosun, would you come with me, and hand up what she needs when I tell you how she is?"

"Yes. Shall I go first, in case it's a trap?"

It had never occurred to me that it might be a trap. I gave Jon Hister a sharp look.

"It isn't," he said. "I wouldn't—"

"Of course, you wouldn't," I said, taking him by the arm. "Just the same, suppose you go first, hmm?"

"I don't blame you. Don't think I blame you, but I'd really rather not."

"Suffering builds character."

He went up the steps and disappeared to the shoulders into the bed bubble. Marissa's outraged shriek, edged with pain, tore right through my head. I hated to think what it must have done to Jon, not to mention how it must have felt on top of a migraine.

Jon scrambled back down the steps. "You see?"

"You're a brave little soldier. Mommie's proud of you."

I called softly to Marissa, to tell her I was coming up. Tiph brought the cloths, and I took them with me.

Marissa had the lights inside the bubble dimmed, but I could see the skin of her face drawn tight.

Old tears had dried, and new ones cut tracks across them. When she saw me, she sobbed and reached for me, as if she wanted me to bend down and hold her.

I pushed her arms aside–but gently. I put the warm cloth on her forehead and wiped her face with the cold one. "Want some water?"

Marissa shook her head. "I'm so glad you came. Darryl said you wouldn't. –Oh, Connie!"

"So, did he? Hurt you? Is that what brought this on?"

"Me? No."

"Honey?"

"No, he never touched her. She was asleep, when we came in last night, and then this morning.... Could I have some water now, please?"

Tiph handed me up the water and Marissa drank.

I hoped she got to the point soon; I didn't want to shake a sick person until her teeth rattled. I always hated Twenty Questions.

"Marissa, did Darryl hurt Honey this morning?"

"No."

"Where did he take her?" Then it came to me. "Did he take her to sell?"

"Yes."

"To Jackie?"

Marissa moved her head back and forth in a painful "no."

"To somebody else in the group?"

Again the "no."

"The Registrar?"

"Yes," Marissa whispered.

"Yes." That figured. It would have been decent to sell her to somebody who knew her, and might care what happened to her.

"And she went? Why did she go? How could you let her? How could you let him do that?"

"My head hurts," said Marissa, in a whine that wanted to be a shout when it grew up. "Don't be so fussy. She went because he told her to, and Honey does what Darryl tells her to. I didn't stop them because I don't care. Why should I? Why should you? When did you become a social worker?"

"I'd have stopped him out of spite. But I don't get it. Doesn't he know we'd find out? How long does he think it'll take Jackie to get to the Registrar's office?"

Marissa whispered something I couldn't hear.

"Act it out," I said. I pulled my ear. "Sounds like...."

"In the village."

"What does that mean? He took her to the Registry in the village?"

"Yes."

"The Omata village?"

She nodded.

"Ha! The Omata village– How pathetic. He only did that for the aggravation. We probably don't even have to go after her; we can probably call and have her delivered."

Marissa groaned. "Don't be so vigorous." Then she said, "He sold her in the village, but she won't be staying there. He's selling her on condition that she be taken to the caves."

"To the caves? But why? I know the way to the caves, that only makes the aggravation a little bit worse."

That was from my point of view, though. To Honey, it would be absolute rejection, hopeless separation, a big fat final "X" to everything she'd emptied herself out to win. Failure, ruin, despair.

"That louse," I said.

"He did it as a warning."

"A warning? Holy Moses, Marissa – A warning of what?"

"That he could do the same thing to me, if he wanted."

That was what had made her sick.

"You should be so lucky. You'd be better off with a cannibal than a missing link. Besides, you wouldn't take that. You'd laugh in his face for suggesting it. Didn't you?"

"The law would be on his side."

"Nobody else would. He could never pull this off with you, never."

"Maybe not, but.... They would laugh at me. All of them. Even if everybody dropped Darryl, they'd laugh at me, and feel sorry for me."

"It isn't fatal. Take it from one who knows."

I stepped out of the bubble.

"Where are you going?"

"I'm going to get Jackie, so we can go get Honey."

"You can't leave me!"

"Sure I can. I just go down the ladder, like this."

"I said don't leave me! How dare you! How dare you! Darry and I will tear you to pieces! You know I mean it! You might as well pack and go home!"

"I'll go home when I'm ready. I've got things to do around here first."

I was thinking of Jackie, and Honey, and my furry friends' wedding, but I guess Marissa thought I meant that as a threat. I guess she thought there was something in it, too.

"Connie, I'll help you. I'll swear Darry hit me and turn myself over to you. Let everybody know, I can face them down, with your help; with me behind you, everybody will follow your lead. You'll be It, Connie, It. I'll give you paper on it. You can have our whole group at your feet, even me, even Zizi, and Darry will have to crawl on his belly to you. – Or I can put you out – out – out! I mean it. If you leave me when I need you, you'll never be invited to another party as long as you live!"

"Party?" Did she really think I'd sell my soul for an invitation to a party?

Of course, she did. Why shouldn't she? *She* would do it, and I had spent the past ten years promoting myself as one of the same. Like my Aunt Bootsie used to say, "If you ain't in business, don't advertise."

"I think I finally graduated high school," I said. "You and your big-haired cheerleader friends can kiss my watered silk bustle cover, and you can hold your parties someplace the sun don't ever shine. –And, even supposing I cared, I sure don't need you, Miss Face, and I'm not afraid of Darryl. I'm so close to being It now, all I have to do is wait for you two social geniuses to screw up one more time."

"All right. You don't need me. But I need you."

"Give it up. Do you think I don't know why you're so set on keeping me here, playing Mother's Little Helper? Control is the name of the game, isn't it? If you can keep me here, when I want to be somewhere else, you own me, pink slip or no pink slip. Well, call me Crispin's Crispian, the Dog Who Belonged to Himself. Honey's the one who needs me. I'm gone."

She blinked at me, but she didn't say anything else.

"Tosun?" I called down.

"Yes, Managlawn?"

"I think she'll be all right, with a few hours' sleep–about four or five."

"I can do it."

Marissa's eyes widened; her pupils dilated. "You wouldn't let him poison me?"

"You can't poison a rattlesnake."

Tosun handed me up the sleeping potion, and I sat with Marissa until it took effect. I mean, she might be a truckload of nothing, but that didn't mean I was going to leave her in pain.

It also didn't mean I was going to let her catch merry hob for spilling Darryl's plan.

I took Tosun and Tiph and went back into Darryl's sitting room, where Jon Hister was waiting.

"Jon," I said, "do you know where Darryl went with Honey?"

"No, where?"

"Marissa says he took her to Muimmea. Is that right?"

"Could be."

I didn't know him well enough to know if he was lying, and he didn't know me well enough to know if I was. But now, when Darryl came back, he'd find Marissa asleep. Jon would either hold his peace, or tell Darryl I thought Honey was back in the city. Either way, Darryl would be off everybody's tails until it was too late.

Moran would pop a seam when we brought Honey back. Maybe he'd stamp his foot three times and sink through the floor, never to be heard from again.

We live in hope.

Chapter 14

I couldn't call Jackie from Darryl's because of Jon, so we three went back to our place. Before we got there, though, I decided not to call him at all.

"Jackie would want to know what's happened," I said, "but.... I'd like to spare him some grief, if I can. I'll bring Honey back, myself."

"Not alone," said Tosun.

"Anybody who wants to come is welcome, but I figure it this way: If we catch up to Honey in the village, we could be back before Jackie knows she's gone. If we have to follow her to the caves, we'll be gone a while. Somebody ought to be here in case Jackie calls or comes by looking for me. Also, if he finds out Honey's gone, somebody should be here to tell him that Miracle Max is on the job."

"Yes, of course," Tiph said. "I'd rather come with you, but somebody should be here for him."

"Shouldn't I take you and leave Tosun? Wouldn't two women be more of a power team than a woman and a man?"

"Ordinarily. But I'm a luxury slave; to tell you the truth, luxury slaves aren't too highly respected in the provinces, not even females. And Tosun is a Shar; the Omata have more respect for Shars than we do, ourselves."

I put on my going-to-the-caves clothes, just in case, and got a couple of credit books.

Tosun said he had some getting ready to do, too. "If we have to go to the caves we'll be dealing with the real back-country people, and they follow the old ways. That means we'll have to meet the Shaman, get permission to do business with Honey's owner, sit around talking about other things, and eat before we get down to business. That's why I'm packing a bag; polite guests bring and cook their own food."

"Better take some gifts," Tiph said. "These knife-swappers always want something on the side."

"What kind of gifts?" I asked. "Beads and trinkets?"

"People who export jewelry all over the Terran Union aren't going to be impressed by beads and trinkets," Tiph said.

"No, I suppose not."

"We'll get something for them on the way out," said Tosun. "I know just what they'd like." While he spoke, he fastened his shield and weapons to his chestpack.

"Why are you taking those?" I asked, afraid of what the answer might be.

"If we go to the caves, I'll need them." Which was the answer I'd been afraid of.

"Where do we go now?" I asked. "The gift shop?"

"The kitchen. The Omata grow some grain and vegetables, and they keep some poultry, and they trade for fish and fruit, but one thing they never have much of: red meat. That's one reason they became cannibals in the first place."

"Oh, no we're not."

"Not what?"

"We're not going to the kitchen and... We're not taking them any...."

"No, not *people* meat. These resorts that cater to you Terrans always have plenty of pork and beef and mutton, raised on-planet, always fat and tender. We're going to take them some cuts of that. They don't serve two-legged flesh at these Resorts. The Health Department would never allow it. You don't know where people have been or what kind of health they're in."

"The other night, the headservitor implied–"

"She was just bragging. A little local color for the tourists. The only time any people meat is served at this resort is if somebody has an accident grating vegetables."

"That's good to know." I made a mental note never to order the cabbage salad.

We had to get Mem Inson's permission to buy some of her joints, roasts, and steaks, and a bag of charcoal for fuel. When she heard we were going to use them to cross Darryl, she sold them to us at cost.

While Tosun and a couple of kitchen slaves packed the meat in bags of dry ice, I kept watch through the kitchen window for Darryl coming back. I didn't want to meet him on the way: I was afraid I'd fall asleep and have a nightmare and thrash around and hurt him by accident.

What I really wanted to see was Darryl and Honey. It was always possible he had only *threatened* to sell her to the Omata, as a kind of refreshing change from physical brutality.

–No, when he came, he came without her, trotting across the floodplain, enjoying the day.

Where did he get off, playing with people like they were plastic action figurines, and only he was real? Like I'd said to him before, I understood the lust for power, because I had it myself, but wanting a candy-apple-red sports car and sideswiping pedestrians with one were two different things.

And he had the nerve to say we were alike. We both grew up poor. We both had to fight to get out of the gutter, and got spit on and stepped on every inch of the way. We both grabbed every chance that didn't see us first, and twisted its tail until it took us as high as we could make it take us. But we were not alike.

Would we have been, if Darryl had had an Aunt Bootsie, or if I hadn't? That was beyond me and, at the moment, I didn't care. I wanted to clean his clock, not find out what made him tick.

Nikki and Lotte were tending the aazzis again when we went out. When I asked if they'd take us to the village, and maybe to the caves, they pretended they didn't hear me. They spoke to each other in what I supposed was Omatan, and snickered. I had forgotten they thought I was a shave-tail. Wearing, that's what it was.

Tosun turned to me, knelt, and lifted his palms.

"I hate it when you do that. Get up."

"Please, my gamba, have mercy on them. They're only ignorant peasants; they don't know a shave-tail from a rich and famous Terran holovision star who could buy and sell this resort ten times over. Please don't get them in trouble with Mem Inson over this."

Nikki and Lotte goggled a bit.

"I promise. Now get up."

He did, and the Omata began saddling four aazzis.

"You have a way of getting to the heart of things," I said.

"That's why I'm a Shar."

~*~

The Registrar's office was on the ground floor of his home. He crinkled up his nose, when we asked him about Darryl.

"He brought in a Terran woman, tall, well-fed. He offered her to me for two credits. Said that's what he'd paid for her."

"Did you buy her?"

"At that price? Of course. Couldn't help but turn a profit. He signed her over and left."

"How did she take it?"

"I can't read flat-face expressions too well, if you don't mind my saying so, but she was red here and here–" across her forehead and cheekbones– "and the rest of her face was a sort of yellow-gray. She had her mouth clamped shut, but she was sniffing–couldn't seem to breathe through her nose – and, every time she opened her mouth to take a breath, she gasped."

Apparently, she hadn't taken it very well.

"Did he say anything to her?"

"Not at first. Neither one of them spoke to the other; she just stared at him and he ignored her. When he left, she said, 'Darry?' And then he said something. I listened carefully, because I'm working on my Terran, and I wanted to see if I could translate. He said – the Registrar repeated Darryl's words, as he had understood them, in Terran, 'This is to teach you a lesson. I'll tell somebody where you are when I think you've learned it. I don't want you. You're holding me back. Nothing is going to hold me back. You have to understand that.' And he left."

To teach her a lesson.

"I asked her if she wanted to challenge the sale," said the Registrar. "I said I'd help her file the papers. She didn't answer me."

"Is she still here?" Tosun asked. "In a back room?"

"No, one of the merchants, Chitamar Peyt, stopped

by on his way back to the caves. He does that, sometimes. He seemed interested in owning an off-worlder –
for the novelty. I told him I'd be up in a day or two to see
if she'd changed her mind about the challenge. Or, I said,
one of her friends might be up after her. I guess that's
you."

"I guess it is," I said.

"He said he didn't plan to keep her long, anyway.
Well, selling her up to the caves was part of the bargain,
but I didn't like any part of this. I ought to tell you, I
passed along my savings to Peyt – I'm not one of those
profit-gougers, like you see in the city – don't let him tell
you different. Still, I did a good piece of business over it.
Any of you others want to teach each other lessons,
Mocaht Robh's is the place to come."

"We'll bear that in mind."

We went back to our guides and aazzis and headed
for the hills.

"Mhrr," said Tosun. "Remember what that means?"

"Peace. Relax. Don't worry. Be happy. That kind of
thing. This is not the time to mhrr."

"Only when you expect attack from no particular
direction can you respond to attack from any direction. A
stone at peace on the tip of a mountain is balanced on its
center. It moves in a blink, at the hint of a breath. But,
aim it at what you think is the enemy, and secure it to be
ready when you want it, and–"

"I get the idea. I think it probably sounds better than it
plays, but I get it."

We pulled into line, then, to go up the rocks, so we
didn't talk any more.

~*~

When we came out onto the plaza this time, we could tell something was up. There was holiday in the air. Children were overexciting themselves while their parents sat outside their caves, shouting and laughing and grooming each other.

"Festival!" Lotte said. "Lucky we came, Nikki. We would have missed it. Yolan are lucky, I always said so."

"Lotte," I said, "what kind of festival is this?"

"Who cares? Somebody's beer is ready to drink, maybe."

"I could use a good, clean beer bash. But first, can you point me towards Chitamar Peyt? I have some business with him."

"You'll have to see the Chief Shaman first."

"Then can you point me towards the Chief Shaman?"

"I showed you before: That one, with the red and white stain around the windows."

"Shouldn't we be introduced, or something?"

"No, go ahead. She won't eat you, you know." Lotte and Nikki thought this was highly amusing.

Tosun and I left them snortling over it.

"You tell me, in Tudolinguo, what you want to say," Tosun instructed me, "and I'll translate it into Omatan. The Chief Shaman probably speaks Tudolinguo, but the extra step will make the bargaining more formal, and hearing it in two languages will make what you say seem more trustworthy."

"We don't have to whittle and spit, do we?"

The Chief Shaman came out to us. She was black, with a brown undercoat. Her long, coarse fur was plaited with gold wire. So many totems and fobs were twisted onto the strands, she tinkled when she moved. Lotte introduced her as Zander. She had an Elder with her, a white male with mismatched eyes. Lotte said his name was Pivi.

Zander said something to Tosun, who translated, "We're very pleased to meet you. Please feel free to stay the night. We're having a feast; there'll be plenty."

I smiled at Tosun and nodded. "Tell the Shaman we'd be delighted to stay for the feast. Tell her that, in the meantime, we've brought our own food."

That went over well. Tosun translated, "She says someone has taught you manners. She invites us to take some refreshment now. She says she has some excellent beer."

"Tell her everybody knows Omata beer is the finest there is. Tell her we beg her to share her beer with us, and that we'll share our vulgar meal with her. Tell her we know it won't be up to her standards, but we can only offer what we have, and rely on her graciousness to make it acceptable."

"Have you done this before?"

"What, pitch bull? I do it all the time, Gramps. That's why I pull down the big bucks."

Tosun stacked charcoal in the small, shallow pit outside the Shaman's door. He pulled a Bic minilasar out of his chestpack and got the fire going.

While the charcoal blazed and burned down, we drank Zander's beer–golden and bitter–and told each other long and involved jokes.

After about an hour of this, Zander said, in Tudolinguo, "What brings you up the trail today, Mem Phelan?"

"A friend of mine was bought in the village down there and brought up here. One of your merchants: Chitamar Peyt. He was told one of her friends might come after her. And here I am. I'd like to buy her back."

"I'm so sorry. Ask me anything else."

"Naturally, I don't want her owner to take a loss; I'll pay her price and some over, and compensate him for his trouble."

"It isn't the money. She was a bargain, for her size."

"For her size? What does her size have to do with–" I felt my jaw go slack. I mean, what was the worst possible outcome of Honey among the cannibals? "Now, wait a minute. Tosun told me you only ate volunteers. Or is that just what you tell the tourists?"

Zander spoke to me gently. "We don't eat the unwilling."

That was all right, then. I apologized. After all, it was a simple statement of fact: Honey had been a bargain, for her size.

"Only a barbarian would eat the unwilling," said Zander.

"I should think so."

"It gives you indigestion. Or so the old ones always said."

"Then, if you'll forgive me for my ignorance, why can't I buy my friend and take her away with me, if she isn't the on the menu?"

"Because, if you'll forgive me for my impatience, she is. But she wasn't forced, Mem, I promise you. Chitamar says she offered herself on the way up from the village."

That might make things more difficult.

"Did she sign anything?"

"Oh, yes."

Oh, yes. She would, wouldn't she? "Maybe, if I talked to the buyer... Where I come from, we have a saying: 'Everyone has his price.' Or her price, as the case may be."

"I could send for him, but I don't think it would do any good. When you give a feast, everyone looks up to you. Chitamar hopes to be an Elder some day, and giving feasts is a good way to get there, eh, Pivi?"

Pivi nodded.

"We'll discuss it," said the Shaman, and she and the Elder went into a huddle.

Tosun unhooked his knife and skewer, and unslung his shield. "Time for these."

"Aren't you being a little previous? Shouldn't we wait and see if they send for this Chitamar? See what he says?"

"No," said Tosun. "Now."

This was sure a swell time for him to go rash on me. "You don't even know Honey. If you did, you wouldn't like her. This is *my* problem. I have to handle it."

"Yes, but I've got to do my part."

"Wait—"

He put his shield, hollow side up, onto the coals, nestling it into them. He pulled a thin flat stone out of his chestpack and some mutton out of his supply bag and began cutting wafer thin slices with his knife. He folded the slices around dried mushrooms and onion wedges and threaded the packets onto the skewer. He wrapped the filled skewer in parchment-like leaves and buried it in the coals. He cut a chunk of pork, and began cubing it.

"Your knife and.... You cook with them?"

Tosun looked at me blankly. "That's what they're for."

"That, and for waving around while you jump all over the living room like a crazy person."

"Right. For balance and dexterity. Like juggling."

"Sure," I said. "Naturally. Like juggling."

He sat back on his haunches, his eyes nearly shut, his tongue showing behind his needle teeth.

"You thought they were for fighting. You thought – just now – I was going to whip them out and go at it."

"Who knew? I'm flying blind, here. Most of what I know

about this place I've learned since I met you. I came here on vacation, for pity's sake, and here I am cutting a deal for somebody's life. Is that fair? And you sit there shaking your head and wheezing at me. Is that fair?"

"I'm sorry, Managlawn. It isn't fair. You're doing beautifully. Rest quietly on your center, and the right responses will practically make themselves."

Tosun tossed the pork into his shield – well, his wok, but it would always be his shield to me – and stirred it with his knife. When it was browned all over, he poured in enough beer to cover it and added some dried citrus fruit and long, clear noodles, as fine as hair.

Zander sniffed, looked around, and said, "We've decided to send for Chitamar."

Tosun pulled a steak out of one of his bags and began slicing it across the grain. He sprinkled it with salt and dusted it with white, black, and red pepper, and sat it near the fire pit to warm.

When Chitamar joined us, Zander made the introductions, but didn't say anything about why we were there. I assumed Chitamar knew; he had the look of a man ready to drive a hard bargain. I tried to look like a woman who didn't really want what he had to offer, but didn't mind passing the time of day haggling about it.

While we ate, we talked about the weather, praised the Shaman's beer, and raved about Tosun's food. Chitamar asked Tosun what sort of meat we were eating, and inspected the raw cuts with encouraging interest.

When we had finished, Chitamar said, "That was quite a treat. Thank you. Now you must come to my feast tonight."

"We'd be delighted," I said. "There's just one slight problem, from our point of view."

"Oh? Is there anything I can do?"

"It seems you bought a friend of mine today. She was sold as a kind of a joke, by a man who didn't realize Honey – that's my friend – would take it seriously. She did, and she got upset."

"She was very upset," Chitamar admitted. "I thought it was because she was selling so cheap. Then Mocaht told me about how it was for some kind of misbehavior, and that somebody was going to come after her and buy her back– Well, here you are."

I nodded. That's the only way to handle these droners, once they get wound up. Don't interrupt; just let them drone themselves out.

"So I thought I'd bring her home and get her in shape and turn a profit when her friends came for her. Then, once we were out of the village, she told me she didn't have any friends. That nobody was coming after her, because 'Darry' wasn't going to tell anybody where she was, and nobody would care, if he did." He held up his palms in a "what was I to think?" gesture.

"And she volunteered ... er ... for the feast."

"It is a painless and productive form of suicide."

"I suppose you pointed that out to her, her being so upset and all."

"I may have mentioned it."

"Yeah. I understand you also mentioned, to the Registrar, that you didn't plan on keeping her for long."

"One way or another...."

"You didn't waste any time. What happened to giving her a couple of days to challenge the sale?"

"She volunteered." I couldn't tell whether Peyt saw nothing wrong with what he had done, or had more brass-faced gall than anybody I'd ever met – even in show business.

"That doesn't surprise me," I said. "She..." I tapped my head, "does things like this sometimes."

"That's too bad." The merchant spoke with apparent sympathy. "But what can I do?"

"You could sell her to me."

"Oh, no. I couldn't do that."

"At a profit?"

"It isn't just her cost; we've been feeding her tsampa all afternoon. That isn't free, you know."

"But it's cheap," said Tosun. He told me, "Tsampa is chopped grain mixed with salt and butter and, usually, strong tea. In this case, it's probably beer."

Chitamar nodded. "Relaxes the muscles," he said, limbering his shoulders. "High in fiber, to cleanse the system. It takes four hours to prepare someone for a feast, and it ... isn't ... entirely pleasant for the prep staff."

Years of dealing with studio lawyers had taught me to smile brightest in the face of the worst provocation. I dazzled them, now. "I'm sure it isn't. Naturally, I would want to make that up to you."

"But what about the feast?" said Zander. "That concerns all of us. We've been looking forward to it."

"I wouldn't dream of spoiling the feast," I said. "I'll tell you what: We've brought these sacks of Terran meat, the meat you sampled just now: suppose we trade you that for my friend? In addition to the price you name for her, of course."

"I don't know," said Peyt. "I was only going to share a

part of her at the feast. Just a symbolic gesture, you know. The rest, I was going to—"

I spilled beer all over myself, and the explanation was lost in the hubbub.

"Then suppose," I said, "I leave this meat, and pay Tammi Resort for more, some of each kind, equal to the weight of my friend, to be issued to you bit by bit as you request it? Fresh, any time."

"Enough of each kind to equal the weight of your friend?"

I had to put a stop to this, or they wouldn't respect me in the morning. I threw up my hands and shook my head.

"Enough altogether," Peyt conceded.

"And what rate per pound do you want for Honey?"

I wouldn't have paid what he asked to get myself out of hock, much less Honey. But he hadn't expected me to. By and by we reached a compromise.

We went over the terms while one of the Omata wrote them down. We shook hands on it; we'd sign formally at the feast, after I'd made sure Honey was all right and they had the food safely on the table.

Tosun took his cooking gear into Zander's house to clean up. There were no leftovers.

I stood, with my hands in my pockets, watching little cannibals merrily at play, while Peyt and the others made small talk in Omatan. I wondered what it would feel like to pick Chitamar Peyt up by the scruff of his neck and heave him over the cliff. I wondered if anyone would stop me, and how much local outrage the attempt would generate. I decided it would probably draw a certain amount of negative feedback. I thought I would enjoy it, though.

Then I'd go get Darryl, and bring him up, and throw

him off, too. And Marissa. Jon Hister, just so he wouldn't feel left out. Maybe I'd jump off, myself, while I was at it.

Volunteered for a painless and productive form of suicide, because she thought – with good reason – nobody would come for her, even if they knew where she was.

Poor old Honey. Poor Jackie. Poor, dumb, Connie. I could see myself, chatting on the phone, a kid tugging at my elbow, me flapping a hand at him and saying "Shhh!" while another kid chokes to death behind me.

I hadn't been quite that bad, though, had I? I had tried, hadn't I? I had tried. But maybe if I'd tried a little harder, I'd have done a little better.

When Tosun came back out, Chitamar Peyt left the others and joined the two of us.

"Can we get Honey, now," I asked, "and tell her she'll be on the other side of the table?"

"On the other side of the table! That's good! Mind if I use that one, myself, sometime?"

I told the merchant he was welcome to it. We followed him across the plaza to a door in one of the brightly-painted walls. He led us into a place very like the demo model we'd seen on the tour, and through a series of arched doorways and rooms with vaulted ceilings. We came to a door that was closed with a curtain. Peyt called to someone inside.

A woman came out. The smoky blue-gray fur on her hands and lower arms was shaved, exposing startling bright pink skin.

"Kitchen slave," Tosun murmured to me. "He's telling her that she's gone through some fairly labor-intensive and highly aromatic hours cleaning out Mem Clayton's system for nothing."

The look the woman gave me would have killed a more sensitive spirit. I could hardly blame her.

Chitamar explained to her, in Omatan, about our deal. He and she and Tosun went back to the kitchen, so Tosun could help prepare the substitute entree.

I pushed aside the curtain, and went in.

The first smells that struck me, you'd expect in a closed place where somebody has just had her system purified with beer and high fiber. Then came the scents of sweet herbs, and hot oil from the lamp.

Honey lay on a pallet on the floor, a bowl of pale green liquid next to her, the skin of her face shining and clear. She was covered with a sheet. Her clothes were in a pile near the door. She was very still.

I squatted next to her and put a hand on her neck. There was a pulse. She was alive but, man, would she have been tender.

I couldn't begin to wrestle her into her clothes, and I wasn't about to try. She wasn't asleep, exactly, just wrapped in a rosy glow. With me coaxing and hauling, she got her things on, and I fastened her up.

It took a while and, before I had her shoes on, Tosun was calling to me through the blanket at the door.

Between us, we walked Honey outside, and sat her against the wall. I wanted her where I could keep an eye on her.

Zander made a short speech, telling everybody who we were and what we were doing there–as if they didn't know. She thanked Chitamar Peyt in the name of the people for the feast. She directed us to feel the presence of the Sacred Spirit, who'd been invoked and invited when Peyt had first proposed the festival, and turned the ceremonies over to the merchant.

Mem Peyt thanked us all for feasting with him. He explained why the menu had been altered at the last minute, and promised more feasts in the future, as he drew against the four-legged flesh I was laying in for him down below.

That seemed to be all of the speeches. Now it was time for the deal to be finalized. I had Honey, and they had stew.

Peyt had estimated Honey's weight and written it in. If it hadn't been for the danger of misunderstanding, this being cannibal country, I would have accused him of having had his thumb on the scales. I knew Honey was a babe with heft, but...

"This weight...." I said.

"I rounded it up."

There comes a time when the bargaining is over, and you either take a deal or you leave it. I took it.

We signed the payment contract and Honey's title transfer, but there was something else. There's always something else.

"It's because the Sacred Spirit was invoked," the merchant said. "Because this was to be a sacred feast. A sacrificial feast, of a volunteer, with the Sacred Spirit and the people sharing the sacrifice. Non-Omata find that disgusting, if not laughable."

"I'm Catholic myself," I said. "But the Sacred Spirit *is* our volunteer."

"So is ours."

That was too deep for me, so I nodded wisely and shut up.

"Because the Sacred Spirit has been invoked, there has to be some sacrifice. Not much, just something to put into the stew; something of the volunteer. Some part."

"How about a fingernail?"

The merchant laughed. "Something edible. Her choice."

I checked Honey. Her eyes were open, and they were both focused, but not on the same thing.

"She's in no condition to choose anything."

"Then you choose for her. Say, some blood for the broth?"

"I can't make a decision like that for her. –Honey! Honey! Wake up!"

Peyt's kitchen slave came and sat by us, with a bowl and a sharp knife.

"Wait a minute," I said. "She's still out of it."

"They always are. No fuss, that way."

"Sweet Liberty! This won't do! Look: Honey's blood is mostly alcohol, anyway. You could substitute beer, and never know the difference."

"It has to be blood. Or something."

"Suppose I won't let you take anything, blood or otherwise. She belongs to me, now; I'm supposed to protect her. The Empress is very particular about that."

"Yes, that's true," said the Shaman, "though I've never heard of anyone carrying the obligation quite so far. The Sacred Spirit will accept your blood in substitute."

I eyed the knife, and said, "Mine?"

"Yours or hers."

"How ... how much?"

"That bowl, full, will do. Just a symbol."

Just a symbol. That bowl, full, would be nearly two pints.

"She volunteered for more than this," Chitamar reminded me.

"Yes, but...."

The kitchen slave reached out for Honey's arm.

"Call the Red Cross," I said, rolling up my sleeve. "I

definitely want my donor card updated."

I passed out as the knife touched me, so I never felt a thing. When I came around, it was all over.

Tosun bandaged my wrist and propped me up next to Honey. "I'm going to get you something to eat. You'll be dizzy and weak; don't move if you can help it."

"Thanks," I said. "–No stew."

"No stew."

I did feel a tad bit ragdollish, now that he mentioned it. I turned my head to see how Honey was doing.

Her eyes were still heavy-lidded, but she was awake, and looking back at me.

"Did he do it to you, too?" she said.

"Who what? When where why?"

"Darry. He sold me; said I was holding him back. He said this was a lesson; to keep away from him from now on. Did he say the same thing to you?"

"You have got to be kidding. He doesn't have to tell me to keep away. The only reason I haven't snapped off his arms and shoved them up his nostrils is because Jackie asked me to help look after you, and I couldn't do that if I was up on charges. I told you I wouldn't have Darryl if he came with a free set of dishes, and I meant it."

"Then why? Why did you ... volunteer?"

"I didn't."

Her eyes glistened, but nothing spilled over. "I wish I hadn't. I wish I could take it back. Do you think Darry will be sorry, when he finds out?"

I started to say, "Of course," but she interrupted me.

"No. He'll be afraid somebody might blame him for it; but he'll turn it around so it's all my fault, and I did it just to hurt him. Nothing is ever Darry's fault; he's always either the hero or the victim. That's why he's a happy man."

I almost exclaimed, "It thinks! It thinks!" but I didn't.

Tosun came back with three aazzi-skin bags of water and two plates of food. "I didn't know what you'd like so I brought some of everything – except the You-Know."

I handed Honey a water bag and a cakk and said, "I have a surprise for you. In case you hadn't noticed, you aren't sitting in a big black pot of hot water."

"I don't understand."

"Management reserves the right to change the Special of the Day with no prior notice."

I tilted up my water bag and drank deeply, while Tosun told Honey that we'd followed her on "information received" and that I'd bought her back.

"No, wait – the blood. I saw them bleed you. What was that for?"

"Honey, when I cut a deal, I cut a deal. That was just something to sweeten the pot – so to speak."

"But yours? Surely it should have been mine."

"It should have been," said Tosun, "but you were still unconscious. She wouldn't let them–"

"Eat," I said. "Protein and complex carbohydrates: that's the ticket."

She ate, the three of us picking out of the same dishes. When the plates were empty, she said, "Connie...."

"What?"

"Why? Why did you come for me? Why did you let them...?"

"What kind of a question is that? I came because I knew. Any of us would have come for you, once Darryl told. I just got here first. Anybody would have."

She shook her head.

This was getting embarrassing. "Jackie would have."

"Yes, Jackie would have. But he isn't one of you. And Jackie's my friend."

She had me there.

"Is that why you did it?" she asked. "For Jackie?"

"Yes."

"No," said Tosun.

"All right." I licked the food juice off of my fingers like a proper little Marneri. "I didn't do it for Jackie. I did it for you."

Honey looked at Tosun, then said, "You mean me? You don't even like me."

"You're right: I don't like you. But that doesn't mean I want to see you on a platter, with an apple stuck in your mouth."

She blinked, startled at the image. It was a bit more vivid than I'd intended, but there it was.

"I owe you my life," she said.

"You don't owe it to me. I own it. My first order is: No more trying to duck out, just because that little dungbeetle told you to get lost and stay lost. He doesn't have that coming to him; not the powertrip, and not the guilt-trip, either. 'Never blame the booster for what the sucker does,' my Aunt Bootsie used to say. Darryl didn't make your life what it is – *You* did. Now, you can make it into something else."

Honey shook her head. "I still don't understand. What is it to you?"

Good question. It wasn't anything to me. So, who was I trying to impress? Jackie? Not hardly; I thought the world and all of Jackie, but bleeding into the soup wasn't a way I would ever have chosen to show it. Darryl? to rub his nose in what he'd done? No; Darryl liked having his nose rubbed in nasty things. The other Socialites? Ha, ha, ha.

"I did it for my Aunt Bootsie. She frog-marched me into a real life, way back when, and she never let me pay her back. Maybe I'm starting to think it isn't too late. –Tosun, can we go politely, now?"

He nodded.

"I can't!" said Honey. "I can't go back!"

"Oh, that's right, Darryl told you not to. Guess you'd better stay up here, then, right?"

She looked around her, almost in a panic. "No! Don't leave me here! It isn't because of Darry. I mean, it is, but not because he told me.... I don't want to! I just couldn't!"

"Well, I'm not renting a cave up here. I'm going back to the resort, where my friends are."

Honey made a scornful noise. "What friends? They're no more your friends than they are mine. Do you know the kind of things they say about you, behind your back?"

"No, Honey, I'm the village idiot– Of course, I know. They say the same kind of things about me behind my back that I say about them behind their backs. We're a charming group, we are. But I wasn't talking about the Socialites; I was talking about Jackie and Tiph. We've been gone a long time. They'll be worried about us. Tosun and I are going back to the resort. You're coming, too. Let's go."

"All right, Connie. Whatever you say."

Chapter 15

Nikki and Lotte didn't want to leave. A couple of pages from my credit book convinced them to let us take three of the aazzis and go alone.

The sun was just setting as we started down. The cave city was still bright; the dancing, laughing people cast long shadows up its walls. Down in the canyon, it was twilight. The rosy-yellow rock looked blue and gray in the dusk. By the time we reached the canyon floor, it was night.

A flat black piece of sky, thick with stars, showed above the gorge's walls. One of those stars might be Sol (astronomy was not my long suit). Sol was out there, somewhere, anyway. Sol, and the Earth, and TerraNet Central, and the cast and crew of CLUB CALIBAN, and the doorman's daughter with the birthmark on her nose.

When we came out onto the floodplain, a fresh wind from the river blew across us. It didn't smell sweet, but it smelled alive.

I felt moved to sing:

> *Oh, give me a home*
> *Where the cannibals roam,*
> *Where the aazzis and Socialites play.*
> *Where Money's the word*
> *And where morals are blurred*
> *And spies whisper loudly all day.*
> *Home, home on the plain!*

Where the aazzis and Socialites play.
Where Money's the word
And where morals are blurred
And the spies whisper loudly all day.

I took a minute to think up another verse, then:

Oh, sometimes, at night,
When the stars are so bright,
And the water is flowing like wine,
I sip on my stew,
And I think, dear, of you.
Part of you, dear, will always be mine.

Tosun joined me in the chorus, which inspired me to continue:

I saw, in a dream,
By the banks of a stream,
A-an art critic, famous and rich.
An aazzi stood near
And you're-way-ahead-of-me, here,
I could not tell which one was which.

This time, to my very great surprise, Honey jumped in for the finish.

I don't know if it was the shock of that, or exercise on top of blood loss, but all the starch went out of me at the end of the last note.

"Wait a minute." I pulled my aazzi to a stop. "Just give me a minute."

"You're all right, aren't you?" asked Honey. "How much did you let them take?"

"Don't worry about that; I'm good for it."

"The tourist village is closer than the resort," said Tosun. "Let's go there."

"No!" Honey stopped her beast and sat clutching the pommel.

"Why not?" I said. "You can go on to the resort, if you'd really feel safer there. I don't feel quite up to it. —I know: bad memories. I'm sorry, Honey, but I can't go much farther. I have to rest, and it's getting cold out here."

Reluctantly, she came with us.

"Do you want something to eat," Tosun asked me. "Something to drink? Or just a place to rest?"

I was getting an idea. "Let's go to Mocaht Robh's."

"Why?" Honey reached over and clutched my aazzi's reins. "Why?"

"I've got a notion, and I need a Registrar to put it over. —Don't worry: I'm not going to slip you the old rubber peach."

She let me go and shrugged.

"I mean it."

"Whatever you say, Connie." She almost chanted it.

We dismounted outside Mocaht Robh's. There was some disturbance inside. The door jerked open. Jackie and Tiph rushed out at us.

"Connie!" Jackie hugged me, and he hugged me hard. "You did it! I knew you would! You are terrific!" He let me go and held out his arms to Honey, while I grabbed my aazzi's saddle-horn to keep from falling down.

"Oh, Jackie!" Honey threw herself into his embrace and sobbed on his head.

"Could we do this inside?" I asked.

Mocaht Robh plugged the doorway. The light behind him made his coarse chestnut fur gleam along his silhouette.

"It's okay, I bought her." I showed him the papers.

"In that case, do come in. I'll send out for some refreshments. You can all split the cost."

"You'll never make Elder that way," I told him, and he wheezed.

"—What's wrong, Managlawn?" Tiph slipped a welcome supporting arm around me.

I tried not to lean on her as heavily as I wanted to. "What makes you think something's wrong?"

"How did you know something was wrong with *me* , on the boat coming here, and that night you gave me sanctuary?" She took me inside. "The heart sharpens the eyes."

"And I always thought it was carrots."

"Jackie," Honey said, still weeping on him as he brought her in. "Darry..."

"I know. Tiph told me, when I came by Connie's room this morning. I almost came after you then, but Tiph talked me into waiting, in case Darryl came snooping around – which he did. I told him Connie and I were fed up with the whole mess and that we were getting ready for a picnic."

"Managlawn!" said Tiph. "Your wrist!"

Jackie set Honey aside and came to take my hand. "What happened?"

"I cut myself. On a doorknob."

Tiph and Tosun found me a chair and helped me sit without thumping.

"It was part of my price," Honey said. "She let them bleed her, in my place. I should have slit both my wrists, myself, years ago."

"Now she tells me."

I'm wounded, and she throws herself a pity party.

"Oh, Jackie," she said, "what am I going to do?"

"Don't ask him. He suggested I join a nunnery."

Honey sank into the chair next to mine. "What should I do?"

"Come back to Earth with us," Jackie said. "Tomorrow."

I gave what I hoped was a look of genuine puzzlement. "'Us'? Who's 'Us'?"

"You said before that you'd go home if I could talk Honey into going."

"That was because I didn't think you could do it. That doesn't count. Besides, I have business here. When that's taken care of, we'll see."

"We had a deal."

"Ah, but she hasn't said she'd go, yet."

"Will you?" Jackie asked her. "Please."

"I..." She looked at me, and back at Jackie. "I just don't know. Give me some time."

"She needs some time," I said to Jackie. "She's got it, now."

Mocaht Robh came back in with a small keg of wine and a bowl of fruit.

I gave him a page of credits.

"That's too much," he said.

"When somebody does me a good turn, I appreciate it. You know what I mean?"

"Not yet, but I have a feeling I will."

"About going back to Earth...." said Honey. "I've decided." She chose a piece of fruit and handed it to me. "I've decided that I'll do whatever you think is best, Connie."

A doormat is a doormat, no matter whose porch it's on. She should have had Please Be Neat and Wipe Your Feet printed on her chest.

"I think you should press charges against Darryl. Tosun, can she press charges against a former master for mistreatment?"

"Yes. And, if she does, he'd better mind himself carefully the rest of the time he's here. That'll be two complaints against him, not to mention your warning. Three actions are a Class Twelve, an Imperial Offense, and that's not something the authorities will wink at for the sake of tourism. A Class Twelve Offense also means automatic divestiture – loss of the ownership of all slaves – in the name of the Empress."

"Who is this, you're talking about?" asked the Registrar.

"Darryl Moran," I said. "You've heard the name before."

"The one who brought you in?" he asked Honey.

She nodded.

"As a Registrar," Mem Robh said, "it would be unethical for me to recommend a course of action unless I'm asked. If it weren't unethical, I would recommend that this Darryl Moran be taken off the streets. But I'm not allowed to say that."

"Honey, do it. If he so much as gooses Marissa, she'll run for cover, and that'll be three strikes – yer out."

"I...." She stared at her hands. "Don't ask me that. I couldn't do that."

"You've got guts, Honey, or you couldn't have lasted with him so long. Why don't you show some now, when he can't belt you for it? Maybe you love him with a love that's true but, even so, you know power isn't good for him."

"I ... I don't know anymore. I thought I loved him, but ... I don't think I do. I don't know. I'm used to him. I don't know what to do without him."

"You can always hit yourself in the head with a hammer now and then, for old times' sake."

She shook her head.

"Are you wanting to be back with him? Do you think, if you don't make trouble for him, he'll take you back?"

"Connie, I...." She shook her head.

So, she wouldn't. She wouldn't do it now, and she wouldn't do it later; that's what she was telling me. I'd have to use the plan I'd hatched on the way. "Mem Robh," I said, "are you open for business now?"

"I'm always open for business."

"Connie, don't make me! I don't think I can!"

"I don't make people do things. I have other needs for a Registrar. Honey, I'm going to sign you back to yourself."

Honey's face twisted, as if she had a sudden pain that hurt more than she could handle. "Don't. Please, don't. Connie, I'm begging you, don't. I *will* go back to him. I can't help myself. And I.... And I want to help myself. Please give me a chance."

"You're begging me to hold you in slavery?" Why was I so surprised? Hadn't she spent the last twenty-odd years of her life doing the same to Darryl?

I threw up my hands. "Whatever. Me, I need a little pink paper, with my name in the Sold space and a blank in the Owner's space. And I need Darryl."

There was a moment of gratifying silence.

Then Jackie said, "Darryl?"

"No...." said Honey. "Why? Not because...." She gave me what is often called "a searching look."

She shook her head. "No, I believe you. You hate him just as much as you said."

"More. –Honey, he can't do like he does. He can't. Somebody has to teach him that he can't. Looks like that's me. I'm going to put the fear of God into him. I'm going to show him a trick worth two of his. –Or Mem Robh, here, can help you hand him a bill for damages."

"It would be a pleasure," he said.

She shook her head. "I know you think I should. And I wish I could do it for you. I know how much I owe you, but... I can't just turn on him like that. It isn't all his fault. I could have stopped him, any time."

"No." Tiph shook her head, her lips pulled back in distaste. "It wasn't my fault he hurt me. It wasn't your fault he hurt you. I tried to stop him; you didn't; he did it, anyway, to both of us. He's the one who did wrong. Not you. Not me."

"If you could just let me think about it for a while."

Think, nothing. What she wanted was time to transfer her clinging vines from Darryl to me. Or to Jackie, or to anybody she could get to stand still long enough for her to take root.

"I can't wait for you to make up your mind. I've taken everything from that cockroach I intend to take, and I've seen all I intend to see other people take, too. Don't worry about it. I can work this without you. You just stand back and think about being kissed off for two credits and enjoy the show."

"Don't, Connie," Jackie said. "Let's just go away. Let's just go home."

"What Darryl does is none of our business, as long as we're okay. Right?"

"That sounds familiar," Jackie said. "Only it wasn't me who said it."

"Don't worry. I'm not taking any chances, here. Trust me."

"Famous last words," Jackie muttered, and lit a cigarette.

"What about Tiph and me?" said Tosun. "What do you want us to do?"

"Take your freedom and get married. Now. Assuming that's what you both still want."

They looked at each other, and Tiph said, "Yes."

"You don't need us, anymore," said Tosun.

"I never needed you. I used you."

Tosun folded his arms, cocked his head, and smiled.

"Don't start that mystic Yolan stuff with me, Granddad. All I want to know is: When's the wedding?"

"Now," Tiph said, "if Mem Robh will perform the ceremony."

"I would be honored."

"I'm legally in charge of Tiph; she took sanctuary with me from Darryl Moran."

"The same Darryl Moran?"

"Yes, thank God. My question is: If I liberate Tiph, will it mess up her case?"

"There's a form you can fill out."

"And a fee?"

"And a fee."

"Oh, well. Okay. I'm giving Tosun to Tiph and Tiph to herself. Wedding presents."

We passed around papers, and signed where we were told.

As each slip left my hand, I felt a stone roll from my spirit.

Tiph and Tosun knelt, with raised palms, while Mocaht Robh asked them questions in Mocskan, and they replied. They stood, the Registrar took a thumbnail-sized seal from his case and impressed both their forms.

"Congratulations," I said. "Best wishes."

Tosun held out his arms. I went to hug him, but he put his hands on my shoulders and licked my nose.

"What the–"

"Now me!" said Tiph. "May the Mother bless you, Managlawn." She licked me, too.

"Will you forgive me," I said, "if I don't.... Where I come from, we kiss cheeks."

"Different places, different customs," said Tiph, and let me perform my strange ritual.

"Anything else?" the Registrar asked. "Do we all belong to the people we want to belong to? Any more weddings?"

"Now, there's an idea," Jackie said.

"It's a lovely idea," I said, "but it'll have to wait."

"Connie–" He glared away from me, at the floor.

"That didn't come out right. I didn't mean it'll have to wait, I meant I hope it'll wait. Because I really do have to do this first. This isn't more important, but it's more urgent. Okay, Dressmaker to the Stars?"

"You're asking? You? Are asking?"

"Could you possibly become a comedian some other time? I'm asking. Are you answering?"

Jackie smiled with his soft lips and his patient eyes, and I'd never wanted anything as much as I wanted to grab him and bug out on the mess, like any other alien.

"Okay, Society Pet. I just hope you know what you're doing."

"You and me both." To Mocaht Robh I said, "I need that little pink paper now. –The one who sold you Honey? The one Tiph took sanctuary from? If I wanted to sell myself to him through you, how would I work it?"

"Supposing you wanted to, you would sign your title and give it to me. I would give it to him, he would sign, and

I would authorize both signatures."

"Honey," I said, "Will you stand on your rights? I wouldn't take the pleasure away from you, if you wanted it."

She wouldn't meet my eyes. "I still.... Connie, I can't say yes! I can't. But, whatever I decide, I promise – I swear – I won't warn him that you're planning some kind of trick."

"Of course you won't. I never thought you would." Which was more in the nature of sympathetic magic than truth.

"Let's do it to it." I filled in the registration's blanks, signed it, and handed it back to the Registrar.

"Just like that."

He looked at it and began to wheeze softly. "I know it's unprofessional, but I didn't like that man. I have a feeling I'm going to enjoy this."

"Now," I said, "Mem Robh, I assume you have a phone link to the resort?"

"Yes. With visual."

"Call Mem Moran. Have him paged, if you have to. Tell him you haven't been able to find a buyer for Honey, and ask him how long he thinks it takes to teach this woman a lesson."

"I can turn the unit like this, so all he can see is me. Do I let him talk to her, if he asks?"

"Tell him I've passed out," said Honey.

"If that doesn't bring him here, we'll have to go to him. While you're making the call, Honey and I can wash up. We both smell like sauna night in a brewery."

"The lavatory's back there. Help yourselves to soap and towels."

"The two of us can split the cost, right?"

"This one's on the house."

There wasn't anything we could do about our clothes, but at least the smell of the local soap gave the smell of the local beer a run for its money.

When we came out, the lights of the village were flaring in through the windows.

"I sent out a tourist alert to the merchants who live in the village," said the Registrar. "Mem Moran is coming. He's bringing a group in the resort 'bus."

"A group?" said Honey. "He's bringing a group?"

"I told you they'd all come," I said, "once he told."

Honey gave a sob that thought it was a laugh. "They're coming to gawk. He wants to show them what he's finally brought me to."

"Well," I said. "What a nasty little man."

Honey almost made it to a laugh, that time. She sat, and bit her lips while we waited.

Outside, the merchants were setting their goods back out and rolling the sidewalks back down. It sounded like a carnival going up in the middle of the night.

The crash of a bottle was followed by a curse and a whiff of musky perfume.

"'Broken in handling'," said Jackie, around a cigarette.

The resort's bus pulled in, dragged at top speed by ten husky Omata slaves. I stood in a corner where I could see who had come before they could see who was here.

It was an exclusive safari; just the nine of the Inner Circle, led by Himself.

They came in jabbering; Darryl in front. He shook a hand at them above his shoulder, making a point. He was happy as a worm in compost.

Marissa was with him, impassive as ever, but too alert to pass for a woman at ease. She noticed me before the others did, and skewed her eyes at me like an animal who knows trouble when she sees it.

I stepped into the light.

"Connie's here!" said Ivor.

"So she is." Darryl gave Marissa a long look. "How did she come to be here, I wonder?"

"How should I know?"

"Quite a coincidence, isn't it?" said Darryl. To Jackie, he said, "This is a peculiar place for a picnic."

"The universe is full of peculiar things," I said to him. "Some, more peculiar than others. –May I have that now?" I held out a hand to Mem Robh.

He folded the pink paper and gave it to me.

"What's that?" Darryl asked.

"None of your beeswax," I said.

Honey moved closer to me. Maybe it was her years in modeling that gave her a sense of drama; maybe it was her years with Darryl.

At any rate, it bothered Moran. His plan had been to bring the Powers out here and take an informal opinion poll. Then, according to which way it went, he'd have bought Honey back, or let one of them assume ownership, or left her again.

But here I was, where I wasn't supposed to be, and I was here ahead of him; undermining his plan, challenging his control over the situation.

He thought it was Honey's paper I was clutching, you see, and he thought he had to have the disposal of Honey's paper, because that was how he'd planned it. A fiery intellect, no.

"Give me that." He held out his hand.

What a pigeon.

"All sales are final," I said.

"What's it worth to you?" Darryl pulled out a book of credits.

Honey took my arm. "Don't do it," she whispered.

"The whole book," I said.

"The whole book? I hardly think that's reasonable."

"Maybe you'll change your mind, after a while. I'm thinking of developing a new show for TerraNet, about this really stupid art critic, but I need a research consultant."

Hurst smothered a laugh.

"Honey's mine." Darryl held out the credits. "The whole book."

I took it and handed him the paper. He signed it. Mocaht Robh signed it, and handed it back.

Darryl tucked the paper in his blazer pocket. "Now tell me, did you really come here by chance?"

"Jon must have told her!" said Marissa.

"No, you told me, Face. Don't you remember?"

"Connie!"

"You aren't mad at her, are you, Darry? She said you'd be mad, but you're not like that, are you?"

Marissa worked up a ghastly smile. "My head hurt. I was sick, and scared. I was afraid you'd do the same to me, and I thought I could talk to Connie. You said I could call her. I thought I could trust her."

"Thought he'd do the same to you?" Zizi asked.

Darryl narrowed his eyes at Marissa. "We'll talk about it later."

Apparently, he still wasn't ready to tell the Inner Circle he was holding title on the Face. A revelation like that needed forethought and set-up. Like the Wicked Witch of the West says, "These things must be done delicately, or you hurt the spell."

Too bad.

"Can I talk about it?" I asked. "She told me all about it."

"Darry," Marissa said, "I–"

"Shut up!" This to the reigning queen of the Good Society.

Now, surely, she would stand up to him. He wouldn't like that; angry as he was now, it wouldn't take much to push him into overload.

"Yes, Darry," Marissa said. "I'm sorry."

I saw a lot of appreciative smiles dead on arrival, as we all realized Marissa wasn't being sarcastic.

"Marissa?" said Zizi. "Is that you? How can you let him order you around like that? Anyone would think...."

Time for the mean part – the part where I used Marissa's greatest fear and the secret she had entrusted to me against her. It should have been my moment of glory. I hoped it was over fast, because I thought I was going to be sick all over myself.

"Anyone would be right," I said. "He owns her. He has, since the day we got here to Tammi Resort."

In the shocked silence, Marissa's small voice whispered, "How could you? Connie, how could you?"

"Consider it a present. As long as he was holding this over you, he could take his time wearing you down." I said to the others, "It was supposed to be all in 'fun,' remember? Like when he 'pretended' he was auctioning Honey?"

They remembered. Credit where it's due: They might laugh at Marissa when the shock wore off and sophistication kicked in; at the moment they were in the grip of primitive humanity, and pitied her.

"He owns Marissa?" Honey spoke more to herself than to anyone else. "Since we got to Tammi? And he didn't tell me? He let her use me for a lady's maid." She looked at me. "And you knew? And you didn't tell me?"

"What good would it have done?"

"It would have hurt me."

She said it so simply, as if it were a cold fact of nature that Connie would do or say whatever was necessary to hurt for the mere sake of hurting.

"That isn't who I am. That was never the idea."

"I hate to break up the girl-talk." Darryl took a step toward Honey and me, his hands loose at his thighs, his body held in a stance of limber menace.

Honey shrank back. She flushed, then stood at her proper height, with proper model posture, and looked through her former lover.

"Strangely enough," she said, "Connie really has been on a picnic today. Not with Jackie, though. With me. You see, when Darry sold me, part of the bargain was that I be taken to the caves. Up where they eat people. Connie came and bought me back. She—"

"Shut up!" Darryl's hand twitched toward a fist.

He wasn't going to hit her again; not in front of me. "You can't tell her to shut up, Boss. You don't own her anymore, remember? You sold her to the cannibals, and you told her she was holding you back, and nobody was going to hold you back. You're really kind of pushy, if you don't mind my saying so."

I'll give him this: He has good reflexes.

He feinted with his right and threw a left. The blow caught me on the right eye and sent me sprawling into the Good Society.

Good reflexes, no brains.

Hannah Hobbs gave a little scream; Marcus held out a restraining hand toward Moran, and Hurst and the countess moved between Darryl and where I lay.

"Sanctuary!" I shouted from the floor. "Sanctuary, in the name of the Empress!"

Jackie pushed through and helped me up. He held me so close he nearly smothered me. "You're crazy. You're a crazy person."

"I told you not to worry."

"You *are* crazy," said Darryl. "You can't claim sanctuary."

"Look at the paper, Slick."

He did.

"Whose name do you see? –You do read, don't you?"

"It's yours...."

"Yes. It's mine. You just paid a whole book of credits for me, Darry darling. And you just knocked me down, in front of witnesses, one of whom is official. –You said you'd get me, and you got me, sweetie."

Honey clapped her hands as Jackie helped me to a chair by the Registrar's desk.

Darryl glowered at her.

"You," she said. "You paid a whole book of credits for the wrong person. Didn't even read the title before you signed it. Even I would have done that, and God knows I'm no genius."

"This is two actions against you, Mem," the Registrar said to Darryl. "I'm obligated to warn you, you don't want another. Three actions mean divestiture – you lose the right to own any slaves unless you're cleared of charges at the trial. And you *will* go to trial on three charges. It's a serious matter, Mem."

The Socialites drew back from him. Bad form, serious matters on vacation.

Marissa started to leave the office. As she passed him, Darryl reached out and wrapped a hand around her upper arm.

"I haven't been divested yet."

She tried to shake him off. "What nonsense. Let me go."

"Since we're so concerned with the law, let's hear what the law says about this. She can't walk away from me if I own her, can she?"

Mocaht Robh wasn't happy about saying it, but he said, "No, she can't." He told Marissa, "You can petition to have the sale voided; in the meantime, unless you have grounds for claiming sanctuary, you stay with him. I can file a Request for Invalidation form for you."

"Yes, do." Marissa struggled against Darryl's hold but stopped when she looked into his face.

"Wouldn't it be better to set me free now? I'll pay. Two credit books – more. Name the price."

"Darling, you don't have a thing to be afraid of. I'd never lay rough hands on you."

Why should he? He knew lots of ways to brutalize; he didn't have to get physical. He'd be better off keeping her than letting her go, now. He had nothing to lose, and might still turn his control of her to advantage before the Season was over. If he couldn't – if this was the social blow I hoped it was – he might as well get what "pleasure" out of it he could.

Tiph, me, and ... nothing. That was it, and it wasn't enough. I'd shot my wad, and all I had to show for it was another black eye.

"Tell the Registrar about the migraine, Marissa. How he left you to suffer. That's abuse by neglect, isn't it?"

"I told her she could send for you. You're her little primary care physician. I won't leave her, the next time. Will you come play doctor then, I wonder?"

"Marissa, just claim abuse–they can sort it out at the trial."

Marissa moved against Darryl's grip again, but he held her firmly. "Please be quiet, Connie, you're making it worse."

"Here's that form," said the Registrar.

Darryl shook his head.

"Never mind," said Marissa.

Darryl put his arm around her shoulders. "Let's go."

"Just a minute," said Honey.

Darryl cast his gaze to the ceiling and sighed. "I don't want to hear it. This time it's really over, Honey. This time, I mean it."

"This time, I want to make sure of it." Honey turned to Mocaht Robh. "I want to lodge a complaint against a former master."

Chapter 16

It was so quiet, you could hear a jaw drop.

"You can't mean that, Honeybunch," Darryl said. "You wouldn't ... betray me?"

Honey sat down with a complaint form and began filling it out. "I'm only supposed to list what he's done to me since he's held my title, right? Otherwise, I'll need more paper."

"That's three," said Mocaht Robh. "Three is automatic divestiture and arrest." He looked at Marissa. "A protest of sale, with particulars, would help the prosecution's case. I would file the protest before I registered the Class Twelve, you see."

I eased Marissa toward the Registrar. "Come on, Marissa. You might as well join the club."

"Divestiture? He doesn't own me anymore?"

"You're free as the little blue birdies. So there's nothing to stop you–"

"I think not," she said. "I'm free, I'm out of it, and I don't care to be involved."

She went to mill with the other Socialites, who were standing stiffly with their hands in their pockets, trying to ignore Darryl and keep an eye on him at the same time.

"You don't care to be involved?" I said. "Honey just saved you from two months in Hell, and you don't care to be involved?"

"You can't make me!"

The Socialites wandered to another corner and re-formed

without her. Their contempt was strong enough to smell. Marissa held her head high and affected not to notice.

Darryl looked around at the shambles of his triumph.

"You still have time to run," I told him. "I haven't signed my complaint form, yet. I'll give you one hour to pack your bags and charter a boat. If you're gone when I get back to the resort, I'll give you another ten hours to get off-planet."

And he smiled at me. He passed close by me as he left, gripped my good wrist, and murmured, "I always knew it would be you and me. I'll see you back on Earth."

Well, I might have known.

"Hold your breath till I get there."

Still, the others stood tense and silent. Honey looked proud of herself, but ready to crumble. I pretended to spit after Darryl and said, "This here planet ain't big enough for the two of us."

The Socialites whooped, the savages. Like I'd told Marissa, all I'd had to do was wait for her and Darryl to screw up one more time. They'd done it, and I'd gone for their throats in the approved Good Society style. The Socialites would have lifted me onto their shoulders, but they were afraid I'd tear their heads off. They settled for truckling, instead.

"You didn't really eat up there, did you?" asked Hannah. "Did they have ... you know...?"

"God! What nerve!"

"I've got to hear everything, start to finish!"

I shook my head. "Run along and play now, boys and girls. We'll join you when we're through here."

"We'll have all the merchants send the bills to you, Connie, shall we?" said Marcus.

"You must be dreaming. I didn't take you to raise."

Rula chuckled. "Then you must stand us to champagne and omelets when we return to the resort."

"If I'm not there, start without me."

They left, Marissa on their fringe.

"It worked," said Mocaht Robh.

I shrugged one shoulder. "I can't enjoy it. I got greedy. I counted on Marissa. When Honey signed on, I thought Marissa would follow up on the migraine gambit, and we'd really have him."

"We do," said Honey. "Tiph, you, me. Three is all it takes, isn't it?"

I pulled my pink slip from my pocket. "This is my real one. Darryl's was a fake: Not filled out properly, not notarized. What you call a dummy, appropriately enough."

I put a hand on Jackie's arm, hoping he wouldn't be angry. "I told you not to worry."

There was a sudden loud and lovely sound in the room. Honey was laughing from her toes up.

"'You still have time to run.' Oh, dear. And he did. But my poor heroism was all for nothing, wasn't it?"

"No, no. Without a 'third' complaint, the bluff wouldn't have worked. When Marissa wimped out, I thought it was all over. Then you thundered up on a big white horse, and I got to thinking Marissa might come along for the ride. Then it wouldn't have been a bluff. Then he would have done time, or at least faced it. Now...."

"If I were sure you Terrans wouldn't drop the charges," said Mocaht Robh, "I'd call the resort Registry and have him picked up on the complaints we do have. Two complaints don't carry the clout of three – no automatic divestiture – but they have a higher priority than one: immediate arrest, at the complainants' requests. You're the one who promised him time to get away, not me, and not the complainants."

"I promised I wouldn't sign the slave-abuse form." I grinned. "I didn't say I wouldn't charge him with simple assault."

"I want to take him to trial," Tiph said. "I want to make an example of him."

"Mem Clayton?"

She didn't answer right away. I didn't want to influence her – didn't even want her to think I was trying. I kept my eyes on Mocaht Robh, and waited.

So I didn't get to see her face when she said, "Call the resort."

"You've got them all where you want them," said Jackie, while Mem Robh filled Emtis Bulfa in on our sales, transfers, shuffles and charges. "All of them – even Zizi – are rolling over and sitting up for you. Congratulations, Society Pet. You've really made it."

"I have? Why, so I have. How satisfying, to go out with a burst of fireworks."

"Go out, how?" asked Honey.

"As my Aunt Bootsie used to say, 'Enough is enough.' –Okay," I said to Jackie, "you were right. I was wrong. Assuming that I really do have them, they're the only thing I ever got in my life that wasn't worth getting. I quit."

Tosun nodded. "The superior person realizes the error of misused energy and rests."

"You must've read my mind," I said.

Tiph, Tosun, Honey, Jackie and I slipped out of the village on our aazzis while the Socialites were still frolicking. I wished it were as finished as it felt. I wished I could fly away to some private place and scrub myself clean of everything.

Honey blew the dream away with a shaky sigh.

"I have to move out of Darry's suite. He'll be gone, but Marissa will still use it, and I couldn't stay there, anyway. I couldn't bear...."

"Sweet memories of days gone by?"

Honey held up a hand, as if holding those memories at a distance. "The trouble is, I'm afraid to be alone."

"Afraid of Darryl, you mean? He'll be in custody by the time we get there."

"Maybe. But he might talk them into just restricting him to the resort. He can seem so sweet and, if they do..." She shook her head. "I'm afraid he'll ... do something ... to make me drop the charges."

"He wouldn't dare hurt you. Not now."

"He wouldn't have to. He's always been able to get around me."

"Aren't you moving in with us?" Tiph asked. "You still belong to Managlawn. There'll be plenty of room. Tosun and I...."

"Of course, Tosun and you," I said. I had lost track, in all the to-ings and fro-ings. "You'll be wanting some privacy. I'll spring for the honeymoon. I don't suppose you want the newlywed suite at the Tammi Resort– They don't seem to get a very nice class of people here."

Tosun said, "I would like...." He leaned across and put a hand on Tiph's, "If it's all right with Tiph, until this litigation is settled and I know which path you choose, I would like to stay close."

Tiph nodded. "Still, a little privacy would be nice."

"The newlywed suite it is," I said.

"Thank you, Managlawn," said Tiph, with the humble grace of an aristocrat admitting a commoner to her circle of genuine friends.

I was touched. I was honored.

"So," I asked Honey, after I cleared my throat, "how about it? As far as I'm concerned, I'm only holding your paper to keep it away from Darryl. Say the word, and it's yours. Ignore it, if you want to; I won't squawk. I do have an empty room right now; it's yours, if you want it."

"Oh, Connie, could I? I'd feel so much safer."

"Naturally, you would. I lead such a quiet, orderly life. I tell you: The next time I pick up a couple of souvenirs, I'm getting embroidered pillows, or t-shirts. Little plastic snow scene paperweights."

I opened the door, so I saw him first: Darryl, lounging on my floor furniture, swilling my liquor. I stopped in the doorway, blocking it.

"Jackie," I said, "take Honey to your room."

"Why?" Honey said, maneuvering to see over my head. "–Darryl...."

"Come in." He waved a welcoming glass. "It's all right. I'm in custody."

Both Emtis Bulfa, the Registrar, and Tabba Inson, the Manager, were with him, sitting in chairlike configurations on either side of him.

"Always surrounded by women," he said.

"What is he doing here?"

"He seems to think this is a joke," Tabba Inson said. "He claims you're teasing him – that the Terrans are, at any rate. We need to clear up any misunderstandings before we proceed. Will all of you please come in? All of you."

"Litigation can be costly," Emtis Bulfa said, as we filed in and stood, in a ragged line, near the open door. "A certain amount of time has already been invested, but it would be better to absorb it now than pursue the case to a more expensive–"

"What the lady is trying to say," Darryl interrupted, "is: Drop the charges now, and all is forgiven; drop the charges later, and the Empress will be very, very cross."

"We're not dropping the charges," Tiph said. "Now or later."

"The game is over." Darryl rose and walked past us to the bar. Jackie stepped out of line and stood between Darryl and the rest of us, like a puppy trying to protect us from a scorpion.

"Honor guard?" Darryl said, with a nasty grin.

Jackie lit a cigarette and puffed in Darryl's face.

"I've always wanted to do that," Jackie said, "but I've never met anyone I thought needed fumigating before."

"Well said," I told him. "That's my boy."

Darryl moved upwind and repeated, "The game is over. They tell me they only have two slavelaw violations against me – that means I still own Marissa, by the way – and I can afford any fine these ladies care to levy."

"This is not a game," said Mem Bulfa. "This is the law. Two violations are not as serious as three; but I, for one, am not inclined to overlook two."

"How about one?" Darryl said, cocking an eyebrow at Honey. "Will your Bureau of Tourism, or whatever you people have, let you throw the book at a harmless vacationer," Darryl placed a hand on his own chest, "who lost his temper once?"

"Twice," said Honey.

"Three times," I said.

"Ahhh...." Darryl winked at Honey. He wagged a finger at me. "But you didn't sign a complaint, did you? And you won't, will you? That would spoil our fun." He spread his hands to include the three of us: himself, Honey, and me.

"Don't flatter yourself, Lover-Boy," said Honey. "Remember how funny I thought it was, when you bought the wrong woman? It gets better: Connie passed you a phony paper. You didn't pay a whole credit book for the wrong person, you paid it for nothing."

"...Is that...?"

I smiled and nodded. "Sucker."

Darryl made no move. Even his expression looked so calm it was almost slack.

His eyes, though.... His eyes had that wide, glassy look you see in pictures of serial killers. And the craftiness.

"Of all the people you have owned, tried to own, or thought you owned," Honey said, "Connie is the only one you never have and never will. And wait till she gets back to Earth. I doubt anybody is going to take your opinion – on art or anything else – very seriously after Connie gets through ragging your reputation. And what will you do, then? I don't think the Employment Office has a listing for gigolos. If they do, take my advice: Don't use Marissa as a reference. Connie threw a wrench in those works, too, didn't she?"

"What is this?" I said. "'Let's you and him fight'?"

Even as I said it, Darryl exploded toward us. Maybe I was still slow from loss of blood. I didn't expect it, but Honey did – maybe, after twenty years on the receiving end, Honey had become extrasensitive to the transmitter.

She stepped in front of me. Darryl's hands went around her throat. Tiph had been half right: Honey couldn't have stopped him, but she sure knew how to get him started. She knew he wouldn't go for her here, where someone else would punish him for it, so she had set him onto me, and walked into his attack.

For an instant, out of old habit, she stood submissively in Darryl's clutch. Then she raised her hands and clawed both sides of his face.

He swung her away from me and punched her in the chest.

I heard the breath whoosh out of her, and saw her face turn grayish-green.

She clutched Darryl's fist as she fell backwards, pulling him away from me and off-balance. She lost her grip, rolled over the rise Darryl had used as a lounge, and disappeared into the hollow behind it.

It happened so quickly – it was as if the fight ran in fast-forward and the rest of the world paused. It ended, and everything snapped back into sync.

Mems Inson and Bulfa stood up. A look passed between them.

The Registrar drew a blue-bladed knife and held it, ready to throw. "When Mem Robh called me tonight, I had a feeling I'd need this. I don't want anybody to move except Mem Inson."

Tabba Inson went around the raised flooring and knelt. After a moment, she said, "I find no vital signs."

I wanted to say, *No!– That's what I thought, too, and there was plenty life left in her!* I couldn't say it. I couldn't say anything. And then I thought, *Jackie. Poor Jackie.*

"I don't believe it!" said Jackie. He moved to Mem Inson's side, taking care not to pass between the Registrar and the rest of us. He dropped to his knees.

"Please don't touch the body," the manager said.

"Do you know what it means to kill a slave?" said Emtis Bulfa. "Do you realize the penalty?"

"Honey," Darryl said. "No...! I couldn't...!"

He turned his back on the place Honey had fallen, his tears gushing and streaming like blood from a wound. He crossed his arms over his chest, pressing them tight, as if trying to hold something close that was bound to get away.

Maybe I should have felt sorry for him, but I had used up all my compassion on his victims.

"Mem Phelan," said the Registrar. "You were her owner?"

Darryl's attention focused on me.

"Yes," he said. "This is *your* fault. We were happy, until you started poisoning her against me. *You* killed her, not me!"

This time, I saw him coming. I met his attack, knocking his arms apart, and butting the front of his head with the crown of mine. He grunted and staggered back, blood bright on his mouth from his cracked lip.

"Somebody grab him!" I said.

"You have the first right," said Tabba Inson, as Darryl shook the stars out of his head.

"Stop him!"

"Nobody moves!" Mem Bulfa shouted.

He came for me again, and got in under my guard, one hand behind my head and one on my chin. I held my neck as firm as I could and popped my open palms against his ears. That's broken many a hold, but it didn't break that one. I drew back my hands; this time I'd catch both sides of his neck with my knuckles.

He grunted again, though I hadn't made my move, and the pressure stopped. His eyelids fluttered, his eyes rolled back, and he collapsed against me.

Tosun was closest; he pulled me away from the wreck as Darryl flopped, face-down, to the floor, Emtis Bulfa's knife in his back.

"I'm sorry," Mem Bulfa said. "It was your right, but he seemed to be winning."

That was a lie. Blood trickled from his ear as well as from his mouth. I could have knocked him senseless, a piece at a time, since nobody had been allowed to protect us from each other. It hadn't had to end with a knife in a vital organ.

"I didn't want him dead. I wanted him arrested. I wanted him stopped."

"He is stopped," said the Registrar.

Jackie hadn't seen it – any of it. He might have been in a different room.

When he spoke, it was to Tabba Inson. "What do you mean, 'no vital signs'? Here – feel her pulse. She's alive!"

"So she is," said the Manager, calmly. "I seem to have made a terrible mistake."

~*~

Jackie, Tiph, Tosun, Honey and I sat in one of the suites on the penthouse floor of the Muimmea Hilton.

We had left Tammi Resort on the first available transport; gone, before the revelers had come back from the Omata village. I wondered if they would finish out the Season.

They wouldn't do it at the Hilton: The Good Society would return from the resort to find all the penthouse suites booked and their own reservations lost in the computer. One of the benefits of having a desk clerk for a fan.

"Emtis Bulfa tells me the Imperial Something-Or-Other is holding hearings," I said. "Some people think off-worlders shouldn't be involved in slavery unless they pass tests and meet a raft of requirements. I've been asked to testify. They want Tiph and Honey, too."

"I'll be there," said Tiph. "I didn't know if you and Honey would. I wouldn't blame you if you just went home and forgot you ever came here."

"Do you think I should stay and testify, Connie?"

"Haven't you heard? Abraham Phelan freed the slaves. Do what you want to do."

"But you are?"

"Yes. I am." I took a deep breath and looked at the coffee table. There was something in my stomach that felt like a knot and a hollow at the same time. "–And, I'll look for someplace permanent to live as soon as this hearing thing is over. I'll have to call TerraNet and let them know, and have the bank transfer my assets."

"Permanent...?" said Jackie.

I felt tears burn in my eyes. I tried to hold them back but two – only two – escaped and rolled down my cheeks. I ignored them. "I'm sorry, Jackie. I'm just as sorry as I can be. But, the thing is, I'm not going back."

"Not going back to Earth?"

"That's right. I don't feel at home there. I can't go back. I don't feel at home here, either, but I think I could."

He lit a cigarette. "You haven't developed a taste for owning slaves, have you?"

"No, but I seem to be developing a taste for liberating them. I know it's part of the culture here, and I know it mostly works. But did you ever hear of a power structure that wasn't sometimes abused? Especially by people who didn't understand it?"

"Like off-worlders, for example," said Tiph.

"Like certain off-worlders," said Honey. "I ... I'll stay,

too. With you, if you'll let me."

I wasn't really surprised. After what she had done–for herself, and for me – she still had less backbone than a four-ounce can of salmon.

"And then what?" Jackie asked. "After the hearings? What do you do with the rest of your life?"

"TerraNet has a Marneri studio – flatfilms for local consumption – about twenty miles west of Muimmea. They can turn CLUB CALIBAN over to the Ariel character if they want to keep it going; I've got a concept for a new show, about this shave-tail Registrar with a heart of gold. Every week she comes up against people crunched in the system, and every week she helps some of them out, with some of the problems held over till next time."

"And...." Tosun prompted.

"And?" said Jackie.

"I've got this other idea. Safe houses, where slaves who don't have anyone to give them asylum could take shelter while their complaints are being processed. Sanctuaries."

"Sanctuaries? What about them?"

"There aren't any. There need to be. I'd finance them."

"I knew you were soft," said Jackie. "I always said so."

"We're going to help," Tosun said. "I know a little about administration."

Tiph laughed. "And I'll see to our clients' comfort. Being a luxury slave might have some value, after all."

"I have a lot to do, too," said Jackie.

"You?"

"I practically proposed. And you practically said yes. If you're staying, I'm staying. It's just what I need: new horizons, new challenges, new markets. The businesses on Earth can run themselves. I'll open branches here."

My heart leapt like a cannibal at a volunteer. Still, could I accept this without making a comment?

Not if my life depended on it – which it did.

"Jackie... Allow me to point out that these people don't wear clothes."

He blew a smoke ring, something I'd never seen him do before. "The shave-tails do."

"The shave—"

"The tourists do. The off-worlders who live here do. And everybody accessorizes."

Jackie put out his cigarette and took me by the shoulders.

And he kissed me–right on the shiny black lips.

"I'd rather lick noses," said Tiph.

About the Author

For as long as she can remember, Marian Allen has loved telling and being told stories. When, at the age of about six, she was informed that somebody got paid for writing all those books and movies and television shows, she abandoned her previous ambition (beachcomber), and became a writer.

Visit the author at her website:
MARIAN ALLEN
Fantasies, mysteries, comedies, recipes
for free reads, recipes, excerpts, and more
http://MarianAllen.com

www.ingramcontent.com/pod-product-compliance
Lightning Source LLC
Chambersburg PA
CBHW070848250626
47159CB00003B/977